LOVE-OBSESSED
Copy

Friends In Crisis Series Book 4

Lucy Appadoo

This book is dedicated to victims of stalking. It is also dedicated to my husband and two daughters who give me unconditional love and support.

Contents

Chapter One

PROLOGUE: ONE YEAR EARLIER

The man bent forward and turned on the tap, waiting for the bathtub to fill up. When the water neared the brim, he turned towards his beautiful girl, her head lolling from side to side where she leaned against the bathroom wall. He stooped low and caressed her dark brown, matted hair. Her piercing brown eyes, beautiful buxom figure, and dainty, delicate hands aroused him.

The girl groaned, but her eyes remained closed due to the medication in her system. He entered the kitchen, uttered a few words to his companion reading on the couch, pulled a jagged knife from a drawer with a gloved hand, and returned to the bathroom. Putting down the knife and leaning forward, he pulled the girl up and gently submerged her in the warm water, the resulting splash in itself a piece of artwork. He smiled and got to work while kneeling beside the tub.

If only she had loved him.

Picking up the knife, he pushed it into her hand and forced her to cut herself. Beautiful. Such artwork. The self-made cuts created a masterpiece, joining the jagged patterns on her wrist, as his hand enfolded hers, forcing it to cut another line. She tried to fight but the medication made her weak. Blood oozed into the water, forming a pattern of whirls and blooms. Aesthetics in the work. He manoeuvred her hand so that the knife in it sliced two gashes into her right leg.

More blood seeped into the water. She was getting weaker and her eyes drooped as he watched her slowly wither away. He was a patient man and could wait.

He sat back against the wall, eyes lit up above a feral grin. *What a piece of artwork.* His front door slammed and his companion yelled out to him.

When the life was gone from her eyes, he pleasured himself until reaching a climax, thinking that maybe one day he would find someone to love.

Chapter Two

PRESENT DAY: THE CLIENT

Gabriella Jamitson ambled up the concrete path, scrutinising a multitude of windows, an arched entryway, and white timber posts. Her eyes flicked towards sunflowers lining the front garden and a well-kept lawn surrounding the brown-brick building with its green tiled roof. Low shrubs and a boulder to the side of the building's entrance gave the local community health centre in Altona Meadows an inviting appearance. She passed the signage and entered through the sliding doors with a quick step, and came upon her first client for the day.

"Hello, Nora. I'll be with you in five minutes." She nodded to the receptionist and walked into her office. She unlocked her filing cabinet, inserted her handbag into it, and took out her client's file and case notes. Putting them on her desk, she threaded her hands through her dark brown hair with its blonde highlights and took a breath. In less than two years, Gabriella would finish her studies and become a fully qualified social worker. As a Drug and Alcohol Counsellor, Gabriella thrived on helping struggling addicts reduce the harm that the substances they took did, and she wanted to ensure she did her duty well.

Wishing she had fewer curves, Gabriella pressed down the wrinkles and folds in her red cotton dress where it stretched over her buxom figure. She stepped back into the waiting room and called for her client. "Come through, Nora."

The young twenty-year-old smiled. Her blue eyes looked tired and her long, red hair appeared unwashed. She wore a stained blouse and a rumpled skirt. Nora had been getting worse over these last few months. Having controlled her addiction and stopped taking too many non-prescription drugs, Nora should have been improving, but instead, she was going downhill. It must have been due to the stress of having to learn to live without something that took away her pain. Or was she lying about ceasing drug use?

Gabriella took a seat in her office while Nora sat opposite in an armchair. She gave her a reassuring smile and leaned forward in her chair to put her client at ease. Nora always needed a bit of time to relax into the session, and Gabriella wanted to make sure that all her clients were comfortable and open. Getting through the usual greetings and breaking the ice with topics like the weather, Gabriella dove into the session. "Tell me about your week, Nora. Have you been working on those goals to mend your relationship with your mother?"

Nora nodded, her hands shaking. "I have, and she's starting to forgive me for all the times I got angry with her. I even practised those self-care activities you gave me. The mindful walking, the rituals before sleep, and calling my sponsor if I'm struggling with temptation. It's all been helpful. Thanks, Gabriella."

Gabriella took notes and uncrossed her legs. "Have you been sleeping?" She hoped Nora hadn't relapsed, and the shaking and bloodshot eyes were a concern.

Nora shook her head. "Not really. I feel tired and drowsy all the time, even first thing in the morning, and I'm jittery and out of breath. I get dizzy and have issues with my memory and concentration. I'm not taking drugs anymore and I don't want you to think I am."

Gabriella gave her a reassuring smile. "You've done great work, and we're at the stage of relapse prevention, given you've abstained for about three months now. But as I've mentioned before, you need to have a medical check-up to rule out anything physical. You seem to be doing everything right."

Nora pursed her lips and stared at her hands. Even her fingernails looked brittle. "I hate hospitals and I refuse. It's most likely me adjusting to my new life since I stopped using." She averted her eyes.

What wasn't Nora telling her?

Gabriella nodded. "Are you sure everything's okay in your life? There has to be a reason why you're feeling this way. You've been off the drugs for a while, and when you did the rehabilitation program, you managed your withdrawal then, so that can't be it."

Nora crossed her arms with pursed lips. "Everything's fine." She gazed past Gabriella as if she was in another place.

Gabriella wouldn't pressure her. She would tell her the real reason for her behaviour in her own time, but something wasn't right. Maybe her friend, Claudia could get her to open up. "Are you sure there's nothing on your mind? I am here to help and won't judge. You've come a long way, Nora, and I am here for you."

Nora averted her eyes. "Hmm. All good."

Gabriella could refer Nora to Claudia who had a different set of skills. There was time for that. "What I suggest then is returning to your previous psychologist, Claudia. She can look more deeply into the underlying source of these issues if you're not willing to do a medical. Will you ring her and make an appointment later today?"

Nora hesitated, her eyes looking past her. "Fine. I'll give her a ring after our session. I guess it can't hurt, and she did help me the last time I saw her."

"Is it okay if I speak to Claudia after you've had a few sessions with her? I'd like us to work together and make a plan to keep you sober."

Nora nodded. "This is the consent form." Gabriella handed her the document and Nora signed it.

"And how's your youth work role? Are you enjoying it?" Gabriella asked.

Nora nodded. "I love it. It's so rewarding to help young kids break through the drug demon after what I've been through."

Half an hour later, they ended their session. "I'll talk to you next week and see how you went with Claudia. Take care of yourself." Nora left with hunched shoulders and Gabriella sat down and wrote her case notes. She believed Nora when she said she had stopped taking drugs, but something else was causing all these symptoms. Claudia might be able to convince her to have a physical check or uncover what was really going on with her.

***

Gabriella left her car in the driveway and lifted her face up to the warm rays of sunshine. She had recently moved into her period home in Spotswood, Victoria, and appreciated having her own space, especially in the spring season. The cottage-style home had latticework and timber posts at the entrance with several small trees in the front yard, a raised walkway to the house, and white, timber-framed windows. Unlocking the front door, she made her way down the narrow corridor, put away her handbag in her bedroom, and headed towards the bathroom. She splashed hot water over her face and wiped it with a towel. Her mind and body were physically and emotionally drained from the day, and she still wasn't sleeping well. The dark circles under her eyes culminated from multiple losses in her life, more recently the death of her friend, Erica, one year ago. It still felt like it had happened yesterday, but she had to move forward and embrace her new life.

She found who she was looking for in the rumpus room past her bedroom and bent down low to pat her grey-furred kitten, Angela, who was lying in her padded bed. Angela greeted Gabriella with a stretch and a yawn, then left her bed to rub against her legs. "You are so cute, Angie, and you are the one bright spot in my day." Having Angela around brought Gabriella comfort and settled her nerves after a challenging day, focusing her attention and giving her an outlet for her nurturing side. She had always wanted a pet, and when her neighbour asked if she wanted one of her cat's babies, Gabriella jumped at the chance.

She rose, holding the kitten in her arms, and pulled out a tin of food from the overhead cupboard. Taking her back to her area filled with soft toys, a water bowl, plastic plates, and a litter box in the corner of the room, she lay her down gently, gave her another pat and rubbed her nose. "How about some food, Angela?" The kitten purred while Gabriella emptied the tin's contents onto the plate and waited for her pet to devour it. Then, giving her one last pat, Gabriella beamed and left the kitten to enjoy its meal.

After dressing in sweatpants and a casual top, she took leftover chicken salad from the fridge, and while eating it straight from the bowl, her phone rang. She put down her fork and answered the call. It was her client, Nora, who didn't normally call her after hours.

"Hi Nora. Is everything okay?" She held her breath.

"All good. I wanted to let you know that I've made an appointment with Claudia for next week. Can we reschedule our appointment to a fortnight's time as I don't want to be too overwhelmed next week? I can only take one counselling session at a time."

"Of course we can, Nora. I'll make it for the same time and day the following week. Is there anything else I can do for you in the meantime?"

"No, thanks. I'm feeling positive about Claudia. She helped me out last time and I'm sure she can help me again."

"Not a problem. I look forward to seeing you in two weeks. You take care." Gabriella ended the call and thought about Claudia. The woman had appeared intimidating to her at first, but once she got to know her, Gabriella realised that she was soft and mushy on the inside. At first glance, people could misunderstand Claudia's behaviour as being aloof and self-entitled, but it was a mask to hide her true emotions. She was a big softy, and they had become friends.

Taking a deep breath, she was thankful that Nora was moving forward to a better life without drugs. She had come a long way. Hopefully, Claudia could help Nora with whatever was going on in her life.

Chapter Three

A DEATH

Three days later, Gabriella and her friend Joy made their way across the grey living room rug, between the blue three-seater couch and the coffee table. They admired the dust motes dancing in the sunlight, coming through the large window and dappling the stone fireplace as they headed out the glass sliding doors to the roofed decking in the backyard.

"Let's sit here," said Gabriella, pulling out one of the steel-backed chairs tucked underneath the round table.

Joy joined her at the table. Her blue eyes glowed in the sunlight and her blonde hair shone. Her slim and toned body was completely different from Gabriella's, and men usually stared at Joy due to her natural beauty. "It's a nice evening. How are you doing, girl?"

Gabriella looked at her strangely. "The same. Why do you ask?" She looked out over the freshly mown grass, recently cut by her stepfather, and the small vegetable garden. This place was Gabriella's safe haven whenever she had anxious thoughts.

"I ask because Jesse's still struggling with Erica's death a year ago. He still seems to think she didn't commit suicide, but there was no evidence to suggest that."

She nodded. "Your brother probably knew her better than either of us. But in those last couple of months before her death, she was acting strangely. She was down and agitated. It's sometimes hard to know what someone else is thinking."

"She was our friend. Why didn't we see it, Gabi? We could've helped if only she had come to us. Christ! I hate seeing him obsessed with this. He refuses to let her go, and I don't blame him. Suicide. Everyone feels guilty and wonders if they could've done anything differently."

When she'd first heard the news about Erica's death, Gabriella had been out for dinner with friends. She got the call from Joy's mother, who couldn't reach Joy at the time. It was heart-breaking to hear that Erica had died in a bathtub, an overdose of medications in her system. She'd also cut herself on her legs and arm and left a suicide note. All it mentioned was, "I can't cope with life anymore." She signed it at the bottom and forensics had proved that it was her own writing. How could she kill herself knowing those who loved her would suffer afterwards? "We have to accept that whatever was going on with her, it was probably bigger than what we could've handled. She needed professional help."

Joy's phone buzzed on the table. She answered the call. "Hey, Jesse. We were just talking about you, bro. What's up?" She waited. "Okay. I'll check it out now." She ended the call and scrolled through her phone, skimming through an article. Her face froze and she looked away while shaking her head.

"What's wrong?"

Joy handed her the phone. "A news story about a young girl who died last night. Tragic, but tell me what it reminds you of."

Gabriella swallowed and took the phone. She read through the article and gasped. "Oh my God!" The tightness in her chest. The palpitations as if her heart was about to explode. Her head spun as if she was about to faint, and her hands shook. She struggled to breathe as she put down the phone and bowed her head. Joy reached out to her and caressed her hand. She knew when to talk and when to remain quiet, and Gabriella was thankful to have such an understanding friend who understood anxiety. Once she recovered, Gabriella turned to her friend. "Joy, this can't be happening. It sounds exactly like Erica. This can't be a coincidence, can it?"

Joy flinched. "This is going to set Jesse back." Gabriella nodded in agreement. "She died in the bathtub, had medications in her system with cuts around her legs and arms, just like Erica. Not similar, Gabi, exactly the same."

Gabriella shrugged. "This can't be true. It cannot be true." A chill permeated her spine. "Do you think this girl's death...Erica's...I mean it didn't make sense that Erica would die by suicide. We both thought that and just accepted her death as the coroner called it. Jesse still doesn't think it was suicide. Could their deaths be related? Could he be right?"

Joy tucked her phone into her pocket. "I don't know, Gabi. Right now, I'm worried about how Jesse is handling this. Hold on." Joy walked inside the house and returned with a glass of water. "Here, drink this. It looks like you need it."

Gabriella picked up the glass and drank it down quickly. It soothed her parched throat, but dizziness hit her like a ton of bricks, and she didn't know what to do next.

"There are coincidences in this world, and it is possible that this girl's death is just that. I'll stay with you for a bit, and then I need to go check on my brother."

***

Jesse Warrier read the news article again, shaking his head. This poor girl had died in the bathtub and they ruled it suicide. He didn't believe in coincidences, and he wondered why it had similarities to the death of his late girlfriend, Erica. He never believed she had killed herself, but law enforcement thought otherwise. Here was the proof he needed. There had to be a connection.

He sat back against his brown chequered cotton sofa and peered through closed sliding doors. The view of the turf yard offered little solace, but Jesse appreciated the low maintenance of it. As the sunlight filtered through the glass, shadows danced on his shiny white living room flooring. Hoppers Crossing had been his home for the past year. The single-front home was modern with a simple landscape garden in the front and a decorative paved driveway that still looked new.

Jesse got up, needing a distraction from the news article. He was letting his imagination get away with him. This poor girl probably did die by suicide, and he was comparing it to Erica's death out of grief. What would he gain by doing that? The police had already ruled Erica's death as a suicide. It was a closed case. Only he continued to struggle to move forward over the past year. Neither his work as a physiotherapist nor his social activities with his friends could deter him from thinking about her death. He suffered from nightmares and was lucky if he got three hours of sleep every night.

Erica's death wasn't the only one he was grieving. Though his sister Mia's passing was thirteen years ago, Jesse remembered her death like it was yesterday, too.

Inside his garage, Jesse distracted himself, tinkering away with an old car, sanding down the body to restore it. He enjoyed buying old cars and restoring them to make them shiny and brand new. Restoration was a distraction from his troubles, and it could make a pretty penny once he sold them to interested buyers. His friend, Derek, had given him the idea.

Jesse's hands became sore after an hour, and he moved his shoulders up and back, rotating them to get the kinks out. No, he refused to think this girl had any link to Erica's death. They hadn't even known each other. He had to get on with his life and find some way to get over the tragedy. It was a closed case and he had to learn to accept it.

Chapter Four

POLICE STATEMENT

G abriella sat inside an interview room with Detective Senior Constables Marco Petrazini and Angelo Ricci, who she knew. Marco and Angelo were boyfriends of her friends Bella and Jamie. Both men were straight-shooters, but Angelo tended to be more impulsive and rougher in his approach than Marco.

"Why am I here, Marco? Is this about Erica? Have you had a new lead?"

Marco gave Angelo a dark look and hidden communication passed between them. He leaned forward opposite with a reassuring smile, playing with his stubble. His hazel eyes bore into her own. "I am sorry to tell you this, Gabriella." He cleared his throat and touched it. "The girl in the news who died in the bathtub.... she was a client of yours. Nora Trueman." The room spun around her as she bowed her head, letting the tears run down her cheeks. A coldness settled in her spine and she quivered. A warm hand rested on hers. "I am so sorry for your loss, Gabriella. So sorry."

Angelo intervened. "I know this is hard, but we do need to ask you a few questions. Will you be all right?"

Gabriella nodded, swallowing. She took a few deep breaths as Angelo held out a box of tissues. Taking one, Gabriella wiped away her tears, straightened in her seat, and steeled herself as best she could.

She had to be strong for Nora, and needed to know what had gone wrong with her.

Marco dove in. "Can you tell us about Nora's state of mind while you were counselling her? Even how she normally presented to you."

She stared into her hands and took a calming breath, fighting back more tears. "I'd been working with Nora for about three months, and she'd abstained from drugs in the last two months. More recently, she seemed to have issues with memory and concentration. She complained of not being able to sleep. I could see how fatigued she was and how she'd get dizzy at times. They appeared to be symptoms of anxiety, but I thought there was something triggering it. She was sorting out family issues and relationships." Exhaling, she continued. "She was taking care of herself with nutrition and exercise and had a generally positive attitude. But something was going on. Only she wouldn't admit to anything."

Angelo's strong, dark brown eyes looked straight through her as he threaded his hands through his short, jet-black hair. "Do you know if Nora had any physical conditions or medical problems?"

Gabriella shrugged. She clasped her hands and briefly closed her eyes, trying to shut out this nightmare of Nora's death. The poor girl had had her entire life ahead of her, and she would no longer be getting the help she needed. "I don't know. She refused to get a physical check-up when I suggested it. I thought with a medical check we could rule out those symptoms if they were physical. In the end, I suggested that she return to more intensive therapy with Claudia. She worked with Nora about a year ago."

Angelo knit his brows making his dimples prominent as he fixed his gaze on her.

"What about medications? Was she taking any?"

Gabriella shook her head. "No, she didn't need medication, in my opinion. But if she had needed it, she would most likely have refused any form of drug because of her history with addiction."

Angelo gave Marco a strange look as if they shared a secret message. "It sounds like you gave Nora a lot of options. Referring her back to Claudia was a good idea." Marco clasped his hands together. "Gabriella. Nora's toxicology report showed high levels of tranquilisers in her system. She also had cut marks on her wrist and leg. Did she have a history of self-harm or suicidal thoughts? Did she ever disclose that to you?"

Gabriella flinched. "No, she never cut herself and was not suicidal, detectives. This is ridiculous if you think she would do this to herself. She had plans to get better and start counselling with Claudia again, so why would she kill herself? Besides, her relationship with her mother was getting strong. She had no reason to do this." Gabriella found her heart palpitating, but she ignored it and waited for their responses.

"It's possible that Nora was too drowsy and disorganised to the point she could've intentionally or accidentally drowned in the bathtub," said Angelo. "She either got the tranquilisers illegally or..."

"Do you think someone could have given her the tranquilisers?" Gabriella said.

"We don't want to speculate at this stage," said Angelo.

Gabriella clenched her fists, wondering if she had killed herself or whether someone had intentionally hurt her. What if she'd missed the signs and Nora could no longer cope with the fight to stay off drugs?

Nora had appeared mentally stable. Sure, she had symptoms, but they were problems that could be fixed. The reality of losing a client this way was a heavy weight on Gabriella's shoulders, and she wondered if her manager would sack her after this. Maybe she would think she was incompetent and should have taken crisis action. She hadn't done a suicide risk assessment as there were no signs. In spite of depressive symptoms, they were manageable and treatable, so she refused to believe it was suicide.

Marco flicked a short, brown strand of hair out of his eyes. "Gabriella. I know this is hard to accept, but without hard evidence to suggest it wasn't a suicide, we can't rule it out. We'll keep digging and see what more we can discover. Octavia will be working with us on this case, but she won't be able to tell you much. Your friendship with her still means she has to abide by the rules with civilians."

Gabriella shrugged. "I understand that, Marco. It's fine."

Marco nodded. "Octavia will be doing what's known as a psychological autopsy which will assess Nora's mental state to determine suicidal ideation and self-harm. We'll look at her social media posts and medical records and interview all her friends and family. We'll get to the bottom of this. Don't worry. For now, you need to take care of yourself, especially after..."

Angelo continued. "You've experienced two deaths in the last year, Gabriella. Make sure you talk to the girls. Hang in there and we'll keep you updated. We might need to request your case notes, but we'll let you know if that's the case."

Gabriella responded to several more questions and breathed a sigh of relief when the interview was over. "Did you find a knife matching Nora's cuts on her wrist and leg?"

Marco nodded. "Yes, we found a knife underneath her in the tub." He cleared his throat. "One more thing before you go." Gabriella waited. "Did Nora ever complain of being harassed by someone at work or by old friends?"

"No, she didn't. As I said before, she was getting her life back on track. She was not depressed and wasn't taking any medications for mental health issues. I still don't believe she would do this." Gabriella didn't sound convincing as she had doubts. Some people could mask their pain well. Angelo and Marco stood up and showed her out towards the exit of the station. "Bye, detectives. Please keep me in the loop."

Angelo nodded. "We will. You take care of yourself."

Marco cleared his throat. "We'll talk soon. Bella will call you."

Gabriella walked out of the building with a prickle of fear running down her spine. Why did she get the feeling that Marco and Angelo didn't fully believe it was suicide?

Chapter Five

FRIENDSHIPS

One week later, Gabriella sat on a small wooden chair at a large table with her friends, Joy, Bella, Liz, Jamie, Octavia, and Claudia. She stared outside the large rectangular windows of the Docklands Cafe, watching passersby. The smells of fresh coffee beans, hot pastries, cinnamon, mixed spice, and nuts filled her nostrils and made her peckish for a sweet dessert. The open counter displayed assorted pastries and various styles of coffee. The women ordered their drinks and pastries.

Gabriella looked over at her friends. Bella, Liz, and Jamie had their own trauma-filled pasts. Octavia, she didn't know much about, having met her through Claudia. On a professional level, she had been impressed with Claudia's clinical skills and had got to know her well on a personal level too.

"A penny for your thoughts, girl," said Joy.

Gabriella turned to her high school friend. "I'm thinking how you guys are great and always help each other out."

Bella lay a hand on hers with a reassuring smile. "We're here for you, Gabriella. Day and night. But whatever is going on in that head of yours, you are not alone. Asking for help is an actual strength." Bella flicked back her shoulder-length brown hair and fixed her green almond-shaped eyes on Gabriella.

"Yes, and know that, whatever the police find out about your client, we've got your back." Liz was the tallest of the women. She had glowing jet-black hair and long, dainty fingers. Gabriella admired Liz who served as her mentor and was a passionate social worker.

"Thanks, Liz. You've always been there for me, but it's going to be hard accepting what happened."

Jamie leaned forward with a frown. "Sometimes going with your intuition is the right thing. Angelo and Marco know what they are doing. They'll get to the truth." Barely a year ago, Jamie had faced a traumatic trial within her own family, but she had survived and now had the love of a good man in Angelo.

"I'll be able to give you general information about my assessments, Gabriella, but not anything that'll compromise the investigation. We will get to the truth." Octavia drew a hand through her long, auburn highlighted brown hair. The mole on her right upper lip and deep green eyes enhanced her beauty. Gabriella often wondered about the burn scars on her hands. Octavia unconsciously covered her hands to hide them.

Claudia toyed with her fingers as if pondering. Claudia's strawberry-blonde hair was tied up in a bun, and she was petite with grey eyes. Her expression turned serious and she looked downcast. "I was looking forward to working with Nora again and couldn't believe what I heard. I know I'll be interviewed next, given my history in working with Nora."

Gabriella shook her head. "I cannot get my head around this. What did I miss?"

Claudia cleared her throat. "Nothing. You did right by Nora. Let the police investigate. We can only tell them what we know and leave the detectives to do their job. I'm certain they'll find the answers soon."

The waiter interrupted, handing coffees to each of them, and a tray of pastries. The women sipped their drinks and dug into their pastries in comfortable silence.

Bella broke the quiet. "How's your brother, Jesse, doing?"

Joy shrugged. "Not too good. He's still hung up on Erica. He cannot accept her suicide, especially with how similar Nora's death was. He's thinking of getting in touch with the police to get them to reopen Erica's case."

Bella nodded. "I know we spoke about this a year ago, but does Jesse have evidence that Erica's death wasn't a suicide?"

Joy's eyes turned a shade darker. "No, he doesn't, but he believes it's the detectives' job to find the evidence if they look hard enough. I know different detectives were assigned to the case back then, but I'm sure they did everything they could."

Jamie squared her shoulders. "Angelo will not rest until he solves Nora's death, Gabriella. He will do a thorough investigation."

Octavia sighed. "It is strange how similar Erica and Nora's deaths are, but we cannot assume anything until we have all the facts."

Bella faced Octavia. "Facts or not, intuition plays a big role in this too. It can lead to finding new evidence, given that a murder can be staged as a suicide."

Octavia nodded. "I hear you, Bella, and I agree with you, but we need evidence."

Claudia touched Bella on the shoulder. "You are an amazing psychologist, Bella, and if only I possessed one-tenth of that strong intuition of yours, especially with what you went through with Marco."

Bella chuckled. "Are you getting soft on me, Claudia?"

"I think she wants to apologise again for how she treated you," said Liz.

Claudia grinned. "I'm glad it all worked out in the end. You and Marco had a close call with that psychopath."

Bella stared at Claudia. Due to a shared harrowing experience, the two women had grown from rivals to friends over the past year. "Thanks, Claudia. I'm glad we both survived. You were a great help then."

Liz put her hands together. "Listen, lovely ladies. How about we change the subject and talk about more positive things like Bella's wedding in the next couple of weeks. I am so excited you're finally going to marry your hunky detective."

Bella's eyes glittered and her cheeks flushed. "I cannot wait, Liz. Fiji here we come."

Gabriella listened as the girls continued their banter and discussions around Bella and Marco's wedding. Anything to take her mind off her troubles.

Chapter Six

A PAST CASE

Jesse walked towards the police station, fixing his gaze on the grey building with its blue and white square patterns above the glass entrance doors. Low brush grew to the side of the doors, and a multitude of square windows clustered above a smaller roof. The signage and patrol car made it obvious it was a police station.

He looked at his friend, Derek, whose brown eyes bore into his own. Derek had dark hair and a short, solid build, and worked out at the same gym as Jesse. "Are you ready to go in and see what we can do?"

Derek nodded. "Sure, man, but...I don't know. Maybe it's best if you leave the past in the past. What can you gain from this?"

Jesse's chest tightened. He thought he'd at least have the support of his friend. "Are you kidding me, Derek? With this new case, they might see there's a connection. I have to at least try to get them to reopen Erica's case."

Derek scoffed. "Whatever. We're here so we might as well go in."

What was his friend's problem? Derek had acted strangely when Erica died too, as if he believed she could've committed suicide. He had known her well enough through Jesse. Surely, he didn't believe her death had been due to suicide?

The sun scorched his scalp as they stood in front of the building before ambling across the road and through the doors. They approached the front counter and an elderly police officer peered in their direction. "Can I help you young gentlemen?"

Jesse cleared his throat and swallowed while tightening his fists on either side of his body. Derek looked agitated, his feet shuffling on the floor.

"Hi, I'd like to see Detective James or Detective Mitch. They worked on my girlfriend's case a year ago. Her name was Erica Winslet. Are they available?"

The officer stood with upright, fixing his gaze on them curiously. "No, they're on a case at the moment. Detective Senior Constable Petrazini is here for the next half an hour. Can he be of service?"

Jesse knew of Marco Petrazini, as he was Joy's friend's boyfriend. He had been invited to his wedding by Marco's girlfriend, Bella. "Sure, why not? The name's Jesse Warrier."

"Take a seat and he'll be with you shortly."

"Thanks." Jesse saw the line getting long, and joined his friend on one of the chairs. His hands fidgeted and his mind raced. What if Derek was right and this was a waste of time? What if they didn't have any new evidence?

His eyes roamed the beige interior as they sat in hard-backed chairs, watching people coming in and out of offices and cubicles. Derek's eyes glassed over, seemingly lost in his own world, and the policeman at reception kept glancing their way. Did he know something about Erica's case?

Jesse was jolted out of his thoughts a few minutes later when Marco called his name.

"Come on through to an interview room." He walked along matte floorboards down a narrow corridor, passing by cubicles which were blocked by tall white cupboards, and led them through to another narrow hallway to a small office. The walls were creme-coloured and patched with dirty smears. They seated themselves while Marco sat opposite with his eyes unreadable.

He turned to his companion. "This is my friend, Derek, detective."

Marco nodded. "Good to meet you, Derek." He faced Jesse. "How can I help?"

Jesse's hands sweated and his throat dried up, but he forged ahead. "My girlfriend, Erica, died a year ago and it was ruled suicide." He cleared his mind. "I'd like the police to reopen her case as I don't believe she killed herself."

Marco stared at him, squinted briefly at Derek, and then refocused on Jesse. "Mr Warrier. I understand how hard it is for any family member to hear about a suicide. Not only are you dealing with grief but also the guilt over the cause of death. It is hard to accept for anyone, and it's only natural to feel that way. Have you had counselling?"

Jesse clenched his jaw. He wasn't here for a psychology course or counselling, so where did he get off putting him down this way? "Detective, I do not need counselling. I am strong and can take care of myself. But I feel there's been a miscarriage of justice here. I won't rest until the police prove that she didn't kill herself."

Derek nudged Jesse. "Listen, man. Why don't we leave? We're wasting his time." Jesse glared at his friend and waited for Marco's response.

Marco looked past him briefly. "Why are you coming back now? What's triggered this decision of yours after one year?"

Jesse leaned back in his seat. "The young girl who was recently on the news. She died in the same way as Erica, and I don't believe in coincidences, detective."

Marco nodded as if understanding. "I see." He fixed his gaze on them both. "We need to look at the facts, Mr Warrier, and not your gut instinct. As much as I'd like to help,

without new information or leads, we cannot reopen the case. Do you have any new evidence which could prove foul play?"

Jesse swallowed. "No, I don't, but with this current case about that young girl, shouldn't that prove a pattern here?"

Marco cleared his throat. "We're investigating all possible leads and doing our job to determine the cause of death. At this stage, we haven't ruled anything out, but please let us do our job, Mr Warrier. If we do come across anything pertinent to your late girlfriend's case, I can inform you. If that is the case, we'll be in touch."

"I'm sure they're two random and separate cases, Jesse," said Derek.

Jesse ignored his friend. "Can I leave you my details?"

He shook his head. "No need. I understand you're Joy's brother. She's friends with my fiancé. Bella explained how she invited you to the wedding, and I look forward to seeing you there. But know this, there are certain pieces of information I cannot divulge either at work or outside work. You're a civilian and anything we tell you can compromise our investigation, so please do not do anything to blur the lines here."

Jesse nodded. "I understand, detective."

Marco stood up. "I'll walk you both out."

As they were walking towards the exit, Derek spoke out. "We are sorry to trouble you, detective. "

"Not a problem, young man. You two take care and stay out of trouble." He walked away, and Jesse strode ahead of his friend towards his car. He contained his angry thoughts and slammed the driver's door.

"I'm sorry, man, but this was a complete waste of time. What did you think would happen? That they'd miraculously work on the case and assume it's foul play without any hard evidence. You know how this works, so let it go and move on with your life."

Jesse hunched over the steering wheel and took calming breaths. "You bastard. I thought I had your support, but you don't give a crap about Erica, do you? She deserves justice, and I know in my heart she didn't commit suicide. She didn't take antidepressants or antianxiety medications, and she would never cut herself. She had no mental health issues so why would she kill herself? Why?"

Derek winced. "How the hell should I know? You were the one who supposedly knew her the best. You were together for five damn years."

Jesse shook his head, fighting the need to punch his friend's lights out. He was tight with Derek, but ever since Erica died Derek had acted strangely, and they'd become more distant. So long as they didn't talk about Erica their friendship was intact, but as soon as her name came up, he clammed up. He needed distance from his friend. "I think we should take a break from hanging out. I don't want to do or say anything which will hurt our friendship." Derek stayed quiet as he turned on the motor and sped off.

Chapter Seven

JOGGING INJURY

Gabriella inserted her earphones and listened to the jazz-fusion sounds as she jogged around the deserted streets of Spotswood and followed the path to the park nearby. She passed through the spacious playground, flowing and towering trees, a sports area filled with soccer players, and other joggers in her path. The music gave her a spring in her step and she increased her pace, savouring the warm sunlight heating up her cheeks.

She hadn't been sleeping lately due to thinking about Nora and Erica, and wondered if it was a mere coincidence the two died in similar ways or if something else was going on. Would the police get any leads and interview her again for either death?

Footsteps behind her prompted her to look over her shoulder as she jogged along the grass in the park. As she turned the jogger changed course and ran towards the street. He wore dark glasses, a beanie covering part of his face, and a raincoat. She stopped for a minute to catch her breath and placed her hands across her waist, panting. Once she was re-energised, she broke into a slow jog and picked up her pace again as she ran back to the streets leading her home. Again, she'd heard footsteps behind her, and sure enough, the same jogger was running behind her. She couldn't see his face properly because of his beanie and glasses.

She ran faster, but the man was catching up to her. It felt as if he was chasing her, but surely he had the right to jog freely in the area. Should she stop or keep going? Testing him out, she took an unexpected path down a dirt track leading to bushes, and the man changed course too. He was following her. No, she was safer to run as fast as her body could muster, but when she turned, her body flew into a huge boulder, and she fell on the ground, twisting her right ankle. "Oh, no!" She moaned in pain as her body lay at an awkward angle until she shifted her right leg out and massaged it. The pain was unbearable as she attempted to stand but her leg wouldn't budge. Her back ached and her mind went fuzzy. She looked behind her, but the man had gone.

Retrieving her phone from her sports jacket pocket, she called her friend, Joy. "Hey, Joy. Can you come pick me up? I've sprained my ankle and I can't walk on it."

"Oh, Gabi. Are you sure it's just a sprain?"

"I think so. It's not that serious, but I won't be able to walk and there's no-one around here now."

"I'm with Jesse and still in my pyjamas, but he's free and ready to pick you up. You know, he's a physiotherapist, so he'll know what to do to make it heal quicker. Tell me where you are."

Oh, great. Now her friend's brother had to see her humiliation and stupidity, but what choice did she have? She gave her the address. "Fine. Thanks, Joy." She ended the call and breathed through the pain while waiting. She massaged her ankle, but the pain was intolerable.

Gabriella thought about Jesse who she barely knew. He was attractive enough but each time she'd seen him at Joy's house, he'd been with Erica and had only had eyes for her mostly. They only ever exchanged polite greetings and nothing more. She remembered as a young teenager when she'd had a big crush on Jesse, but he had always had girlfriends and was busy living life. He had barely noticed her then and was too busy courting his own ladies. He had always been her best friend's brother, with nothing more on his part. She was over him now and that was a long time ago.

Gabriella scrolled through her phone, checked her social media pages and emails and took deep breaths to avoid the pain. A passerby stopped to ask her if she needed help, but she explained she was waiting for someone to pick her up. If only she'd seen her earlier, she wouldn't have had to ring Joy. She became more anxious each time someone stared or offered help. *Hurry up, Jesse!*

Twenty minutes later, a familiar figure approached. "Gabriella. Are you okay? You don't look too good."

She stared at Jesse who wore tight-fitted jeans and a baggy t-shirt. "I think I sprained my ankle. I tripped over the boulder over there and twisted it."

He nodded and moved closer to her ankle, feeling around it. "Is that sore here?"

"It is painful, and I can't walk on it." As he touched her upper leg, she ignored a tingly sensation in her stomach. She remembered Joy telling her he worked out, and it showed in his ripped muscles."

"It does look like a sprain, which is lucky for you because a fracture would mean I'd need to take you to the hospital." He placed his arm around her back and lifted her up slowly. "Lean on me and we'll walk to my car. It's not too far from here."

Gabriella nodded. "I'm sure I can manage." How could she not notice his square jaw and how his blonde highlights shone in the sun? It was cut short and revealed his handsome, chiselled face and full lips. She leaned most of her weight on Jesse and fought back the pain with each step.

"How did this happen exactly? I mean, how did you miss the boulder? It's pretty obvious." Jesse's eyes lingered as she turned to face him while they walked.

Gabriella shrugged, not wanting to explain her paranoia about the man jogging behind her. "I was distracted, thinking about something and didn't see it. But I appreciate you taking the time to get me. I didn't want to call an ambulance and Joy's one of my best friends. And I forgot you were a physiotherapist." Why was she rambling?

His eyes glistened as he held her snugly with his strong arms. "It is no problem, Gabriella. Any friend of Joy's is a friend of mine. I'm happy to help a damsel in distress." Oh, please! She was anything but. "I'll take you home and get you settled."

Gabriella ignored her fragility and focused on being pampered by a handsome man who she was sure had always seen her as a little sister.

Chapter Eight

TENDER LOVING CARE

J esse drove onto the paved driveway of Gabriella's weatherboard house, his eyes lingering

over the drab front garden which featured loose dirt and wood shavings, with two small wilting trees and a taller one in the middle. If he lived here, he would've planted colourful flowers and new plants which were low enough not to block the front window. Was he distracting his mind from the sensual experience of having her arm around him? How did he not notice Gabriella's soulful, dark brown eyes and her feminine curves before? He'd never actually had a proper conversation with her over the years she'd been friends with Joy. He was too busy socialising, going out with other girls before Erica, and dating Erica for five years. He'd been twenty-one years old when he first started dating Erica until her death a year ago, but he'd had his fair share of fun before committing to the five-year relationship. He had loved her and hoped that they could've been married. It was a pipedream until that fateful day.

Gabriella unlocked her front door as she leaned on his body. He helped her along the small foyer leading to the living room. A coffee table on a square rug could be a tripping hazard if she wasn't careful. A blue sofa matched the decor, and sunlight streamed through an open window. He spotted a romance novel on the table, and her slippers beside the sofa.

Jesse eased her onto the sofa and lifted up her legs. "It's important that you rest your ankle and not put any weight on it for a few days. I suggest you either get a crutch or take time off work, so you give it time to heal. Limit the time you need to walk on it at least." He walked to the fridge and found an icepack, then wrapped it around a tea towel. Placing it over her ankle, he pressed gently onto the pain. "Let's leave this on for twenty minutes then I'll get you a bandage. Do you have one in the bathroom?"

Gabriella nodded. "In the middle cupboard, you'll find something, but it might be a bit ratty. It's down the corridor on your left." He strolled towards the bathroom and rummaged through the cupboard. He was curious and came across a bottle of anti-anxiety medication on the counter. He would never have figured Gabriella to have anxiety. She'd always appeared confident. Not that he knew her well. Erica had normally socialised with Joy and Gabriella without him, and he hadn't wanted to tag along on their usual girls' nights out. But was that the real reason or had he found Gabriella attractive and wanted to keep his distance? *Crazy!* Grief could make you have such thoughts. He missed Erica and vowed to get justice for her.

Jesse returned with a bandage and checked his watch. "It's only been five minutes, so we'll wait until it's time to put the bandage on." The awkward silence was unnerving, and he wondered what she was thinking.

"Help yourself to a drink. I would get it myself but I'm otherwise indisposed." She chuckled, and he loved how her eyes lit up when she smiled. He looked away and gave her a reassuring smile. *Say something, man!* Why was he nervous?

"I'm good, thanks." He cleared his throat. "So, you like jogging? How often do you go?" His eyes landed on her lips as she bit the bottom one.

She knit her brows. "Sundays and a few times during the week, but sometimes less, depending on my work schedule or social life. Do you exercise?"

"Derek and I go to the gym a few nights a week, depending on our schedules too. I've noticed you like reading. Romance, ha?"

Gabriella blushed. Was she embarrassed to be reading romance? "I love reading as it stops me from thinking about the past, you know. It's an escape, but I like thrillers and psychological suspense too."

He leaned forward, aromas of lavender and flowers coming from her. He imagined only smelling sweat, but it was as if she hadn't even jogged such a long way. "I like reading thrillers too, but I don't always get the time with my work, going to the gym, and restoring old cars. That's a passion of mine."

Gabriella's eyes darkened. "My father, before everything changed, loved restoring old cars too. He was a mechanic." She averted her eyes, and he wondered why it made her withdraw all of a sudden. *Oh, Christ!* He remembered Joy telling him how her dad had been in prison and was violent, but he hadn't been interested in the details back then. His life had been too busy, and it had revolved around Erica. Why was he suddenly interested in her life now? He wasn't but he had to make conversation.

"I am sorry about your father. Joy told me some of the story." She remained quiet, and he unrolled the bandage and gently wrapped it around her foot and ankle. Gabriella flinched, her eyes looking the other way as if she wanted to hide her pain. "Is it too tight?"

Gabriella stared at his tanned hands, and her cheeks flushed again. Her skin was soft, but he couldn't think about that as he had a job to do. "No, it's good. Thanks for taking the time to help. You were probably busy."

He laughed. "I didn't have anything else to do. I was lazing on the couch with Joy, who was still in her pyjamas. We were watching a breakfast TV show, so I didn't miss anything." He swallowed. "Later tonight, elevate your foot, and as I said, try not to walk on it for a while. I'll get Joy to come over and she can cook you dinner." He could have offered to cook her dinner, but he didn't want to overstay his welcome.

"Thanks, Jesse. That would be great if she could come over."

Jesse turned when a grey kitten made its way towards Gabriella. As she spread out her arms, he picked it up and handed it to her. She wrapped her arms tightly around it. "Who's this? It looks as if she wants you." Her eyes lit up as her pet shifted a little in her arms.

"This is Angela, my pride and joy. She understands me, and I love her like my own child. My neighbour gave her to me, and she's my rock." She smiled at him. "Would you mind checking her water and food in her room? It's over there, past my bedroom."

Jesse's heart warmed. "Of course not." He picked up the kitten, walked over to the room, and took care of her needs. He could see how much the kitten meant to Gabriella. He soon returned to the living room, satisfied when the kitten was drinking the water and eating the food. "I'll come by tomorrow night and check on your ankle again." Their eyes lingered before he steeled himself and rose from the couch. "Take care of yourself, and I'll see you tomorrow. Is there anything you need? Groceries, toiletries. Anything?" She shook her head.

He gave her a reassuring smile and walked out the door with hesitation.

Chapter Nine

IN A NEW LIGHT: 18 YEARS EARLIER

"Hey, sweetie. Why don't you go get mummy a beer? I could really use one."

The young boy wandered over to the fridge, picked out a bottle, and handed it to his mother. She scoffed. "How am I supposed to drink it from the bottle? Put it in a damn glass." She shook her head as he took back the bottle. "God, I raised a dummy. You really don't know anything, do you?" She smoked marijuana, the fumes surrounding the living room.

The boy coughed and fought back tears. "Sorry, Mummy. I'll get a glass for you. "He returned with a glass of beer, but he filled it too high and some of the liquid fell on the tatty carpet. In one fell swoop, she slapped him hard across the face. He started crying and bowed his head, turning away from her after putting the glass in her hands.

"Can't you do anything right? What is wrong with you? I swear, sometimes, I feel like selling you on the dark web. You're that stupid. But I guess if I was rich, someone might take you off my hands. Now get the hell out of my sight!"

The boy nodded and rushed to his room. A wave of fury washed over him, and he vowed that one day he would be in control, and not his mother.

***

The next evening, Gabriella hobbled to the front door and welcomed Joy into her house. She put her arm around Gabriella and walked her back to the couch while shaking her head. The TV blared in the background.

"Damn, girl. I didn't think you were this bad." Joy carried a bag of food. "You look like you're in so much pain." Gabriella nodded as she elevated her leg and fought back the pain. "Sorry I couldn't make it last night, but you did order take-out, didn't you?"

"I did. It's all good. What did you bring? It smells delicious."

"I made lasagna for us to eat tonight as you shouldn't be doing much of anything until your ankle's healed. I take it you called in sick for the next few days?"

Gabriella nodded. "I've taken the rest of this week off. My manager wanted me to take time off after what happened to my client anyway, but I told her about my ankle, too. She thinks I should get counselling to deal with Nora, but I told her I was managing."

Joy scooted closer to her friend. "It's worth considering, given how horrible it is to lose a client like that. You've got nothing at all to lose, Gabi."

"I've had counselling before and it doesn't work for me. I have my own ways to work through anxiety. I will get through this in my own time, Joy."

"Fair enough, girl. I'm going to ice that ankle, so stay put and do not move." Joy ambled to the fridge, picked up an ice pack, wrapped it in a thin tea towel, and undid the bandage. She placed the ice over the sprain and Gabriella winced from the cold. Her ankle was much better today, and she had managed to sleep on the couch last night to limit her walking. Should she have got a crutch? No, her sprain would heal soon.

Joy rested back on the couch. "Any more news about your client?"

Her chest tightened and she took deep breaths. "No, nothing since my interview at the police station. I imagine they're still gathering evidence and talking to her family and friends. I wish I knew where they were at, Joy. She didn't deserve to die at such a young age. I still don't believe she could kill herself like that."

Joy wrapped her arms around her. "I know it's hard, and you need to stay strong. Think about yourself and let the police do their job." Gabriella didn't know what she'd do without Joy and her other friends, and she was thankful for them each day.

A knock on the door broke her reverie but as she moved herself up, Joy pushed her back down. "I've got this, girl. No weight on your foot, okay?"

Joy returned with Jesse by her side. Gabriela's stomach flipped as her eyes took in his taut arms and confident stance. He wore a fitted white t-shirt and black jeans. She tried not to stare at the few strands of chest hair showing though his open neckline as his eyes brushed her from head to toe. Joy watched her brother and lifted an eyebrow in Gabriella's direction. He carried a pair of crutches in his hand.

"Hi, Gabriella. I'm just here to check on your ankle. How is it today?"

Gabriella couldn't help blushing at his intense gaze. "Much better. Joy iced it five minutes ago, and it's feeling better than yesterday."

He sat down on the sofa next to her and lifted up the ice pack. "I'll have a feel and see if the bruising has gone down." His fingers trailed her ankle and pushed around it. Gabriella took deep breaths to ignore her pain, but her heart fluttered at the way his fingers showed tenderness and care. "It looks a bit better than yesterday, but I want you to use these crutches in the meantime, so you're not forced to bear weight on it. At least you'll be able to get around in the meantime. It'll heal quicker if you don't put any strain on it."

Joy intervened. "How did you fall anyway?"

Gabriella frowned, not wanting to mention her paranoia about the man behind her. "I got distracted and didn't see a huge boulder in the park."

"Distracted how?"

Gabriella averted her eyes. "I had other things on my mind and didn't look where I was going and twisted my ankle. It can happen to anyone."

Joy watched her with curiosity. "I guess it can."

A commercial filled the TV screen of a young female actor looking downcast. She spoke to an older lady, and the narrator said, "If ever you're experiencing symptoms of depression or anxiety, seek out your doctor or psychologist for service support referrals. A phone call can save your life."

The awkward silence made them stare at the screen long after it ended, and Gabriella broke the tension. "How about we put the bandage back on."

Jesse's eyes turned a shade darker as he nodded. "Of course."

Joy lightened the mood as she usually did. "Jesse, my brother. You can have lasagna with us for dinner, and I'm not taking no for an answer." Gabriella was thankful to Joy for inviting her brother over for dinner as she didn't have the courage to do it herself. Surely it was a good thing to get to know Jesse as her best friend's brother? Nothing more to it.

"Sure, I'd love to pick on how bad your lasagna is." Joy hit him across the arm. He put up his hands in surrender, turning to Gabriella. "Only kidding. Her lasagna is the best."

Gabriella forgot about the commercial and decided to enjoy good company instead. She refused to let her client or the commercial bring her down. After what she'd been through with her family, she could deal with anything.

Chapter Ten

A WEDDING

Over a week later, Jesse shouted instructions to Gabriella. "Move your ankle up and down." Gabriella obeyed. "That's it. Nice and slow. Now up and out. Do it a few times." He nodded. "Great. Now rotate your ankle. I want nice, big circles." Gabriella followed his instructions easily.

"It's healed, Jesse. I don't know why I need to keep doing these exercises, especially today of all days. Aren't you going to Bella and Marco's wedding this morning?"

He nodded. "Sure, but we still have a few hours. Plenty of time." He moved further away from her. "The goal of these exercises is to strengthen your ankle. If we make it stronger, you're less vulnerable and it puts you at a lower risk of re-injury. But it looks as though you can walk on it now. It's been a week and your sprain wasn't too severe." He rose from the couch. "How are you getting to the wedding?"

"I figured I'll drive as I don't drink much. Joy, Liz, and Jamie are tagging along with me. What about you?" Should she invite him to go with her to the wedding? She did have room for one more in her car.

"I'll find my way there. I do drive, you know." Before he turned away, he faced her. "Joy mentioned it was your client who died recently. I wanted to say how sorry I am. It must've been hard for you to accept. I read the article but had no idea you worked with her. Do the police have any leads?"

"Not that I know of."

He grinned, but it didn't reach his eyes. He was floundering as if he wanted to say something. "I'll see you at the church later." He walked off before she could reply, and she wondered why her home seemed suddenly empty.

***

Gabriella sat in the same row as Joy, Jesse, Octavia, and Claudia while the priest recited his sermon about the lifetime together and joys of marriage. Marco and Bella sat in their respective seats after reciting their vows to one another. Liz and Jamie both stood in as Maids of Honour in the front pew, given that Bella couldn't decide between either of them. The groomsmen consisted of Marco's two friends. With love in Marcos's eyes, he said, "I, Marco, take you, Bella, to be my wife, to have and to hold from this day forward, for better, for worse, for richer, for poorer, in sickness and in health, to love and to cherish, until death do us part. This is my solemn vow." Bella repeated the vows then ended with. "I love you so much."

Marco leaned in. "I love you more, beautiful."

Gabriella's heart warmed. She only wished she'd find a love as beautiful and deep as Marco and Bella.

Jesse was a few seats away from her and watched her with a brief smile. He faced the front, but she could've sworn she'd seen a flicker of interest in his eyes, or was it wishful thinking? No, after what she'd been through with her ex-boyfriend, she couldn't risk her heart again like that. It wasn't worth it when he would most likely hurt her. She could only protect her heart and never risk loving anyone again, at least in the short-term.

Bella's wedding dress had thin straps and was fitted from chest to the knee, where it flared out with tulle, and it showed a little cleavage. Lacework draped over the fitted part of the dress, sequins lined the back, and a tiara with a long veil perched on her head. She looked beautiful and sensual, and her cheeks glowed with adoration for Marco. He stared at her with as much yearning and longing, making them a gorgeous couple.

Holding the ring in his hand, Marco placed the wedding ring on Bella's finger. "Receive this ring as a sign of my love and fidelity. In the name of the Father, and of the Son, and of the Holy Spirit."

Bella did the same with the ring. "Receive this ring as a sign of my love and fidelity. In the name of the Father, and of the Son, and of the Holy Spirit."

Their wide smiles were infectious as the priest uttered his final blessing then faced the couple whose eyes were fixed on one another. "You may now kiss the bride." The guests clapped and roared with laughter and applause when Bella and Marco kissed.

The ceremony ended with Marco and Bella walking out holding hands and smiling, and greeting everyone as they reached the exit. Once the church was clear of guests, Gabriella reached Bella and wrapped her arms around her. "Congratulations, Bella. You look absolutely radiant."

Bella's eyes shone and her cheeks glowed. "Thanks, Gabriella. I am so happy. I cannot even put it into words."

"You deserve it," said Gabriella who envied her in that moment. She moved aside to let Joy, Jamie, Liz, Octavia, and Claudia greet her. She moved over to wish Marco well, wrapping her arms around him. "Congratulations. You're a lucky man."

Marco chuckled. "Thanks, Gabriella. She does look gorgeous, doesn't she?"

"Of course she does, and she is so happy, I can feel it a mile away. Treat her well."

Marco nodded. "Listen, Octavia will be in touch with you soon. I'll be gone for a couple of weeks, but Angelo and a few others might speak to you too. As soon as we get back from our honeymoon, I'll be investigating the case. Hang in there."

Gabriella was pushed to the side when friends of Marco shoved him on the arm, congratulating him and sharing banter. She joined Liz and Jamie who were talking to Camilla and her six-year-old daughter, Mariana. Camilla was Liz's boyfriend's sister. She had had issues with drugs but had been clean for the past year.

Camilla wrapped her arms around herself as she looked up at her. "Hi, Gabriella. I didn't get a chance to talk to you earlier. I am so happy for Bella and Marco. It was a beautiful ceremony."

Gabriella gave her a wide smile. "The best, Camilla. You look great." She bent down low and wrapped her arms around Mariana. "Hello, sweetie. Are you enjoying yourself?"

She pursed her lips. "Don't know. Too many people here, Gabi."

She nodded as she touched a strand of the child's hair. "I know, but I do see a few other children here, so later you can play with them when the real party starts."

Liz touched her on the shoulder. "I noticed Jesse staring at you with interest?"

Jamie intervened, shaking her head. "Oh, leave the girl alone, Liz." She turned to her boyfriend, Angelo, who waved her over. "Angelo's calling my name, ladies. I will see you at the park shortly."

"Where's Mathew?" Gabriella asked.

Liz cleared her throat. "He's on a shift but he'll be free later tonight."

Joy and Jesse soon joined them, and Gabriella's skin tingled with goosebumps. Jesse wore tight black pants and a crisp white shirt that displayed his pecs and masculinity. His woody cologne sent her mind racing, too, as his eyes flicked over her from head to toe as if he was undressing her. *Hell!* She was so aroused she could sense her face heating up exponentially.

Joy noticed the exchange, her eyes unreadable. She introduced Jesse to Camilla and Mariana who were whispering to each other. "Let's head off to the park, Gabi." She looked at Jesse. "We'll meet you there, bro."

Jesse leaned forward, grazing Gabriella's bare arm as she fought back yearning thoughts. "I have a client I need to see, but I'll see you at the reception later." He walked off, and Jamie and Gabriella made their way to their cars and said goodbye to Camilla and Mariana. She passed by Octavia and Claudia, waving to them as they left the church grounds.

As she entered her car with Joy in the passenger seat, Gabriella noticed something about her car. It was a combined smell of lavender and citrus. "I can smell something in here, but it's not your perfume, is it?"

Joy shook her head as she fitted her seatbelt around her. "I am wearing musk perfume, but you're right. I can smell a fruity scent."

Gabriella turned on the motor and drove towards the park. "I guess the smell could be anything."

She realised that when they first drove to the church, she hadn't smelled anything apart from their own perfumes. *Strange!*

Chapter Eleven

A DANCE

Gabriella walked into the reception centre to her allocated seat with Joy and Jesse, admiring the silk drapes hanging loosely to the ground. Candelabras and orchids decorated each table, and cotton floral padded chairs surrounded the room. The bride's table featured flowing orchids and several black and white strips of fabric that flowed to the floor. The large dance space was opposite the bridal table, and a band was arranging their musical equipment while waiters bustled about with baskets of bread to be placed on the tables.

When the music started playing she sat back in her seat next to Joy, and focused on the slow jazz sounds, smelling herbs and spices that made her salivate. She turned around and spotted Angelo, Matthew, Camilla, and Mariana heading towards their table. Greeting the guests, she shifted in her seat as Jesse sat two seats away. Octavia and Claudia sat opposite her and beamed her way while Marco's mother and aunt strolled towards a nearby table.

New music played, and the Master of Ceremony stood near the microphone on stage and introduced the bridal party a half-hour later. When it came time for the bride and groom to dance to the bridal waltz, Jesse's eyes lingered on hers, and her heart fluttered as she watched the sensuality of their movements, wondering if she could ever have such lasting love. Poor Marco and Bella had endured their own trauma through a stalker and serial killer a couple of years back, both having been close to death. But that experience had only made their love stronger.

Waiters brought over trays of antipasto. Gabriella picked at her slices of meat, olives, and sundried tomatoes and put them on a piece of bread. Their entree consisted of prawns and avocado, and jugs of soft drinks, juice, and water were placed on the table.

Joy's eyes roamed. "I wonder who'll be the next person to get married. It definitely won't be me."

Camilla clasped her hands together while chewing on a piece of cheese. "It has to be Matthew and Liz, don't you think, Matthew?"

He turned a strong shade of red in the face. "Do not put me on the spot. If Liz was here right now, she'd curse you." He slapped Angelo on the shoulder. "It is most likely Jamie and Angelo next."

Angelo chuckled. "I'd marry that beautiful woman in a heartbeat, but she is not ready, given what she's been through. I'll let her take the lead on that one. What about the younger ones here? It could very well be them."

Joy shoved an olive in her mouth then took out the pit, placing it into a small bowl. "It could be Gabriella."

Gabriella blushed. She could kill Joy right now. "Not me. Definitely not me. Can we change the subject, please?" She looked over at Jesse who was staring into his plate, all quiet and withdrawn. She wondered if he was thinking about Erica as they would've been planning their wedding by now. She wanted to take his pain away, as she knew exactly what it was like to lose someone you loved. She had loved Nick and he had betrayed her as her father had.

"I am married to my job," said Claudia.

Octavia lifted up her hands as if surrendering. "Do not look at me, guys. I am also married to my job. I don't think any man could measure up to my expectations." Her eyes became downcast as if remembering something. What was Octavia's story?

Mariana waltzed over to another table and talked to another girl. Slow music came on after they'd eaten their main course of alternating plates of roast beef and creamed chicken breast. Camilla moved off with Matthew to dance, and Angelo got up and walked over to find Jamie at the bridal table. Joy whispered something to Jesse, and he shrugged, but she kept shoving him on the shoulder.

Jesse leaned forward, cleared his throat, and looked over at Gabriella. "How about a dance? Joy here's pushing me to dance as I don't normally dance at weddings. I had better prove her wrong."

Gabriella shot daggers at her friend. Was she matchmaking? "Fine, but only to stop Joy from hassling you. Knowing her, she never takes no for an answer."

Joy waved them off. "Go on, lovely people. I have Octavia and Claudia to gossip with."

Jesse approached Gabriella, ignoring the stares of all three ladies at the table as they wandered over to the dance floor. He put one arm in her hand and the other around her waist, ignoring the heated desire between them. His hand was warm against her back, and she could hear his breathing with his face inches from hers. His lips were rosy and inviting, but she looked away and focused on the crowds of guests dancing around them.

***

Jesse breathed in her musky scent and focused on the softness of the skin on her arms. She looked beautiful in her fitted, silky black flowing dress with its thin straps. The split on the side showed toned, tanned legs which he yearned to run his hands over. His heart beat fast as he looked into her glistening eyes until she turned away to stare at the crowd. Her hand shook slightly, and he wondered what her bright pink lipstick would taste like. He wanted to run his hands through her blonde highlights and hold tight onto her sensual curves. No, this was too soon. He still loved Erica and often dreamed about her. The banter at the table showed how Gabriella had become withdrawn and quiet after the topic of marriage came up. Joy had mentioned how her ex-boyfriend, Nick, had betrayed her, but she hadn't gone into any details. He imagined she wanted to give Gabriella privacy about the sensitive matter. He pulled apart from her when the song ended, and they made their way back to the table as waiters placed dessert on it. He wanted to know what was on her mind, but did he truly want to get closer to her?

Chapter Twelve

A PSYCHOLOGICAL PROFILE

Gabriella ambled inside the police station and asked for Octavia. She'd been called in for further questioning about Nora. Her mind kept drifting to Jesse and how he had held her so tight and yet gentle. The way his eyes searched hers as if needing to see through her very soul, and the way his hand fit her own like a glove. Images of his face distracted her from her current troubles.

She shook the thoughts away as she watched others lining up in the queue, staring in her direction. Why was she suddenly paranoid when people looked her way lately? It must've been the man jogging behind her or the strange smell filtering in her car at the wedding. That was crazy! Smells came from everywhere, so she didn't need to make a federal case about it.

Octavia called her name. "Hey, Gabriella. Thanks for coming in. This shouldn't take too long, hopefully." She was led into an interview room and Angelo sat in a seat opposite.

"Hi Gabriella." He rubbed his hands together. "We wanted to get a bit more of a profile of Nora, given you'd worked with her for a few months. Some things have come to light and we need to fill in the gaps."

Gabriella's body tensed up. What leads had they found, and did they mean that Nora hadn't committed suicide? Not that they would tell her at this stage, but they wouldn't be questioning her again if they were sure that she had killed herself. They must've had doubts. "It's fine. I'm happy to help in any way I can."

Octavia took the lead. "I'm going to ask about the specifics in regard to Nora's personal details and her state of mind at the time of her death. Your responses will most likely be repetitious, but we need to ask them again to look for particular patterns and to recheck your memory. With the right questioning in a psychological autopsy, we can extract a lot more details. It might also trigger your memory about things that appear trivial but could have a huge bearing on the case. Are you ready?" Gabriella nodded and rested back against the hard-backed chair.

"I've looked at your case notes, but I'd like your initial impressions of Nora. Can you backtrack to the first time you met her?"

"Nora was referred because of a history of drug and alcohol addiction." The image of her sweet face came to mind, but she had to brush it aside. "My first impression of her was that she was introverted. She struggled to open up about her real feelings to family members who exposed her to violence, emotional and physical abuse, and neglect. She explained how each time she opened up or answered back, her father would punish her by getting her to swallow boiling water fast." Gabriella winced at the idea and took a calming breath. "It had the desired effect as she was unable to talk after that."

"Could you verify the information or was it a lie?" Angelo asked.

"It was confirmed through her medical records which showed she'd been admitted a few times at the hospital for burns and abuse until her father was arrested when she was about sixteen. The mother was submissive and struggled to defend her daughter. If she tried, the father would punish her in worse ways. She hated her mother for a lot of years, but more recently, she came to understand her. They had a way to go in their relationship but they were growing closer."

Octavia nodded. "Did she have any other bad relationships, friendships or enemies?"

"Not that I knew of. She had two close friends who supported her." She took another calming breath. "In terms of her other stressors, it was her constant struggle of coming off the drugs, which were her way of coping with her emotions as she wanted to be numb to them. More recently, she'd studied youth work and worked as a youth worker. She loved her job. Her case was on the news, and she was involved with the media a lot when her father got arrested. Nora wanted her side of the story to be told, and didn't want the media to portray her mother in a bad way. She also didn't want to be judged because of her drug history."

Angelo interjected. "You mentioned she was abstinent from drugs and had no abnormal mental health symptoms. Is that right?"

"Yes, as I said before, she had issues with concentration, memory, and dizziness, but she didn't want to get a medical check. She hated hospitals, as you can understand, because of what she'd been through with her father. She was in drug rehabilitation and had experienced withdrawal symptoms there, but afterwards, she got clean. She had no other stressors and wanted to seek out counselling with Claudia. She was looking forward to it."

Octavia looked at Angelo. "We have a woman who was clean of drugs for at least a month, had a great support system, was returning to study and worked part-time, and was seeking out further help. Did you ever do a suicide risk assessment?"

"Of course, but even in the beginning, there were no signs of suicide, and more so in the latter stages. Are you guys doubting her suicide?"

Angelo cleared his throat. "We've been looking at her medical records, family history, and social media pages. We've interviewed most of her family and friends, and they all mention the same thing.

She was not suicidal. We are waiting on the autopsy report, which could take a few more weeks, and it might tell us why she was having those symptoms you mentioned."

Octavia leaned forward with a reassuring smile. "Did she have any recent arguments with a family member or friend?"

Gabriella shrugged. "It's possible, but she didn't tell me anything. Why?"

Octavia ignored her question. "Was she a generally neat person or messy?"

Gabriella processed the question, not sure of the answer. "It's hard to say as I never asked her that question."

"Tell me your impressions. We got responses from her family and friends, but we need your professional perspective."

"She was groomed and well-dressed, so I'd say she was most likely neat, but who knows about her house."

"What do you know about her brother?"

"Only that they weren't close. He was envious of her because her mother seemed to show her more affection than him. He was abused too, but he still harboured those feelings."

Angelo leaned in and fixed his gaze on Gabriella. "Was the brother abusive towards her more recently?"

Gabriella shrugged. "Not that I know of. She never mentioned it. Claudia might know if he'd been abusive in the past as she saw her over a year ago."

"Angelo's spoken to Claudia but we need a more recent assessment."

Octavia and Angelo asked her further questions about any other stressors, including self-harm. The one thing that struck Gabriella were the cuts. Nora had no reason to cut herself in the bath even with high doses of medication in her system. Could a friend of her father's have hurt her after she testified against him in court? Or was it her brother?

At the end of the interview, she walked outside the building; her mind focused on the questions they asked her. Why did they ask about neatness? How was it relevant to the case? She took a breath and walked straight into a man's chest. Gasping, she came out of her reverie and saw Jesse holding her gently by the arms and straightening his posture. She ignored the flutter in her chest as he smiled. "What are you doing here?"

"Angelo wanted to see me, but I'm not exactly sure why. I think it has something to do with Erica. I gather they asked you about your client?" Gabriella nodded, but before she could respond, a voice called for Jesse.

"Jesse. Come on inside. Thanks," said Angelo.

Gabriella waved to Jesse, wondering why they'd need to see him straight after her. What was going on? Did they have leads on both cases? They couldn't be connected, right?

Chapter Thirteen

HACKED ACCOUNT

The following Saturday, Gabriella woke up, had breakfast and read a few pages of her romance novel before putting on her jogging shoes and sportswear. She entered the rumpus room and sat across from Angela who was sleeping peacefully. Instead of patting her as she usually loved to do, she watched her for a few minutes sitting on the floor crossed-legged. The soothing rhythm of Angela's breaths calmed Gabriella. When her legs grew numb, she rose, moving over to the cupboard and retrieving a tin of food. Opening it up with the can opener, she placed it onto the plate, careful to be quiet. Gabriella checked the feline's water bowl, and comforted that it was full, was able to continue with her morning routine.

Her hand hovered over the door handle. Yesterday, she thought a man was following her, but she talked herself out of it. The park was a popular public place. He probably just chose the same trail as she did and she was just being overly cautious.

Inserting her earphones, she stepped outside her house and started jogging around the block. She waved to her neighbours and smiled at passing strangers who either walked or jogged in the opposite direction. She wasn't ready to jog to the park yet, but at least she was getting her exercise. Another two blocks and she could get home and shower as she was already puffing after not jogging for the past two weeks, given her ankle injury. While jogging, she peered behind her, but nobody was following her. Her anxiety was getting the better of her.

It was strange how Jesse made her feel safe. She wondered why he had been called into the station. She wanted to ring Joy about it, but what if Jesse didn't mention talking to the police? What if she was interfering where she shouldn't? She was sure to find out what was going on from Joy, even if she yearned to see Jesse again. That was a mistake as she was happy with her life the way it was.

Once she returned home, she showered and made herself a light lunch of cheese on crackers with a piece of fruit. Sitting on the couch, she turned on her laptop and checked her emails. Nothing interesting. Only junk mail. She checked her social media pages and tilted her head at a post on her page. *Strange!* She hadn't posted anything on her page late last night, so what was this? It read: 'I wanted to reach out to my followers about the intense topic of suicide. I had a client who recently engaged in the act, and what I have learned is that if you're thinking of hurting yourself, please speak to someone and share your thoughts. Call the crisis lines. Speak to your family. Speak to anyone. Reach out! Help is only a phone call away. I know if I'd truly listened to my client who was suffering with depressive symptoms, she might still be alive today. I should've known she'd kill herself if only I asked her the right questions. I don't want to make the same mistake again. A huge apology goes to my client's family and friends. If only I had saved Nora. Please forgive me!'

Gabriella's body went numb, the room around her spinning. She couldn't think and remained frozen in the spot for many minutes. This couldn't be happening. Who had posted this on her website and how many people had seen this already? Christ! She was in big trouble and wondered if she should delete it. Pacing the floor, she took calming breaths and gave herself time to think before acting impulsively. Rash actions gave her bad results, and she'd learned to take her time with events that could have serious consequences. No, this was evidence of someone taunting her, wanting to get her into trouble. But who would do such a disgusting thing? She retrieved her phone and took a photo of the post, noting the time and date. Then she copied the post and sent it to her email inbox. She deleted it too.

Her phone rang. It was her manager, calling her on a Saturday. "Yes, Joan. What's wrong?" She already knew the answer.

"I saw your social media post which tagged me. What is going on? Why would you tarnish your reputation and that of the centre?"

"I swear to you, I didn't write that post. Someone posted on my page, but it wasn't me. I think I've been hacked."

"Why would anyone do that? Is it a family member upset with you, blaming you for the suicide?"

Gabriella wondered the same thing. "It's possible, but I've taken a copy of it and will send it to the police. They have ways of finding the source."

"Okay then. I guess it's a good first step, and I believe you when you say you didn't post it. Although, I think for the time being, take another week off until the hype from this dies down. A few of your clients have cancelled appointments anyway."

Gabriella was nauseous. "Are you serious? This wasn't even my fault, Joan. Let me explain it to the clients. I'm sure I can make them understand."

"Listen. If it was up to me, I wouldn't have worried so much, but the council members feel this is the best way for the time being. Catch up on your reading and take time out from what you've been through with Nora. Let the excitement of it all die down."

Gabriella's chest tightened, her heart breaking. She didn't want to take more time off. Didn't it show her running away from the problem? She was innocent in all this. "Okay. If that's what I need to do, I'll stay home. I'll see you the following week then."

"You take care of yourself, and I am sorry for this, but when you're dealing with board members and council funding, we have to adhere to certain rules and policies. The words are out there, and it's tarnished your good name and the centre."

"Okay. Thanks, Joan." Gabriella ended the call with her head bowed, staring into her lap. Shaking her head, a chill permeated her spine. Who would do this to her?

After an hour, she rose from her seat and peered through the Venetian blinds. A fleeting shadow caught her eye and footsteps stomped outside her front entrance. Quickly, she opened the door and ran towards the footpath, staring into the distance. She saw no-one, but she could've sworn she heard footsteps.

As she turned back into her home, she saw an A4 envelope protruding from her letterbox. Pulling it out, she ripped open the yellow envelope and took out a note. *"I admire your beauty from afar. One day soon, we'll be together and can make great art together. With love, your one and only."* For a split second, Gabriella wondered if Jesse or Joy was playing a joke on her. Surely this was a joke. Who would send her a poetic love letter?

Chapter Fourteen

HIDDEN THOUGHTS

J esse increased his pace on the treadmill for five minutes, then lowered the speed and slowly got off. He wiped his sweaty forehead with the towel, drank from his bottle, then hopped onto a cross-trainer for the next two minutes. This was followed by the dumbbells and upper limb exercises while watching Derek do light weights. He stared through the long window into the nearby park and took a few deep breaths. His mind flashed to Gabriella who he hadn't seen since the wedding. The intimacy they had shared in their dance filled his dreams, and the beauty of her quiet grace made him yearn for her more each day. He had wanted to reach out to her when he'd heard from Joy about the hurtful social media post.

Jesse brushed away his thoughts and joined Derek on the exercise bikes, his legs moving in a steady rhythm. "I need to talk to you about the police, Derek. Once we finish up, let's head over to the nearby cafe and grab a bite."

"Sure, but we have to work on the latest car. I know someone who wants to buy it at a higher price than we planned to sell it for."

He nodded. "That's great. We can work on it after we get a light lunch." They got off the bikes, wiped off their perspiration, and took a five-minute walk to the cafe. A small group of people chatted at the counter and tables as they entered. Seeing one table empty, they sat down opposite each other and placed an order for a chicken wrap for Jesse and a beef burger for Derek.

His friend started off. "So, what did the police question you about the other day?"

Jesse straightened his body, watching customers come and go as the cafe became more crowded. The smells of assorted meats, herbs, and pepper filled his nose as he watched Derek, who looked worried. "They asked me about Erica and wanted to know if she was seeing anyone else or if she had enemies. They wanted to know if she was on medication. She was never mentally unwell, so I don't know why she'd be on medication. I answered these questions a year ago, but I guess Marco and Angelo weren't the ones in charge back then."

"They wanted a new perspective a year later," said Derek whose hands fidgeted. "Are they still ruling it as suicide?"

Jesse shrugged. "I don't know, man. But I still wonder why she had high doses of anxiety medication in her system when she wasn't an anxious person. If it was an accident, why dose herself so much? If she was suicidal, she might've taken a lot of pills, but she wasn't suicidal, and never had a history of self-harm. And why the cuts? A lot of this doesn't make sense, and I'm sure the police are realising there might be more to the story."

"But there was a suicide note, Jesse. That shows intent."

"I don't know. That's what I find strange. I am trying to rack my brain over everything she did and said which might've suggested she was unhappy with her life, but I cannot think of one thing. She was a journalist and had spent time overseas. She loved her work and we were going to get married. She had her friends. She had everything she could have wanted, but for some reason, she ended up in a bathtub with cuts on her legs and drowned? I don't believe she would kill herself that way or any way."

"Did the police find out anything else about her? Did they mention any new leads?"

Jesse was curious about Derek's strong interest in the case. "When I asked, they ignored my question and said I might need to go back to the station for more questions. They said if they had further news, they'd let me know. In my opinion, I think the police know more than they're letting on. I even saw Gabriella coming out of the police station. They must've wanted to ask her about her client, the one who recently died." He wondered if there was a connection between the two cases. Hopefully, he'd find out what was going on.

Derek grimaced. "You like her, don't you?"

Jesse's face flushed as he turned away. "She's only a distant friend. I barely know the woman, man. You're crazy."

He scoffed. "You've known the woman for years, but you chose to ignore your attraction to Gabriella because of Erica. I think you felt obligated to your girlfriend in the end. But I could see the way you looked at her when she was around."

Jesse drew back. "I can't believe you're saying that, Derek. I loved Erica and we were planning to get married. I was one hundred percent committed, and you know that."

The young waiter brought over their food and smiled. "Enjoy."

Derek bit into his burger. "Are you sure that's what both of you wanted? I mean, you guys had been together for five years without really committing to anyone else"

Jesse took a bite of his wrap. He angled his head. "Did Erica say something to you, as she sure as hell didn't tell me anything about not wanting to get married."

Derek put up his hand, averting his eyes. "No, I didn't mean that. It's only that you guys were still young. Who gets married in their twenties nowadays, man? You've got to live life and enjoy women. Why commit at such a young age?"

Jesse shoved his friend on the shoulder, sometimes hating his immaturity towards women. He still had a lot of growing up to do. "You won't say that when you've found the right girl, Derek. Talk to me then about commitment."

Jesse wiped his hands with a napkin after putting down his wrap. Why did he get the feeling Derek was hiding something?

Chapter Fifteen

REMINISCING

On Saturday, Gabriella walked with Joy across a nature strip that led to a concrete-paved path towards Jesse's house. He wanted to explore a summary of events they might have missed before Erica's death.

Jesse's house was a brown brick building. Pebbles surrounded a crème letterbox in the front yard. Conifers and assorted trees stood in the front garden on the right side of the house along the edge of a steel fence. Two white posts stood on either side of a crème-framed screen door with a welcome mat laying in front.

Joy rang the doorbell and waited with jumpy feet and fidgety hands. Her friend was never one to stay still. But, at this moment, she wondered if Jesse had got new information or leads from the police. Had they missed something about Erica a year ago, and could things have turned out differently?

Gabriella ignored her upset stomach and flushed face, wondering whether it was the prospect of talking about Erica that made her nervous or if it was about seeing Jesse again. Lately, he'd been on her mind, but she had to push him out of it.

Jesse swung open the door and smiled at both of them. "Hello, ladies. Thanks for coming. I've made lunch."

Joy pecked him on the cheek and pushed ahead of him inside the foyer. "I don't know, Jesse. Your cooking leaves a damn bitter taste in my mouth." Gabriella laughed as Jesse nodded in her direction, his eyes lingering. His abdominals stood out underneath a white fitted t-shirt, and his short sleeves displayed tanned biceps. His jeans hugged his lower body just right, and she swallowed and turned away to look at the rest of his house.

"Practise makes perfect, sis. Don't knock it until you've tried it."

As they passed by a large kitchen and ambled into the living room, Gabriella's eyes roamed. "Nice place." She adored the glossy white tiled flooring and double glass doors with a view of the backyard. A large screen TV sat opposite a chequered sofa, and a low glass coffee table covered with car magazines, recipe books, and health magazines was placed a short distance from it. It said a lot about Jesse who obviously loved cars, enjoyed exercise, and had to cook for himself.

"Thanks, Gabriella. My parents have been a great help as I know yours have been too. It was hard with them for a lot of years, but they're learning to live again." Their sister had died thirteen years ago, and their parents had struggled with the loss for many years. At least now they'd found her killer.

He walked into the kitchen while Joy and Gabriella sat on chairs in the middle of the room. A jug of a colourful liquid glistened as Jesse put it on the table with three glasses. "It's my famous brew of vodka, lime, and cranberry juice. Would you like a glass?" They both nodded, and Jesse poured it into their glasses.

Gabriella took a sip of the drink which soothed her parched throat. "It's good. I've tried this mixture before. Cranberry and vodka always blend well."

Joy drank it all down and wiped the remnants of juice from her lips with the back of her hand. "I'm having another, bro." She poured herself another glass while Gabriella drank hers slowly to enjoy the tangy flavour.

Jesse chuckled and sat opposite them. "I wanted to talk to you guys about Erica and about your client too, Gabriella, if that's okay?"

Joy intervened. "Listen, bro. We assume the two cases might be connected, but unless the police get evidence, it doesn't mean anything. We might never get justice for Erica, and you might need to accept that." She briefly looked at her friend. "Do not set yourself up for failure. Consider both options." She touched him gently on the shoulder. "I think, for now, keep the good memories of Erica to heart. Can you do that?"

His eyes lit up as if being in another place, another time. "I do remember something funny." He stared into the distance. "I remember, I had to pick up Erica from her Christmas party one night a couple of years back. She had her car but got so drunk she called me to pick her up. And not only was I picking her up, but I was also picking up her friend, Marie, who was the receptionist at her work. Even her colleague, Arthur, was drunk and came with us. Erica was making me laugh with these jokes about Marie and Arthur both getting drunk on purpose so they could hook up. They were so out of it that they didn't even understand what she was saying. I dropped them off home and literally had to carry Marie into her house, and then Arthur. To this day, he claims he doesn't remember me doing that. But he had such a fancy federation-style home, and I thought one day, I'm going to get Erica a house like that. I dropped him off, and he mumbled something about other houses close by which were more affordable. There was no way I could afford homes like that in Williamstown. Who knew we'd never get that future?"

"That's a nice memory," said Gabriella.

Jesse sat cross-armed, squinting as if annoyed. "I'm sure you guys remember she was acting strangely in the last few months like she wasn't herself."

"That's true, but we'll never know why," Joy said. "She must have been going through something we didn't pick up on."

Jesse leaned in, gripping his glass tight. "She wasn't exactly depressed but jittery, as if she was scared of something."

Gabriella's back ached, wondering if they'd missed something with Erica. "Can you be more specific?"

Jesse peered into the distance and turned his body away. "She was jumpy, forgetting things all the time. She even called me a few times in the middle of the night because she couldn't sleep. She was worried about something, but she wasn't on any drugs or medication. At least, not until the day she died. She wouldn't let me take her to the hospital, saying she was overworked. I asked her countless times if it was more than that, but she said it wasn't. It has to mean something, surely."

Gabriella leaned forward. "I remember the few times we saw her just before she died. She was a bit hyperactive and jumpy, but I put it down to overwork initially. I knew she was ambitious and always over-researched issues. It might have been a lack of sleep and fatigue. When you don't sleep, it causes all sorts of issues. I did wonder if something was going on, but she denied any problems. She even refused to cut down her hours at work, saying she wanted to move up in the firm." She turned to Joy. "You thought the same thing, didn't you?"

Joy nodded. "She was stubborn, that's for sure. And if you told her to do something, like see a doctor, she resisted even more. She had to do things when she was ready. And we hardly saw her anymore, Jesse. You barely saw her just before she died, but we need to figure out if more was going on with her."

Jesse shook his head. "Her stubbornness might have got her killed, Joy. She wouldn't listen to anyone, and I hated her for that for a long time. I wanted to protect her, but I couldn't because she wouldn't let me." He fought back a tear.

Gabriella cleared her throat. "I am sorry, Jesse. I wish we could have done more for her. We're as much to blame for not getting to the heart of her issues. But she made her choices and we tried to help." Jesse gave her a reassuring smile. "Did you tell the police any of this?"

"I did, but I don't know what they're doing with the information. I told Marco and Angelo this, and those other detectives when Erica died."

Joy touched her brother on the shoulder. "I know you miss Erica and were planning to marry her, but let the police do their job. If they find a connection between Erica and Nora, I'm sure they'll let us know. They'll most likely have more questions."

Gabriella knit her brows. "I'm sure they'll find something, Jesse. I agree that both cases seem to be similar. But as Joy said, the police need hard evidence."

Jesse's eyes turned hard. "The police have been damn hopeless so far, Gabriella. It wasn't an accident. Something was wrong, and someone did this to her." He sighed. "Most likely, something suspicious happened to your old client as well."

Joy downed the remainder of her drink. "Why don't we have lunch? What's on the menu?"

"Steak and salad." Jesse's eyes misted. "It's been too long since we visited Erica's grave together. Why don't we go after lunch?"

Joy nodded. "I'm game. It has been a while for me. What about you, Gabi? Care to join us after lunch? We can honour her one-year anniversary."

"Of course." Gabriella loved Joy for being able to get out of sticky situations; as for now, Jesse's hands clenched tight, and his eyes looked downcast. What was the point in ruminating about possibilities when the detectives were on the case? She didn't want to mention the note she'd received as Jesse had his own concerns with Erica. She was curious about the reason for Erica's behaviour as they had hardly seen her in those last few months. Each time they had tried to get together, she had been busy chasing up a story or was busy with Jesse. If they had seen her more often and figured out what went wrong, would Erica be alive today?

***

Gabriella sat on the dirty ground of the cemetery with Joy and Jesse as she lifted a bottle of a mixed cocktail towards Erica. She watched as Joy pushed in a bunch of flowers on the side of the plot while Jesse slid a rag over the back of the grave.

"Let's toast to Erica. In memory of an amazing woman who left this world too young." Gabriella picked at a few blades of grass and rubbed them between her fingers. "I remember the first time we met Erica in school. It was my first day and she came up to me and said, "I like you. You can be my friend." She turned to Joy. "Then you approached Erica and me, and we became the best of friends. She was there for us whenever we needed her: through our fights with family, boyfriends, and issues with my dad. I loved her so much, and I miss her." She stared at the headstone with a mournful look. "And she loved her mum's home-cooked meals. She'd mention how sometimes she hated going out because the food wasn't as great as her mum's."

Joy sat beside her and put a gentle hand on her shoulder. "She sure did love her mother's cooking." She took a breath. "I remember one time she forced me to leave school to buy fish and chips at the local shop. You didn't want to come with us, Gabi. Then we were caught out by one of the teachers after we bought our food. He took it away from us and started eating it himself. We got detention, but Erica made it fun by doodling all these crazy animations of a few of the teachers at school. Boy, she was smart and loved writing, didn't she? Not surprisingly, she became a journalist."

Jesse put down the rag then picked up his bottle of beer and took a quick sip. "I remember when Erica and I went out to dinner. This guy who was so drunk, started arguing with me just because I was looking at him. He approached and punched me for no apparent reason. Erica straight away called the police but they let him go with a warning. Later that night, she tended to my wounds and looked after me. She had a big heart."

"To Erica," said Joy.

"To Erica," said Gabriella.

"May you rest in peace," said Jesse.

It gave Gabriella comfort to know that she was no longer suffering. But she would one day get her justice.

Chapter Sixteen

OFFICE LOVE NOTE: 16 YEARS EARLIER

"*Oh, darling. I love you so much. So much. You've made me so happy with this money. You're the best, sweetie.*" *She wrapped her arms around him and smothered him with kisses.*

"Thanks, Mum. I love you too." He inched forward slowly. "Mum, I was wondering. The next time I get money from the paper round, can I buy myself some pencils and pens?"

His mother's eyes turned a shade darker. "No, son. I need my medicine to make me feel better."

In a quiet voice, he said, "Please, Mum. I promise I'll be good."

She pulled him towards her and caressed his hair. "Hmm. How about we make a trade, son?" She undid the buttons of her shirt. "How about you make mummy happy, and I'll get you those pencils on your next paper out?"

The boy cowered. "But Mummy. I don't want to do that. It hurts me."

She swung out her arm and hit him hard across the head. "You never say no to me." Her eyes got hard. "I can easily sell you to some loser who won't think twice to bash your brains out. Now make mummy happy." She smiled and pushed him towards the bedroom as he nodded sullenly.

***

Gabriella rested her back against the chair in the conference room while her manager ran through the agenda. She gripped her notebook as she readied herself to take notes.

Her manager, Joan, was a woman in her fifties with greying hair on the sides and a solid stature. "The first item on the agenda is the upgrade of the toilet facilities." Gabriella's mind focused on Jesse who struggled to accept the death of Erica. He desperately wanted to believe she hadn't killed herself, but did the police have any leads? The symptoms he'd described were similar to Nora's, but were they only seeing what they wanted to see or were these suspicious deaths?

Joan clicked her fingers. "Gabriella, are you with us?"

She broke out of reverie, blushing as others around the table fixed their gazes on her. "I'm sorry."

The manager nodded. "Okay, then. Next item on the agenda is completing and reminding ourselves to do a suicide risk assessment with each client." She looked at Gabriella with concern, as if she didn't want to get into this topic but had to. Gabriella understood how important this topic was and it needed to be addressed. "Even if a client doesn't appear to present with symptoms, we will still need to ask the questions to rule it out. Many times, these symptoms are masked, and we need to dig deeper to get to the root of the problem."

Gabriella's heart beat fast as she knew this topic had come up because of Nora. If her client was suicidal, then she didn't do her job properly. She would have to rethink her career in social work, too. But what other career could she take? It was a hopeless situation as she didn't want to do anything else. She loved helping people and found it rewarding. Helping others who had experienced violence and abuse as she had was the purpose of her existence. Throughout the remainder of the meeting, Gabriella participated and offered suggestions to better the needs of the clients. They were developing improved assessment reports and arranging guest speakers to talk to them about suicide risk and the psychology of behaviour. She didn't need this as she was studying psychology as part of her social work degree, but having different perspectives and refresher training couldn't hurt.

Joan uncrossed her arms and rose. "Okay, back to work, everyone." She turned to Gabriella. "A word, please."

Gabriella joined her on the other side of the table, standing awkwardly. "Yes."

"Are you sure you're okay to return to work today, given what you've been through? I know it's been rough, and you've been working hard with your other clients, but I wanted to check in. I need to make sure you are totally focused on your clients."

Gabriella appreciated her care but didn't want the focus to be on her when she had so much going on in her head. "I'm fine, Joan. I know I did the best I could with Nora, but I still feel guilty." She exhaled. "At least the police are still looking into her death."

Joan tilted her head. "I thought it was ruled a suicide."

"I don't know, but I guess her family want them to investigate to explore all avenues."

She nodded. "I guess that makes sense." She gave her a reassuring smile. "If you need to talk, come to my office. My door's always open, okay?"

"Of course. Thank you." Joan walked out when the receptionist walked into the room and handed Gabriella her mail. She strolled towards her office and checked the two smaller envelopes that involved support service referrals she'd made for two clients. A larger A4 envelope caught her eyes and had no sender's address. Slowly unsealing the envelope, she took out the note and scanned through it. *"Oh, Gabi. I love the way you help others in need. Words cannot express how much I admire your beauty and sympathy towards others.*

The lust I feel for you goes deep into my loins. One day soon, my love. One day soon."

Gabriella dropped the note as if it was on fire. Her body sat frozen, and her mind knew it was the same person as the first love note. Who the hell was this? It had to be a joke. Nausea filled her, and she rushed over to the bin and retched. Taking a deep breath, she picked up a tissue from her desk and wiped her mouth. She took a sip from the bottle of water on her desk. Her heart raced and chills ran up her spine.

She closed her eyes and made a phone call, knowing that Marco was back from his honeymoon. He answered after three rings. "Marco. I need your help. Can I come to the police station during my lunch break in about two hours?"

"Of course, but if I'm not in, Octavia will be here, and she'll be able to help. What's this about?"

"I'd rather discuss it in person. I'm at work now. Thanks, Marco." She ended the call and stood up from her desk. She drew the curtains at the side window and stared outside, but she didn't see anyone lurking around. Even when she passed the waiting area, the few people there appeared innocent. She walked over to the receptionist who had bright blue eyes and long, frizzy hair. "This large envelope I got. Who gave it to you? It wasn't sent by post."

The receptionist looked at her for a moment as if sizing her up. "I don't know. I went outside to get something from my car and noticed it by the door. It must have been placed there when we were in the meeting, so I don't know who it was."

"Okay, thanks." She walked back towards her office, pushed the matter from her mind, and retrieved a case file from her desk. Then she made her way back to the waiting room and called out her client's name.

As she smiled and walked back inside her office, she refused to let the mystery of the note distract her now, and focused on her client. She didn't have control over her stalker situation, but she still had control over her work.

Chapter Seventeen

INCIDENT REPORT

Gabriella slowed down as she approached the entrance to the police station, her foot bumping against the low brush as she reached the door. She carried an envelope of her love notes and loose diary entries that recorded her strange sensations of being watched. She also carried a copy of the social media post. She wasn't sure if it was worth reporting the love notes as they appeared harmless enough. He was an admirer from afar who didn't sound as if he planned to hurt her. Or was she wrong?

Accessing the front counter, Gabriella shook off her worry, took a deep breath and stood behind the few people in the queue towards the front desk. It was slow-moving, and her mind brought up an image of Jesse who made her feel safe. The way his muscles enhanced his looks. The way he threaded his hands through his dirty-blonde hair when he was nervous. The well-defined arms which could keep her safe if she was wrapped in them. *Stop it!* She was on a mission, and nothing could deter her from checking out whether her admirer was harmless or dangerous.

One foot further took her closer to the front, and her mind ruminated about the most recent note. Who would have had the courage to drop off an envelope in front of the door, knowing that he could be seen with such an implicating note? It was daring and brave, and she realised that this stalker might not be afraid of anything. He was living in a fantasy land, thinking they would be together. It couldn't be anyone she knew, surely?

Turning back, a few new people joined the queue, and police officers walked in and rushed through in teams as if they'd been on an exciting patrol experience. They whispered and shoved each other on their shoulders as if they'd had a successful morning. Once she reached the front counter, she smiled at the officer. "I'm Gabriella. I have an appointment to see Marco."

The young officer with a grin said, "Of course. He mentioned you were coming in and decided to wait for you before he left. Please take a seat in the waiting area and I'll call him in."

"Thank you," said Gabriella. She made her way back and seated herself in a chair next to a young man whose eyes lingered too long in her direction. Now she was being paranoid. Not everyone who looked at her was the person harassing her. Turning away, she crossed her arms and stared down at the floor, wondering whether it was worth reporting the notes. What if it was a waste of time, which was not time that Marco had, considering he was busy investigating Nora's case, and most likely many others.

When Marco called her name, she got up and grinned at him. "Thanks for seeing me. I know you're busy, but this is important."

He smiled. "I am never too busy for you, Gabriella. Bella's friends are my friends too." He ushered her down the corridor and straight into his office. Angelo sat in a chair opposite her and nodded to her in greeting.

She angled her head. "I didn't know you'd be here, detective."

Angelo looked at his partner and slouched in his chair, processing. "We needed to ask you a few more questions about Nora, but I understand you have something to report." She nodded.

Marco sat beside him, focusing on her with curiosity. "Why don't you start from the beginning, and I'll take notes." He scribbled something on a pad. "It'll be added to the official report later on."

She placed her documents on the table and clenched her hands. "I feel I'm being watched, and I had a social media post appear which I didn't put there. I also had a couple of strange love notes. I don't know what to make of them, but they're odd."

Angelo fixed his gaze on her. "How about you take it step by step and tell us when this started, and what exactly happened? We need dates, times, and specifics of events. Then we will take those documents from you."

"Of course." She recounted her jogging incident, the times she felt she was being watched at home, the love notes, and the social media post. She handed them her manila folder of love notes, social media post, and diary notes.

Marco left the room and came back with a set of gloves. He picked up the documents and searched through her paperwork with a keen eye. Angelo scanned them too, giving Marco a strange look. What was she missing here? Did this mean something, or were they being curious? "Okay, leave this with us, and we'll hand it in to forensics who can check for any fibres or fingerprints. They might even be able to analyse the typed script."

"Hopefully, they'll find something." She hunched over. "Any leads on Nora's case or anything else I should know about?"

Angelo shook his head. "Not at this stage, Gabriella, but we'll keep you in the loop." He pressed his lips together and touched the base of his throat. "If you can avoid going anywhere alone, it'd be great. No outings at night especially, and take note of any further strange occurrences. If you can stay with Joy for a while, it'd be even better, or you might have someone stay with you."

Marco intervened. "I'll get Bella to check in on you. She'll give you further insights about how to take care of yourself. Any questions?"

Gabriella shook her head and got up. "No. Thanks, guys. Keep me informed about Nora. I need to know what's going on."

Marco rose and wrapped his arms around her. "You take care of yourself, Gabriella, and stay safe. We'll be in touch."

Angelo gave her a wink. "Don't take any unnecessary risks, Gabriella." She nodded, and they followed her towards the exit with a wave. As she was walking back to her car, she realised that Angelo hadn't asked her any questions about Nora. Had the situation changed after reading through the notes?

Chapter Eighteen

BIRTHDAY CELEBRATION

The following Saturday night, Gabriella stood on the terrace of a rooftop bar enjoying a glass of champagne with her friends, Joy, Bella, Liz, Jamie, Octavia, and Claudia for her birthday celebration. She leaned against a steel rail as she took in the view of the city of Melbourne with its high-rise buildings and attractions. The warm breeze feathered her cheeks as she listened to Bella talk about an upcoming housewarming party.

"The party won't be for a month or two; until we settle in, but you all need to come. I'll text you the date soon." Bella's eyes glowed. She had had a permanent smile ever since she returned from her honeymoon.

Gabriella moved away from the rail and leaned closer towards Bella. "You look absolutely radiant. Marriage seems to agree with you."

Joy lifted a thumb. "I second that, girl. I bet you're not letting Marco have any rest, are you? He must be more exhausted than usual."

Jamie shook her head, her strong, brown eyes boring into hers. Her vibrant red hair shone in the final rays of the sun. "Joy, that is Bella's business, not ours. Leave the woman alone and let her enjoy the novelty of marriage."

"Come on, Jamie. Let's have some fun with this while we can." Liz downed her cocktail as if there was no tomorrow. She could always hold her alcohol.

A group of people got up from a brown timber table with long benches across the room, and the ladies quickly scooted themselves over to sit there rather than having to stand all night.

Octavia threaded a hand through her auburn highlights. "It was a beautiful ceremony, Bella, and I for one, can see how you and Marco deserve all the happiness you can get." A sadness in her eyes made Gabriella curious.

Bella gave Octavia a reassuring grin. "Thanks, Octavia, but I'm sure you'll find someone special soon too. You can't be all work and no play, even if you're amazing at your job." Octavia drew into her shell and looked away.

Claudia squeezed Octavia's shoulder and they shared a look. "I believe the waiter's bringing in the birthday cake for Gabriella. It is time, isn't it ladies?"

Gabriella cleared her throat, her eyes roaming past them and towards the bar. "Camilla just sent me a text. She said she's five minutes away. We can get the cake, but we'll wait for her to get here. Is that okay?"

Liz nodded. "I can call over the waiter but we'll wait for Camilla." Her eyes looked down for a moment. "I'm glad she's become a part of our group. I love her like a sister." She gestured over a waiter who approached and whispered to him. He rushed off into the interior of the bar. Liz turned to Gabriella and Claudia. "Is there any new information about your client?"

Claudia interrupted. "I haven't heard anything, Liz. It is still ongoing." She faced Gabriella. "Have you heard anything?"

Gabriella didn't want to ruin the exciting vibe of the night. "Nothing, really. At least not anything I wish to talk about tonight.

How about we make this a fun night with no talk about anything negative. Is that okay?"

Joy clinked her glass with Gabriella's. "I'll drink to that. No negative talk." The waiter returned a few minutes later with a three-tiered birthday cake slathered with fresh cream, and strawberries on top. Chocolate icing was spread around the sides. He handed them matches and the candles Gabriella had brought while another waiter set down plates, spoons, and napkins.

Jamie touched her neck. "Camilla and I have become close and she was somewhat nervous about coming here tonight. She needs time to get her confidence back after what she has been through."

"We'll make her welcome, Jamie. Don't worry." Bella searched in the distance. "Camilla is a kind-hearted person and she's come a long way. Oh look, here she is."

Camilla was a vision in her black wedged heels and a black fitted top with loose white pants. The blonde highlights in her hair gleamed as she smiled nervously at the group. "Sorry I'm late. I had to wait for the babysitter." She kissed all of their cheeks and fixed her eyes on Gabriella. "Happy birthday. It is your twenty-third, isn't it?" She handed her a small, wrapped gift box which Gabriella put aside.

Gabriella nodded. "It is, and you look great, Camilla. Thank you so much for the gift, but you didn't need to bring anything."

Camilla smiled and peered into the distance with her arms crossed over her chest. "It is a pleasure, and thank you for inviting me." Jamie walked over towards her and touched her gently on the shoulder.

Joy and Bella stuck the candles into the cake and Liz lit them. A beautiful fiery glow surrounded them. Gabriella stood in front of the cake and took in the smiles of all her friends, who had been so supportive during her ordeal over Nora. She didn't want to think about her client nor about Erica, which made her think about Jesse.

The group sang out, "Happy birthday to you. Happy birthday to you. You look like a princess and you smell like one too."

"Ha ha, funny, girls." She bowed down and blew out the candles and they all clapped. One by one, they wrapped their arms around her, practically choking her to death.

"You are so young, Gabriella. I feel old around you," Claudia said.

Bella stared daggers at her. "Oh, come on, Claudia. You're only twenty-nine and that is still young in my book."

Liz put up her hand. "I agree. Once you turn forty, you might as well call it a day and get your affairs in order. But you've got another decade for that."

Claudia laughed. "Thanks, Liz and Bella. I crave for your reassurance."

Gabriella cut the cake, placed slices on plates, and shared them around. The ladies enjoyed banter and small talk until a familiar figure came onto the terrace. He was standing with two other men. Oh, Christ. What was Erica's brother, Nigel, doing here? She didn't particularly want to talk to him, but their eyes met and she couldn't ignore him. Nudging Joy, she smiled at him heading in her direction. He whispered to his friends, and they nodded while moving off towards a corner, no doubt wanting private words with both Gabriella and Joy.

His cold, grey eyes fixed on Joy. His crew cut made him look like a hard soldier about to go to war. He was solid yet short and wore long, dressy beige shorts with a crisp white shirt which showed his pecs. "Fancy meeting you and Joy here."

Gabriella struggled to give him a genuine smile. "Hi, Nigel. How have you been?"

He shrugged. "I am fine, but my parents are still struggling over Erica. You'd think they'd be over it by now. Even in death, she gets more attention than me. Who cares anymore?"

Joy's eyes darkened. "How can you say that about your sister? She deserves respect." The group watched the exchange without saying anything. "I'd introduce you but what's the point?"

Gabriella looked at Joy and shook her head. "Nigel, please give your parents my best. I haven't seen them since..."

He put up his hand. "Yeah yeah, whatever. You were always a bit more decent than Joy over here. At least you have manners and a less sharp tongue, but know this. Erica was weak for doing what she did, and I am sick of my parents going over the same thing. About how they should've supported her and how I should've been closer to her. All the same damn shit. I thought things would've changed after she died, but I'm still invisible." His face turned red, and his hands tightened into fists as if he was holding back rage.

Joy stood inches from him. "She did not kill herself, Nigel, and you are still a pathetic, jealous brother who thinks he's better than everyone else. If you need more love and attention from your parents, then get off your high horse and be a better person."

He scoffed. "You bitch. I always hated you, but Gabriella I can tolerate."

Gabriella pushed Joy aside. "Leave it, Joy."

He chuckled. "Don't worry. I'm leaving. I have more dignity than to argue with the likes of you, Joy, but if you get in my face again, I will..."

Joy challenged him with her eyes. "You'll what? Hurt me? Kill me? What is it, Nigel?" He moved away and stormed off towards his friends.

Gabriella picked up Joy's hand. "He's not worth it, Joy. Let us get on with our positive vibes and not let him ruin our night." The way Nigel looked agitated and angry made her wonder if he could get violent. How could he have so little empathy towards Erica, who had been a beautiful person on the inside and out. Had he been that deprived of love that he needed to taunt Erica in death, too?

Chapter Nineteen

DISEMBODIED VOICE

Midweek evening, Gabriella ambled along the curving concrete walkway of her university, with its tall green trees rooted around rectangular garden beds amidst the tall buildings. She dodged groups of students and staff members heading to evening classes from one building to the next. Rolled up flags fluttered in the wind above low brush and hedges. A steel enclosure fenced in part of the university grounds, and white and red cedar trees covered a grass covered hill.

Gabriella climbed the steps which led to a large lecture theatre, the building covered with dark glass that hid the interior. She had a couple of years of part-time studying left on her social work degree, and studied both online and face to face when required. Luckily, she had managed to gain credits after completing her community services course when she was working with Liz in her social work clinic over a year earlier.

She made her way to the lecture theatre and greeted a few students before grabbing a seat. She looked at the male lecturer who was flicking through documents while standing at the podium. He leaned his body in towards the microphone and started to speak about social work ethics and policy. Taking out her notebook and pen, she scribbled down notes, ignoring the chill of the air conditioner against her back. Her mind got distracted by an image of Erica's brother, Nigel, at her birthday party. His glaring eyes had seemed so threatening. Did he really hate his sister to the point that he had no sense of loss after her death? He seemed to loathe Joy with a vengeance, and she wondered if it was only due to her challenging him. Gabriella didn't see any point in arguing with a self-entitled, self-absorbed man who was much older than Erica, and should've had more emotional maturity through life experience. But he didn't have it. Nigel harboured a lot of anger, and she wondered where it came from. She was concerned for Joy, who had no regard for self-preservation when she thoughtlessly spoke her mind. It could get her into trouble one day.

Focusing back on the lecture, she leaned forward in her seat and watched a few people to the side of her dozing off while others listened with rapt attention. She noticed a man in a chequered coat in the lower seating area walk out of the lecture. How rude to leave the theatre before the end of the lecture.

An hour later, she rose from her seat and exited the building. She settled on the fresh, green grass, leaned back against a gum tree, and took out her textbooks. The warm grass tickled her legs, and the setting sun on her face made her squint. The smells of gum and grass brought her closer to nature. Pungent spicy and wood scents from the trees permeated her senses. She had a half-hour to spare before her final psychology lecture on "The Fundamentals of Human Behaviour." She flicked through the textbook and read through points she'd highlighted, particularly about the primitive roots of behaviour as well as the neurological structures and processes responsible for mental life. She wondered about Erica and Nora who were both different in their behaviour and must've had different wiring of their brains. Erica was well-educated, a journalist, and took responsibility for her life, but she had been sheltered by her parents and had felt stifled by them. Nora wasn't well educated, was a drug addict, and had felt abandoned by her family until she made amends. Two very different women died in the same way, but what did they have in common? Erica had no reason to kill herself, and neither had Nora when her life had been about setting new goals and taking responsibility for her mistakes. But they had both presented with strange symptoms before their deaths.

She was making her way to her final lecture when the man with the chequered coat came back into view. He must've had another lecture to attend, and headed towards another building. He looked directly at her, as if realising she was staring at him. There was something about the way he appeared in these surroundings that made him look lost, as if he didn't fit in with the student vibe. Gabriella shook the feeling off as she walked up more steps, and passed through a building and the cafeteria before she made it to the lecture theatre.

Two hours later, she left the theatre and walked through other buildings until she reached the stairs which led to the top of the parking space. This part of the area had few cars and was deserted until a few people made their way to their cars and drove off. Around the corner was another row of cars. Her car was two minutes away, but she suddenly hated the quiet because darkness was approaching.

Quickening her steps towards her car, a muffled voice and a cough rang out. Turning back, she didn't see anyone in her line of vision. It must've come fron the lower level. She ignored it and hastened to her car.

"Hey Beautiful."

She stopped in her tracks and then rounded the corner away from her car. There was the other car parking area. Taking slow steps, her eyes darted in all directions and her lower lip trembled. There were a few people walking to their vehicles in the other area, and she didn't see anyone acting suspiciously. This was ridiculous. So many students filled this area. Anyone could have said that to their loved one. What was she thinking? Not everything was about her.

Shaking her head, she walked back in the other direction to her car and noticed something on the ground close to the steps. Was that a recording device? Rushing towards it, she narrowly missed a sporty red car whizzing past her towards the lower level. She hadn't noticed that car before and remained frozen on the spot. Who was in it? The windows were tinted so she couldn't see who was inside. The car disappeared from view. She turned back to the recording device, but it had disappeared.

Chapter Twenty

CONFRONTATION

Jesse was standing inside Derek's garage, hunched over a small yellow second-hand car. He was removing window glass, slicing the rubber seal with a knife. He wiped his brow and stood upright while Derek sanded the car's paint on the other side.

When Jesse had removed all the glass, he took out his clipboard and pen and wrote a list of parts they needed to restore the car. He remembered working with his father on cars, but it had stopped when he was thirteen years old, which was the time his older sister had died. He missed those bonding sessions with his father, but he was slowly coming around to engaging in his old interests again. It no doubt had to do with the fact that, over a year ago, his sister's killer had finally been caught. His parents got their sense of justice and could live in peace with her death.

Derek rubbed his back. "Oh, hell. I think we could use a break, man."

Jesse nodded. "Sure, but I have to make a list first. Let's see. We need to replace the panels." He wrote it down. "And we need new body paint."

Derek interjected as he continued to sand the paint. "We need a high build primer, too, and gaskets, and rubber seals."

"Of course." Jesse scribbled further items on the list then put the clipboard back on the shelf. He followed Derek inside his house to the kitchen.

"I have salami, cheese, and tomatoes to put in a roll. Is that okay?"

Jesse nodded. "Sure. I could probably eat a horse right now. Thanks, Derek." He proceeded to cut the roll which Derek loaded from the pantry and added a slice of cheese on top of his salami and sliced a tomato. "Do you have lettuce?"

Derek reached inside the fridge and handed him a lettuce leaf. Jesse washed and dried it and put it underneath the cheese. They sat on chairs and devoured their rolls, washing them down with bottles of beer.

"How's work going, man?" asked Derek. "Are you still working with the guy who was not likely to walk again?"

"I am, and he's progressing, but I imagine if he listened to those doctors, he'd most likely never think about walking. They literally said he would never walk again, but he proved them wrong. It is mind over matter."

Derek wiped his mouth with a napkin and scrunched it up on the table. He sipped his beer and set it down. "You make the difference, too, man. It's your passion that shines through. Not many can do your kind of work and give people hope."

Why did Jesse get the feeling that Derek was trying to butter him up for something? "It takes training and passion to do physiotherapy, but I love it. As you love your work as a mechanic. I appreciate you teaching me so much about cars." His mind flicked back to the first time he'd met Derek at school. Jesse had been shy at the time. Derek had taken a chance and had been the first person to speak to him. They'd become fast friends, but ever since Erica died, they had become distant, mainly from Derek's side.

"Your dad had a hand in it, too. Maybe he'll get back into restorations and sell them at top dollar. Not that we can, but we can easily make a bit of a profit reselling this car we're doing. We've got to recoup our costs on everything we order."

Jesse dusted breadcrumbs off his chin, satiated from the roll. He finished the last drops of his beer and stood up. "I have to go to the bathroom. I'll be back."

Derek yelled out after him. "Can you go to my bedroom afterwards? My top bedside drawer has a document with a list of cheap suppliers for parts. And don't take too long. We're on a deadline, Jesse."

"Sure thing." Jesse made his way to the bathroom and noticed that the bathroom cabinet was open an inch when he was rinsing his hands . Closing it completely, the door bumped into something. Reaching up inside the cabinet, he pulled out a small bottle. Out of curiosity, he read the label—Alprazolam. Wasn't that for anxiety? Okay, so it must've belonged to one of Derek's family members. Nothing strange about that. Jesse shook the thought away when he remembered that he had to get that suppliers' document from Derek's top bedside drawer.

Walking inside his friend's room, Jesse bent down, pulled out the drawer and grabbed the document. When he closed it, he turned around and saw something sticking out of the walk-in closet. Opening the closet door, Jesse noticed something familiar on the ground. It was a grey scarf that had printed images of newspapers and cameras surrounding it, a symbol of journalism. This scarf had belonged to Erica, so why in hell was it sitting in Derek's closet? Could Erica have given the scarf to his mother or sister to borrow? There had to be an explanation for this. He assumed that the medication belonged to either his mother or sister, but what if it had something to do with Erica having medication in her system on the day that she had died?

No, that was crazy. Derek would never have hurt Erica, but why did he have her scarf? Derek had a lot of explaining to do.

He rushed back into the kitchen while Derek was washing the few plates. He turned around to face Jesse. "Did you get lost or something, man?"

Jesse put the document on the table and waited until he turned off the tap before confronting him. He held the scarf in his right hand and swallowed. "Explain this to me."

Derek's face paled and his eye twitched. Noticeable signs of guilt. "What is that?"

Jesse scoffed. "You must know this belonged to Erica, Derek. So why was this in your bedroom closet? You must have an explanation."

Derek moved towards a chair with his head bowed. "From memory, Erica came by one time, and she asked me about a journalist friend of mine from New York. She wanted a contact when she did her foreign reporting. She had a coffee and spilled it over her top. She went in the bathroom then grabbed one of my tops from the closet. She got changed in there and must've forgotten it in the room. I don't notice women's accessories, man."

"Right. I find it hard to believe that a scarf which got stuck in the door was not noticeable. And why is it the first time I'm hearing this?"

He lifted up his shoulder. "How should I know? I guess I forgot about it. Erica should have explained this to you, man. Her scarf stayed in the closet and I didn't realise it was there. I didn't think it was a big deal."

Jesse wasn't convinced of his story. It sounded fabricated, but he would go with it for now. Erica's scarf didn't have to mean anything, did it? "I bought her that scarf for her birthday, so I would have thought it meant something to her." He pushed down his fury, not having the energy to continue this discussion. "I have to go, but I'm taking this scarf. You don't need to walk me out. I'll be in touch."

Before he left, he turned back for one more thing. "I noticed anxiety medication in your bathroom cabinet. I didn't realise anyone in your family took it. Whose is it?" Derek flinched and avoided his eyes without responding. If it did belong to his mother or sister, he didn't want to know their business. "Goodbye then."

Derek nodded. "We can finish working on the car another time. I'll be seeing you, Jesse, and I'm sorry I didn't tell you about the scarf."

As Jesse walked out of the house, he ruminated about the scarf as he twirled his hands through it, remembering the time he'd bought it for her. It was her twentieth birthday and they'd been together for one year at the time. She'd worn it often and loved the symbolism of journalism and the softness of the silk on her skin.

A car drove into the driveway as he walked out towards the kerb. "Hey Mandy." Derek's sister rolled down her window and smiled. She had long, curly hair with a short fringe which covered part of her hazel eyes. She was twenty and beautiful enough to be a model, and he knew she'd had a crush on him years ago.

"Hi Jesse. You're leaving just as I'm coming in?"

"I have to go." He could check in with the truth from Mandy. "Listen, did Erica ever visit Derek here without me on one occasion?"

She drew back, hesitating. "It was a few times, Jesse. I thought they were friends and you would've known about it."

Jesse ignored his tight hands. "Right. And does Derek have a journalist friend in New York? Or somewhere overseas?"

Mandy laughed. "Where did you get that idea from? His friends are all from Melbourne, and he's never mentioned a journalist friend in New York to us."

His chest squeezed tight. Jesse waved goodbye and entered his car, wondering why Derek would lie to him about New York. Or maybe he never mentioned his friend, but he didn't buy his story about the scarf either. He would not jump to conclusions until he could dig deeper into this.

Chapter Twenty-One

A REQUEST

G abriella made her way inside the local library, walking along the grass-lined concrete path. The pitched roof and brown brick made it look like a small house. Tilting trees, hedges, and bushes framed the front of the building. The gentle breeze feathered her cheek as she pulled open the glass door and stepped inside the quiet space. She walked over to the fiction section of books, searching for books on contemporary romance, which she could read at night before bed.

People sat at computers or read inside cubicles while others bowed their heads to work with piles of textbooks at their sides.

She picked up one a romance novel, turning the book over and read the blurb. She put it aside and focused on another, but as she put it back, she spotted a gloved hand in between the books on the other side of the shelf. The person was roughly shoving several books on the shelf and dropping several of them.

Gabriella moved away and made her way to the non-fiction section, holding her romance novel under one arm and her bag strap over her shoulder. She wandered over to the computer catalogue to search for textbooks on social work case studies, and keyed in her search terms on the computer. A few items on case studies came up, and she made her way over to the section and scanned through the item codes until finding the one she wanted. She flicked through the pages and put it back on the shelf, when the same gloved hand pushed through and continued to drop books on the floor. She peered through the gap on the shelf but couldn't see the person's face. What were the odds of having the same person who had been in the fiction section now move over to the non-fiction section? It was possible as the library was quite small. She was being ridiculous and letting her imagination get the better of her. No-one was following her around the library. But out of curiosity, she walked over to the other side and spotted the back of a figure leaving. He wore gloves, a beanie, and a thick jacket and dashed through the door without looking back. What was his hurry? He didn't even have any books.

Gabriella left the area to head back to the fiction section. She found another romance novel to read, scanned the books, and printed off the library receipt. As she turned, she wondered if she'd seen the person wearing gloves out of the corner of her eye, but it ended up being someone else. Shaking her head, she exited the library and walked to her car, which was parked on the other side of the road. Footsteps sounded behind her and she quickened her steps, thinking that it might be the person from the library following her. Should she dare turn around and see who it was? The person coughed and she turned around and flinched. *Derek!*

Gabriella smiled at Jesse's friend, wondering what he was doing close to the library. "Hi Derek. What brings you by here?"

Derek's eyes roamed as if he was waiting for someone. "Oh, hi Gabriella. I dropped off my sister at Scienceworks so was in the area. What are you doing around here?"

"I was at the library, borrowing a couple of books. I'm a reading buff and cannot get enough of books. If I didn't need to sleep, I would read all night."

He grimaced. "I hear you, but I am just the opposite. Get me a tool and a car and I would rather ditch anything involving paper." He cleared his throat, standing in the street not far from her car. "How about we go to the local cafe for a coffee?"

She shook her head. "No, I can't. I have to work on social work assignments and am a bit behind. But thanks for the offer."

Derek's eyes turned serious. "No problem."

"I'll see you around." She turned to move towards her car and stopped short when footsteps continued to follow her.

"Wait up, Gabriella. I will follow you to your car." She faced him, nodded then ambled back towards her car. She stood by her vehicle with Derek standing opposite. His eyes were unreadable.

"Before you leave, I wanted to talk to you about Jesse." She angled her head, waiting. He obviously had something on his mind and it couldn't wait. "I know you have been seeing him lately, especially after what happened to your client." His eyes flickered towards the ground briefly. "I want you to convince him to stop this crazy notion about Erica. She was depressed and killed herself, and he has to get on with his life. He is living in the past and it's not healthy."

Gabriella's spine tingled at the mention of Jesse. But what influence could she have over Jesse when she barely knew the man? "I don't know how I can convince him, Derek. He has his own mind. Besides, it's not like we are that close. We only talk to each other because of Joy. You'll need to talk to him yourself."

Derek looked over his shoulder as if he was expecting company. "He will not listen to me, but someone needs to drum the idea into his head. You can be objective and tell him to let Erica's death go."

Gabriella got the feeling there was more to his story. "Why is this bothering you so much? If that's what Jesse believes, then who are we to change his mind? We don't have real facts to the contrary."

Derek shook his head. "Are you telling me you believe in the same crap too?" He scoffed. "I thought you would be different and see sense."

Gabriella wandered over to the other side of her car. "Erica was my friend, and you didn't know her as well as we did, Derek. She was not depressed and had no reason to kill herself. What makes you think otherwise?" She placed her hand on the car's door handle and waited for a response.

Derek averted his eyes. "Nothing. I only want Jesse to live his life and let this go. We sometimes cannot know what is going on in a person's head. There are just things you would never understand."

What did that even mean? Before she could respond, he rushed accross the road with his shoulders drooping. That was weird. Where did his notion about Erica come from, and why was letting this go so important to him?

She got inside her car and started the motor with a heaviness in her chest.

Chapter Twenty-Two

ROSES ARE RED

He squinted through a set of binoculars, adjusting his focus to get a close-up view. She had just arrived home from work but moved straight to the kitchen. She was watering an indoor plant by the kitchen window with such grace that he wanted to take her now. But no, it was too soon. Plans couldn't be rushed. She drew the curtains, and instantly, he smashed the binoculars onto the ground and waited. Why did she have to close those damn curtains? Now he would not see her reaction to his lovely surprise. But once she called the police, he could savour his work. All in good time and she would be his.

***

Gabriella filled up a glass with water at the kitchen sink after watering her indoor plant. She drank it down to soothe her parched throat after a tiring day. She had had two at-risk youths today and had contacted their doctors and next of kin about their suicidal thoughts. Both parties planned to monitor their movements and would get them checked into a mental health facility to stabilise their symptoms. It had become harder for Gabriella to manage those with suicidal tendencies, given that she'd lost her friend and client within a year of each other. She had supervision with her manager often, and it helped, but she still didn't feel right about Erica and Nora's deaths. It was as if there was no closure. She was thankful it was Friday and she could enjoy her quiet weekend.

Rubbing the back of her neck, she closed her eyes briefly and put the glass in the sink. She peered through a gap in the kitchen curtain, a reflection of light appearing before her as if a spotlight had shone on her house. Who knew what was in the distance? She didn't need to concern herself right now. What she needed was to get changed into her casual clothes and have a light dinner so she could take a break from thinking about her clients.

Angela wandered towards her with a purr, and she bent down low and held her tight while staring into her big eyes. She stroked her warm fur and rubbed her nose. "Hey, Angela. Am I glad to see you." The kitten purred again then plunged out of her arms and made her way back past her bedroom, no doubt wanting to play with her toys.

Gabriella's mind turned back to Derek and how he'd acted strangely about Erica. Why did it bother him that Jesse would not let Erica go when there were so many unanswered questions? There had to be more to her story, but in what way did it impact him? She would need to talk to Jesse about his odd behaviour.

Gabriella entered her room and gasped for breath. She stood frozen in the spot; her body numb from the image in front of her. Her blue bedspread was filled with red rose petals. The petals were in two rows, one close to the pillows and the other underneath. Two words were spelled out with the rose petals. *Together Soon!*

Running out of her bedroom to the bathroom, Gabriella wretched into the toilet and wiped her mouth with the back of her hand. With muscles tensed, she walked back into the kitchen and drank more water, her legs becoming unsteady. Grabbing a knife from the block, she gripped it tight and wandered through all the rooms to check for any intruders. The house was empty.

Taking a calming breath, she sat down, picked up her phone on the kitchen table and placed a call to Marco. She hated calling him after hours, but this was an invasion of her privacy. She no longer felt safe in her own home. Whoever did this had been here earlier today while she was at work. "Marco, it's Gabriella."

"Hey Gabriella. Is everything okay?"

Her whole body shaking, she said, "Someone's broken into my house. They left rose petals on my bed."

"Are you hurt?"

"No, I'm fine, Marco."

"Is there anyone in the house? Are you safe?"

"I checked the house and I think the person's gone."

"Do not touch anything, Gabriella. I want you to go to your neighbour and wait for us there, just in case the perpetrator decides to return. Go now and I will stay on the line." She exited her house, rushed down her driveway and walked to the front door of her neighbour's house. "I am here now, Marco." She ended the call.

Her neighbour, Marjorie, was an elderly widow with smiling blue eyes, a stooped posture and short, grey hair. "Hello dear. Is everything okay?"

Gabriella shook her head. "Can I come inside? I will explain everything."

Marjorie's eyes darkened as she opened the door wider. "Of course, dear. We will have a nice cup of tea and you can tell me all about it."

Gabriella managed a half-smile. "Thanks, Marjorie. I appreciate it." With unsteady legs, she walked inside. Her eyes widened at the stacks of books lining the floor of the walkway and the mounds of boxes blocking the way towards the kitchen. The house was dark, with all the curtains closed as they passed the living room.

Marjorie pushed the boxes aside and created a path to the kitchen laden with piles of newspapers, magazines, and dirty tea towels. "Take a seat, love." She proceeded to switch on an electric kettle, placed tea inside two mugs and poured boiling water into them. Turning, she set a cup of tea in front of Gabriella with a jug of milk and a sugar bowl. "Now tell me what is going on, Gabriella. You look extremely pale."

Gabriella didn't want to scare the woman by telling her she was being watched, so kept her reply general. "Someone broke into my house and I am waiting for the police. I'm worried they're still around so the police will check it out. They wanted me to stay with one of my neighbours and here I am. You've always been nice to me, Marjorie. Thanks for being here."

Marjorie leaned forward and touched her hand. She shook her head and pursed her lips. "Oh, dear. Who could it be? Are you alright?"

Gabriella sipped her tea without sugar or milk and set it aside. "I am feeling better now. Thanks." Her phone buzzed. She checked her message and it came from Joy asking her if she wanted company tonight. *Christ!* Now she'd have to let Joy know what was happening. She ignored it for now. "Marjorie, did you see anything or anyone earlier today?"

She tilted her head. "I might have seen someone behind one of those trees, looking through their binoculars. But then a car came by and he got in and disappeared. He must have been a tourist with an interest in the surroundings. I'm sure they were just having fun. I don't think there was anything suspicious about that."

Gabriella wondered if it was her stalker, but there was no way of knowing. She remembered her phone message. "I am sorry. I need to reply to this message."

Marjorie nodded. "You go right ahead, love. I will go check on my cat and be back in a jiffy. Take your time." She got up and walked towards the back of the house.

Gabriella sent off a reply to her text. *Sorry. I had a break-in and waiting for the police. Cannot do anything tonight.* She heard Marjorie returning.

"Here, kitty kitty. Here kitty kitty." She approached Gabriella. "I have no idea where my cat's gone. She always stays in her little basket outside but she is not there now. I guess the police will have an extra job to do today."

Gabriella rose. "I will help you find her." They walked back outside but there was no sign of thecat. As they came back inside, she had a thought. What if her stalker spotted her coming next door and kidnapped the cat? If that was the case, she had just got a poor old woman involved in her problem.

Chapter Twenty-Three

PROCESSING A SCENE

G abriella wandered back to her house from Marjorie's place hugging her body tight as if she was cold. Answering the doorbell, she took a breath as Marco and Angelo greeted her, with a crime scene van and police officers approaching behind them.

She led them to the living room and stood near the couch while forensics entered her house. She showed them to her bedroom then walked back to the detectives. "One of the officers will stay with you outside for a few minutes. We'll sweep the whole house just in case. You said it was in the bedroom?" Marco said.

She nodded. "I don't see anything else touched, but it would be great to check anyway. You know I'm not a stranger to depravity or sick minds."

Angelo intervened. "Forensics will check for DNA and fingerprints. Before you go outside, can you give us the rundown of everything you did when you got home?"

Gabriella explained the events. "I even saw a spotlight in the distance over by the park. My neighbour, Marjorie, said she spotted someone from the reserve across the road, using binoculars. Someone picked him up afterwards."

Angelo leaned in. "Do you think your guy was watching you in the house?" He gave Marco a serious look.

"It's possible." She cleared her throat. "And my neighbour's cat's gone missing. You don't think the stalker did that, do you?" She shivered in the evening's setting sun and looked over at Marjorie next door who was watching her with curious eyes.

"We will get an officer to speak to her, and they can canvas others in the area who might have seen someone suspicious lurking around," Marco said. "Someone else might have seen this guy with binoculars." He took a breath. "Listen. Stay with a friend tonight. I doubt he'll come back, but just to be safe."

Gabriella nodded. "I can do that. I'll get a bag once you guys have finished."

Angelo touched her briefly on the shoulder. "Are you sure you don't know who might be doing this to you?"

She shook her head. "I don't think so. My ex-boyfriend Nick is in prison and my dad is no longer a threat."

Marco pressed his lips together, gripping his notebook tight as he looked at her with concern. "What about friends of your father or Nick? Could they be seeking revenge against you for testifying in court?"

Gabriella's heart raced. "I don't know. Not that I know of, Marco. Oh, God! I hope not." She peered at the ground, her face heating up exponentially. She could not go through that again. She wouldn't.

Angelo gave her a reassuring smile. "We are only fishing here. It could be anyone at this stage, but we need to rule these things out first." The slamming of a car door made her jump. He moved over to the front door at the sound of the doorbell. Gabriella joined him and Joy fell into her arms. "Hey, girl. Are you alright?" She pulled away from her and noticed Jesse standing near her letterbox.

Gabriella followed Joy to her brother outside while Marco shouted instructions to two police officers. "Head over to the neighbour's house and find out what she witnessed today. Canvas this entire street and find out if anyone in this area noticed anything suspicious between the hours of 8:30 and 5:30 today. I want this done quickly. And check if anyone has a personal security camera." The officers nodded and made their way to Marjorie's house when Marco rushed back inside. A stout and elderly police officer stood near the entrance with his arms crossed and eyes roaming the area. He ushered the onlookers in the street back to their homes.

Joy asked, "What is going on here?"

Jesse stood silently near her letterbox. His body was present but his mind appeared to be elsewhere. "Are you all right?" He looked up at her with such tenderness that her whole body tingled. She was in fear for her life and should not be having such reactions to his glances.

At that moment, a white van stopped at the side of the road. A nerdy-looking man and an older lady exited it. Both of them had reporter's tags around their necks. The man was tall and lanky with ginger hair, a moustache, and glasses. He was plain-looking and barely stood out as a journalist, but he looked familiar. On closer inspection, she remembered him from Erica's workplace, but she didn't remember seeing the woman before. She sported shoulder-length vibrant red hair, a model-like body, and wore a revealing white blouse with two buttons undone and a long grey pencil skirt.

The tall man spoke, turning to Jesse. "Hello, Jesse. It's been a while."

The woman gave him a warm smile. "Jesse. It's great to see you again." She held out a notepad and looked at the front of the house with curiosity. Then she turned back to her colleague.

Jesse nodded. "Hi Arthur. Janey. What are you both doing here?"

He lifted his shoulders and moved closer to Gabriella. "We just need to talk to Gabriella over here." His eyes softened. "I was out of town during Erica's funeral and am so sorry for your loss, Jesse. I wish I could have been there."

"No worries, Arthur," said Jesse.

He turned to Gabriella. "So, Gabriella. You were Erica's friend, weren't you?"

She wasn't happy to have a reporter here but would play this out. "I do remember you from Erica's work." Her hands were shaking, but she held it together. She kept ruminating about the person harassing her, but she didn't want to show her fear.

He looked at Joy with curiosity and put out his hand to Gabriella which she shook. "I worked closely with Erica. I am sorry for your loss."

Janey smiled. "It is nice to meet you, Gabriella. Arthur mentioned you had lost your friend about a year ago. So tragic, and I am sorry for your loss, too."

"Thank you." She didn't want to get into a conversation. But she had to put on a brave face, as surely this stalker didn't plan to hurt her. He had to be harmless with his expressions of adoration. Perhaps, having the media might scare him off. She turned back to Arthur. "I must've seen you a few times at her work when Erica and I had lunch." She looked at Jesse who kept sighing while Joy stared at her feet, looking bored.

He turned to his lady friend. "We would like to help if we can. We got a tip from our police consultant about a break-in."

Arthur faced the crew, coming in and out of the van. "I was on my way home when I realised we could cover this story for tomorrow. Can I ask you a few questions for the newspaper? It won't take too long."

Before she could reply, Joy intervened. "I don't think so. You can speak to the police,

Arthur. I am sure they have a media liaison person you can speak to."

Jesse cleared his throat. "It really isn't the best time, Arthur. I'm sure the police will give you the facts. Gabriella's in shock here."

He nodded with a smile. "I suppose I can wait if Gabriella's not ready to talk." His eyes were friendly. "I hope this all gets sorted out, but if you don't mind, I will speak to that policeman over there."

"That's fine. The detectives can steer you in the right direction," said Gabriella. He scurried towards the stout police officer who had resumed his position.

Joy looked at Gabriella. "Let's talk in the car while we wait." They followed her to Jesse's car, and sat on the back seat with Jesse in front. "Now, Gabi, tell us exactly what happened and what was taken?"

Gabriella shuddered at the thought of what he had taken. Her sense of security. Her private sanctuary was tarnished, ruined. She was no longer safe in her home. "My bed was filled with rose petals which spelled out, *Together Soon*."

Joy sat in shocked silence. "Are you serious? My goodness!"

Jesse banged his fist on the steering wheel. "What the hell, Gabriella? Who is doing this to you? An ex-boyfriend? A jilted lover?"

She drew back, surprised by his anger. "I don't know, Jesse, but don't get angry at me. It's not my fault this is happening." Joy glared at him.

"I am sorry. I'm not angry with you, but at the situation. Something about this doesn't feel right. And it's just bringing up...never mind."

"I'm sorry, Jesse. You didn't have to come today, but I appreciate it." She turned to Joy. "Can I stay at your place?"

"Of course, love. I'm sure my parents won't mind. I can give my mum a call later and let them know."

Gabriella pushed back her tears. "Who is doing this to me, Joy, and why? I have never hurt anyone, and I refuse to believe it's connected to my past."

Joy held her hand. "I wish I knew, girl. Did Nick have any shady friends?"

Gabriella shook her head. "No, not that I know of."

Jesse twisted his body to get a better look at Gabriella. "Why don't you stay at my place instead? You will get more privacy and not be hounded by my parents every second of the day. My mum is a worrier of all sorts, and my dad might make you uncomfortable with his silences and stares."

Gabriella winced, not expecting such an invitation. She could not stay at his house, with him thinking she was weak. "No, I am sure I'll be fine with Joy."

Joy squeezed her shoulder. "You know what. He might have a point. Jesse's studied karate and will know how to protect you. You do need privacy and my parents won't give you any. I am struggling living at home myself."

"So you don't want me to stay with you, Joy? Will it be an issue for your parents?"

Joy scoffed. "What a silly question, girl. You know I love you like a sister. It is not that, but I worry after everything that has happened with Erica and your client, Nora. I don't know how safe you'll be at my home. If your parents weren't on holiday, you could have stayed with them, but they won't be back for weeks."

Gabriella understood her point and staying over with a guy she barely knew was daunting, but she needed to feel safe. If he had studied karate, then maybe he was the best choice. "I don't know. I really hate imposing on anyone. This is madness." She looked out of the window and saw the crime scene staff loading up their van as if they were almost finished. "I'm sure I can stay home if they have a patrol car out front. They did that with Jamie."

Joy grunted. "And look at how that turned out when she stayed home? A patrol car does not guarantee your safety, girl. Jesse even has an alarm in his house so that would trigger any sort of invasion."

Jesse leaned in, his eyebrows lifting. "Come on, Gabriella. I could use the company and I promise I will not bite."

Gabriella could try it for a few days and then go back home. "Fine, Jesse."

His eyes lit up. "Great. I have a spare bed you can use."

Gabriella waited in the car until forensics and the police left, then hurried back inside to get her belongings.

Chapter Twenty-Four

NIGHTMARE

Jesse exited his car in the garage and waited for Gabriella as she walked towards the side door with a travel bag slung over her shoulder. He unlocked it and entered with her following behind. He wondered why he'd asked her to stay with him. Was it a good idea, given the way she looked right now? Tense, distant, and hands quivering, she put down her bag as her eyes roamed the house with awe.

He had asked her here because nobody had the right to invade anyone's home and she needed to be safe. He couldn't protect Erica but he could protect Gabriella. He would've done the same for Joy if she was in danger. It was in his nature to do what was right and serve justice. That was all this was.

He brought himself back to the present. She stood awkwardly, with her hands in the pockets of her jeans, which she wore well. He forced his eyes away from her feminine curves and the tightness of her thighs and butt. Even the way her t-shirt showed a little bit of

cleavage and clung to her full breasts. *Stop it!* "I will give you the grand tour before I show you to the spare bedroom." He walked her through his kitchen and living room, and stepped out to his backyard with its empty fountain, low brush, towering trees, and paved path. "I plan to fix up the yard once I've saved up for a landscaper. They're pricey."

"Hmm. What do you plan to do here?"

"I want conifers, flowers, more low brush, pebbles surrounding more trees, and these particular palms that can put up with Victoria's crazy, changeable climate. I am not much of a gardener but a landscaper would know what's low maintenance."

Gabriella nodded, keeping a safe distance away from him. Did she think he would bite? "I hear you, but I'm not great in the garden either. Although, I did manage to grow parsley, thyme, and basil on a few occasions. They didn't die on me."

He chuckled. "Good for you." He pressed his hands together. "Let's go back inside and I will show you to your room."

As he slid open the glass door, a hint of fresh, floral perfume permeated his senses, and he could hear her soft breathing behind him. He walked up the corridor and strolled to the room after she had grabbed her bag. "You are welcome to settle into your room or I could make you a coffee before bed."

"Coffee would be nice. Thanks. White with no sugar."

Back in the kitchen, he turned on the electric kettle, reached up for two mugs, and spooned in a teaspoon of coffee into both of them. The silence was comforting while he waited for the water to boil, his mind churning over how he had panicked after hearing that her house had been broken into. When Joy rang him, he could have kicked himself for not checking in with her sooner.

He set both mugs on the table and sat opposite her with a hint of a smile. She took a sip, and he wondered how the mug felt with her lips encased over them. Her shyness in his house was endearing. "I'm sure the police will catch whoever did this to you." He placed his hands around his own mug, staring down at the table. "Joy mentioned that you've been getting love notes. Are you okay?"

"As good as can be, considering. I am a fighter, Jesse, and I will be fine. I appreciate you taking me in. Thank you." She hesitated, as if wondering what to say next. "I know you like your privacy, and I will stay out of your way. I'm sure, in a day or two I'll be cleared to go home."

"Let's take it one day at a time." He ignored the ache in his chest. "Has anything else happened?"

Gabriella shifted. "Yes, I saw Derek near the local library." She cleared her throat. "He told me to tell you to let go of this obsession you have with Erica. He thinks you need to live in the present and forget the past."

Jesse could have killed his friend. How dare he go through Gabriella to pressure him about the past? He didn't want her involved in their conflict. "I am sorry. He shouldn't have tried to go through you to get to me. I'll speak to him."

Gabriella leaned forward; her hands squeezed together. "Is everything okay with Derek? He seems worried about something."

He nodded. "I think so. He just worries about me." He remembered his sister telling him that Erica had been to their place a few times and that Derek didn't have a friend in New York. He wasn't convinced that Derek was purely worried about Jesse. More was going on.

Once they finished their hot drinks, Jesse wandered over to his closet and got her an extra pillow. He entered her room and handed it to her. "The pillow on the bed's a bit hard. This one's softer." As he gave it to her, their hands brushed, and he had to push down his urge to grab it. Her hands were so soft and dainty.

"Thanks, and goodnight," said Gabriella. He walked off with a deflated posture. He didn't want the night to end, but they needed to sleep.

***

Gabriella was deep in sleep, running down a narrow corridor as a faceless man raced after her. Heart thumping and her legs aching, she pushed through to get away. A door was within easy reach to the exit. She fumbled with the knob as the man gained on her and shoved her to the ground. She crawled away, but a large hand reached for her and viciously pulled strands of hair out of her scalp. The man held a knife. He swung it up high and was about to stab her when a familiar disembodied voice rang through. "Save yourself now." She woke up screaming, beads of sweat peppering the back of her neck. Sitting up in bed, she took calming breaths. Her door opened and Jesse rushed in.

"Oh, my God! I thought you were being attacked. What happened?"

She leaned back against the headrest and fully opened her eyes. "Just a nightmare. I'm sorry for waking you up."

"Don't be silly! I panicked because I...I didn't know what was happening. Can I get you a drink or anything?"

"No, I'll be fine."

"Do you want to tell me about the dream?" His body edged close to hers and she felt safe.

"A faceless man was chasing me. He was about to stab me when I heard a voice, saying 'Save yourself now,' then I woke up."

He frowned. "A voice. Who was it?"

Gabriella's heart broke as she thought about that sweet girl, taken too young. She swallowed down her tears, not wanting to cry in front of Jesse. "It sounded like Nora."

Jesse moved his body forward and caressed her shoulder. "She protected you in the dream, but what do you think it means?"

Gabriella swallowed hard. "What if Nora really did kill herself? I couldn't save her, Jesse. That gets to me every day. If she did kill herself, how could I have not seen the signs? How could I have failed her? I am so stupid." She couldn't stop the tears anymore.

Jesse wiped them away. "Come here." He pulled her into his arms and stroked the small of her back. "You are not at fault here, Gabriella. You have no responsibility for other people's behaviour and you did the best you could. She saw Claudia too, and it sounded as if she was getting better. Do not blame yourself."

Gabriella sank into Jesse's arms and savoured his strong yet gentle arms around her.

Chapter Twenty-Five

BONDING

J esse rubbed his eyes as he entered the kitchen, listening to Gabriella on the phone. "No, I am fine, Bella. Let Jamie and Liz know I am not in the mood to go out. I just saw you guys at the cafe for dinner last night. You do not need to keep checking up on me. I am not alone here." She blushed, and he wondered what Bella had said to cause it. Once she ended the call, she turned to him with a warm smile. He couldn't help but get lost in her striking dark eyes.

"Good morning, Jesse." She sighed. "I have to put up with clingy friends. They wanted to go out tonight, but I told them I just wanted a quiet weekend. I hope you don't mind if I laze around here." She looked away. "I've got my laptop as I've got an assignment to work on. Can I do anything around here for you?"

He shook his head. "No, nothing."

She put up her hand. "Please, do not wait on me hand and foot. Do your own thing and I will do mine. Let this be your normal Saturday routine. Don't you sometimes work on cars with Derek on the weekend?"

His heart warmed at her generous nature. "I do, but plans can change."

Gabriella moved towards him. "I don't want to stop you from following your routine, so please go to Derek's place. I will be fine. I'm sure the stalker doesn't know where I am."

He squared his shoulders. "I am not taking that chance. Besides, we can do things together. Now, how about I cook us breakfast?"

Gabriella put down her phone on the table. "I can do it. What would you like?"

"No, you are the guest, so go sit down and relax. You can turn on the TV if you like." She didn't want to argue with him, so she sat down on the couch and turned on the TV. A news program came on, and she immersed herself in the stories while Jesse cooked up scrambled eggs. His eyes stayed focused on Gabriella. She crossed a toned leg over the other one, the light cotton dress she wore flowing down to her knees, displaying her slim body. He saw her eyes darken as she watched the news, which was mostly negative. He was so wrapped up in concern for her that he accidentally dropped an egg on the floor. He shook his head and avoided stepping on it. Gabriella got up, picked up a few sheets of paper towels from the counter and wiped up the gooey mess. She threw it into the bin then wiped down the floor with fresh, dampened paper towels.

"I am such a klutz." He picked up another egg, but Gabriella took it from him, his heart stopping at the gesture.

"I make a mean scrambled egg. Let me." He sat on a chair and watched her as she bent down to search the fridge. The back of her legs showed as she reached down for a tomato and a packet of cheese. She expertly chopped up the tomato, grated the cheese, cracked four eggs and scrambled them on the stove while adding the tomatoes, cheese, and seasoning. She put the eggs on plates and poured coffee, and they sat down to eat in comfortable silence.

He had a sudden thought. "Did something happen in that park when you hurt your ankle? When I came over to your house, I got the sense that something had distracted you."

She put down her fork and wiped her mouth with a napkin. Her eyes flickered as if she was deciding whether to be truthful or not. "It was the reason I fell. I thought someone was following me. I got distracted, ran too fast, and hit that boulder."

He nodded. "I wish you had told me, Gabriella. It might have been when all this started." She remained silent, wrapping her full lips around her food. "This is delicious, by the way. You sure know how to cook."

"My mum taught me, in spite of having a husband who constantly abused her. She was an amazing mother, and I am thankful that she survived that bastard."

Jesse's heart went out to her. What she must've endured with domestic violence, followed by an ex-boyfriend who'd betrayed her. She was stronger than she thought, and he admired her resilience and strength. "She raised an amazing daughter who loves to help others. What attracted you to social work?"

She chewed the last bit of her eggs and sipped on her coffee, pondering. "I didn't want anyone to experience what I experienced. The pain, the degradation, the unpredictability of not knowing the type of person you'd be dealing with from day to day. Would my father be the sweet, caring, and charismatic father, or the sadistic, violent, and manipulative father? I vowed that I would help others who suffered as I did so I could stop their pain. I can relate to so many of my clients. I was even suicidal once." She cast her eyes down to her hands and rubbed her knuckles. "I thought of my mum, and how I couldn't do that to her, so I stopped myself." She exhaled. "I remember one time how my mother put too much salt into the pasta." She fought back tears. "He slapped her a few times then grabbed the jar of salt and poured it down her throat until she almost choked to death. I tried to stop him but he pushed me down. Eventually, he stopped and laughed about it. He had no remorse for anything. And what that bastard did to Liz. It's madness."

Jesse felt his own tears sting his cheek and reached for her hand. "I am so sorry, Gabriella. I don't know how anyone can put up with that kind of violence. You and your mother got through it, and now you have an amazing stepfather."

She smiled, averting her eyes. "He is kind, gentle, and giving, and I love him like my own father. He is my true father, Jesse."

They finished their breakfasts and continued to drink their coffee in silence for a few minutes when Gabriella looked up at him. "You have your own demons with your sister and Erica. Not to mention how hard it was for your mum."

"I got through it with my family and friends. My mum got into a car accident not long after Mia died. I was thirteen years old. I saw her at the hospital, and my dad told me she had smashed into a tree and injured herself pretty badly. I watched her still body, then later saw her do rehab and couldn't bear feeling helpless. I wanted her to get better. I wanted her to feel better, which is why I studied physiotherapy. It's rewarding to know I can help ease people's suffering a bit. I can get them to walk again if they're in a wheelchair. I can help to ease their chronic pain. It's not a magical cure but it helps."

"It's an amazing profession, Jesse, and I am sorry about your mother. But she has come a long way since then."

He nodded. "We later found out that she had tried to kill herself because she had all this guilt about not being able to protect Mia. They had had an argument the night before, and she wondered if they hadn't fought, whether Mia would have still gone out that night."

Gabriella leaned back in her chair. "That is crazy. Joy told me that Mia was a rebel, so whether they had an argument or not, she still would have gone out to meet her friend. No doubt. She was young and wanted the freedom to go out. Nothing would have been different. I hope your mother knows that."

Jesse clasped his hands together. "My mum understands that now, and she is sorry for doing that to us. She got help and is fighting fit now." The doorbell rang. "I wonder who that is." He rose from the table and answered the door.

Marco stood awkwardly with a stern expression. He nodded in his direction. "Jesse, can I come in? We need to talk."

He lost all breath, wondering if someone else had died. "What is it?"

"I have a few more questions about Erica and Nora." Jesse swallowed, a prickle of fear running down his spine as he ushered him inside the house.

Chapter Twenty-Six

PATTERNS

G abriella rose and kissed Marco on the cheek when he walked in. He sat at the table across from her beside Jesse. "I am sorry to interrupt your Saturday but this couldn't wait."

Jesse nodded. "Can I get you anything to drink?"

"No thanks. I'm good." He ran a finger across his knuckles, hesitating. "We have had developments in the case of Nora and Erica."

Gabriella looked at Jessie who shrugged. "What kind of developments?"

He rubbed his stubble and turned to Jesse before ploughing in with the news. "I cannot give you specifics, but we discovered that about ten years ago, a woman was killed in the same way as Erica and Nora. It was ruled a suicide and there was no further investigation. Then another young woman was killed in the same way about five years ago. This was considered a suicide too. These cases were in Queensland, and we're cross-communicating with law enforcement over there to get more details."

Gabriella's face paled and she cowered in her seat. She briefly closed her eyes and took deep breaths. They no longer believed these were suicidal acts. "What makes you think they're not suicides or accidents, and are related to these recent cases?"

"The cases are too similar to rule out, given a particular pattern occurring here. Murders staged as suicides, using the exact same method. We have also interviewed family members of both women, and they stressed that their daughters were not suicidal." He took a small notepad out of his back pocket. I have questions to ask you both about Erica and Nora.

Jesse frowned. "But I thought we answered everything about Erica? What more do you need to know?"

Marco shifted in his seat. "Sometimes trivial things can tell us a lot." He fixed his eyes on Gabriella, then Jesse. "We can look for more patterns similar to those cases in the past." He took a breath. "I know you mentioned that Erica was behaving strangely in those last few months." He looked away briefly and clasped his hands as if he didn't want to bring something up. "Was Erica seeing someone else at the time? Or someone who might have taken an interest in her while you were going out?"

Jesse tilted his head and sighed. "Of course not. As I said before, she had isolated herself, always wanting to stay home and not go out. She said she'd been burned out from work and refused to get medical help."

"And did you know about any news stories she was working on?"

Jesse searched back in his mind, peering into the distance and realised that he hadn't given any thought to her work in those final moments. Why hadn't he noticed that something was off with her? "As far as I know, they were local stories. Nothing scandalous. I don't think she could handle that much when she looked so tired and forgot conversations we'd had the week before. At the time, I thought she was recovering from the flu, but maybe it was more than that."

Marco turned to Gabriella. "Did you know of any news stories she was working on in those final days? Or whether she was worried about anything or anyone?"

Gabriella moved her body forward, ignoring her coffee which had turned cold. "No, nothing. The foreign news she reported on happened a couple of years earlier, but more recently, she had worked on local news. We never talked about work, and Joy and I had only seen her a few times. She was a bit withdrawn and mentioned that she was mostly fine, apart from having a few things on her mind, like work issues and her plans to marry Jesse. But I didn't believe her, and if I'd pushed harder, she..."

Marco jotted a few things down then looked up. "This is not your fault, Gabriella. Erica made her own choices, and she decided to be quiet about something."

Jesse swallowed. "Those other two women who died. Did they experience the same symptoms a few months before their death?"

Marco squinted. "I will only say we need to look deeper into things, but we are no longer suggesting suicide as the cause of death. It appears that whoever is doing this is staging a murders as suicides. We might need to reinterview her circle of friends, colleagues, family members, and acquaintances."

Jesse leaned forward. "What do you know about Erica? There's something you are not telling us. What is it?"

Marco sighed. "Jesse, I cannot tell you anything more as this is an ongoing investigation. I needed your views on the situation and now I have them. That's all I can say at this stage."

Gabriella asked, "Are we looking at a serial killer, Marco?"

Marco pressed his lips together and tucked away his notebook. "Octavia seems to think so, given the multiple kills in the same manner." He got up. "Gabriella, you should not be at home on your own. You can either stay here a little while longer or get someone to stay with you. As long as you are not on your own."

Gabriella's eyes darkened. "Are you telling me you think my stalker is the serial killer? Is that what you're saying?"

"I do not want to speculate at this stage, but we need to proceed with caution just in case. These kills were organised, planned, and had meticulous steps to the murders which suggests that it is possible he stalked them first, got to know their routines, and picked them at their most vulnerable. They would have been on their own and available for him to kidnap initially. But your stalker is different. He appears to be a love-obsessed type, and they don't always wish harm on their victims."

Gabriella's body shook and her eyes stared down into her mug. "But why target me? What did I do to this guy to want to stalk me this way? Are you sure he won't try to kill me?" Streams of tears ran down her cheeks. Jesse rushed to her side, sat in the chair beside her, and put his arm around her.

"It's going to be okay, Gabriella. You are safe here with me. And you do not need to go anywhere. I will protect you."

Marco's eyes turned a shade darker. "I am sorry, Gabriella. I didn't mean to upset you. It's just that I want you to be on your guard and take this seriously, just in case. I know it is hard to hear, but as I said before, your stalker may not be the killer. He may be an admirer, but you still need to take precautions, and I will not bet with your life. It is best you know so you can be careful and stay with your loved ones. I am telling you this for your own good and not to scare you." He pursed his lips. "We need to be prepared for the worst possible scenario."

She looked at Jesse briefly then turned back to Marco. "But this all seems connected, Marco. What more do you know?" He remained silent, staring. "I need the truth."

He gave her a reassuring smile. "I am sorry, but I cannot say anything to a civilian. I need to keep the boundaries between our social lives and my work. If I don't, my sergeant will likely pull me off this case. Right now he hasn't because we're doing our job. Trust me on that."

Gabriella sat frozen in the spot when Marco moved over to her side and gave her a gentle squeeze on the shoulder.

"Please take care of yourself, and I will be in touch. I'll see myself out, Jesse."

"Thanks, Marco."

Marco walked out of the house and Gabriella looked at Jesse with a fleeting smile. He leaned over and played with the strands of her hair as they sat there in silence. She abruptly rose from the chair and rushed into her room, hearing a rush of breath coming from him. She didn't need Jesse's pity when someone was possibly wanting to kill her. She had to be strong.

Chapter Twenty-Seven

PANIC MODE: 13 YEARS EARLIER

His chest constricted looking at the rose petals on his mother's bed. They spelled, "I love you." No doubt from her mother's boyfriend. He turned at the sound of his mother's heels behind him. She gasped at the sight before her. "Oh, my God! Gerald loves me. He did all this? Where is he?"

He smirked. "Oh, I just saw him. He had to leave, Mother."

His mother glared. "What? Why would he leave after this beautiful gesture?"

"You have to understand, Mama. He wanted to get between us, and I had to tell him that I am the only man who can love you. Not him."

His mother moved forward, her long fingernails digging into his scalp. "What the fuck did you do, dummy?"

He hyperventilated, not wanting to experience his mother's wrath, but he could never lie to her either. She would always know when he was lying. "I am sorry, Mama. I had to tell him."

She pushed him hard on the bed, the petals flying in the air. "What did you tell him?"

"I told him that you and me have special times in this bed, and that we love each other so much. I did it for us, Mama. For our love."

She picked up her heel and hit him hard in the chest, striking blow after blow while he tolerated the knocks in silent pain. "You bastard!

You are not man enough for me, and what we have is our own little secret, and you go telling my lover. How could you? I'll kill you. I'll kill you." She stopped when the phone rang.

***

Gabriella huddled under the blanket on the spare bed a few days later, a chill settling in her body as she thought about Jesse being in the next room. She was still reeling about the possibility that her stalker might be a murderer. But what if he wasn't? The police kept investigating and her friends had visited over the past two days to check in on her. Octavia explained how it was possible that her stalker was only a secret admirer and nothing more, and she had to believe that. But Marco had told her to be on her guard just in case.

Jesse had been a godsend, but he was a distraction to her mission to find out who was doing this to her, with his striking beauty and masculine physique. She felt helpless and itched to do something, but what? Was she willing to risk her own life to find out the identity of her stalker if he was the murderer? She had to get her anxiety under control. Each creak, footstep, overhead plane, or bird chirp caused her to cower in her room. Every night, she had eaten a silent dinner with Jesse and later locked herself in her room, not wanting to stay with him longer than necessary. Last night, she had skipped dinner after work and stayed in her bedroom. Jesse had called out to her but eventually gave up. How could she pretend that everything was okay and engage in light conversation with him? Her life was no longer normal.

Getting up from the bed, she drew the curtains at the window and watched a man walking his dog and a woman pushing a stroller down the footpath. Their lives were routine, and she wished for the same thing instead of being holed up like a prisoner in Jesse's home. There had to be a way to get back to her place, but did she want to spend police resources on her situation when they were investigating two murders? What if their investigation was related to her situation? How could she be sure it wasn't?

Hugging her body tight, she answered her phone when it rang. Gabriella didn't want to talk to anyone, but she had to make the effort and not close herself off completely. "Hey Bella."

"Gabriella, we were wondering if you would like to go out for drinks tonight? The girls and I can come and pick you up."

"No thanks, Bella. I am not up to it tonight, but thanks."

"You said that Sunday night, too. You cannot stay locked up in that room. It is not healthy to stay indoors this long and let that stalker win. Come out with us. You'll feel better."

Gabriella sighed when a knock on her bedroom door startled her. "Come in." Jesse walked inside her room and sat on her bed. She resumed her conversation. "I appreciate your efforts, Bella, but I am not feeling the best." She waited for a response but it got quiet. Jesse frowned and shook his head.

"Now you listen, girl, and listen good." Liz came on the line. "You will go stark-raving mad staying closed up like a hermit, and I love you too much to allow you to become a recluse. Do not let this bastard win. We have your back and you will be safe with us, girl. Marco and Angelo will get to the bottom of this, so don't worry."

"I love you, Liz, but I am not ready to socialise. I have to stay safe, and right now, I am only safe in this room. Please understand. I would be bad company and I don't want to take the risk. I am sorry."

"Okay, Gabriella. I understand, but eventually, this has to stop. We'll give you time to process everything. I know it's been a bit of a shock with the home invasion. "She paused. "You take care, girl, and we'll be in touch."

"Thanks, Liz. Say hi to Jamie and the others." She ended the call, put her phone down and remained standing by the window. She didn't need another lecture from Jesse but she knew she'd be getting one. In the last two days, Jesse had dropped her off at work and picked her up, then he was with her during the nights. She appreciated his efforts, but a part of her felt guilty overburdening others with her insecurities. Despite insisting she could drive to work on her own, he would not budge about letting her go alone to work. She was impacting his normal routine.

Jesse smiled. "How long are you going to lock yourself in this room, Gabriella? You've been here since Saturday night and it's Tuesday now. Let me help you get through this. I can keep you safe if you want to go out."

She scoffed. "And how will you do that, Jesse? Do you have the power to stop this creep, or do you know something I don't? Because from where I'm standing, he won't stop anytime soon. If anything, he's likely to escalate. But maybe if I marry the guy, it'll work out."

Jesse drew his brows together, his hands smoothing out a crease on her bed. "It has been quiet the past few days so it might have stopped."

"Hmm. I doubt that. And I want to be on my own, so you can leave now."

Jesse drew back. "You are being ridiculous. You have friends and family who care about you, and here you are, shutting everyone out. If this keeps going, you won't have anyone left. Is that what you want?"

Gabriella's heart clenched in her chest. How dare he try to control her? She didn't need anyone controlling her, not anymore. "You could never possibly understand what I am going through. None of it."

"I understand more than you know."

"Please leave, Jesse. I am not in the mood to talk to you or anyone. Do not pretend you are happy with this situation, me cramping your style. Go out with Derek and your other friends. I am sure you're missing out on meeting someone you can care about after Erica. I will be fine here. I do not need babysitting."

Jesse stood up with his hands on his hips, taking a step towards her. "You are being ridiculous if you think I'll leave you here on your own. I am happy where I am. It's not like I want to meet a girl. I am not looking for any relationship right now, if ever."

Gabriella stared at him for a minute, her body tightening up. What did she care if he never wanted a relationship? Neither did she. "You know what. I do not care what you do or don't do. Just leave me the hell alone. Get out of here." She shifted her body towards the window so he wouldn't see her eyes. Footsteps moved away from her.

"Fine, but you don't have to be a bitch about it." He slammed the door. She turned around, staring at the closed door for a few minutes, wondering why her body had turned cold. What the hell just happened, and where had her anger come from?

Chapter Twenty-Eight

NEWS

Jesse stretched out his arms the next morning and pulled the quilt off his body. He yawned, got up, retrieved clothes from his drawer and stepped into the shower, hoping to miss Gabriella this morning. His mind still reeled over the way she had angered him last night. Did she not care what he did? Was she okay if he decided to have sex with another girl or meet someone else? Not that she was looking for a relationship either, so what set her off last night? He was doing his best to keep her safe and this was the thanks he got? She could go back home for all he cared. Jesse shook the idea away, thinking it was too dangerous. If something happened to her, he would never forgive himself. But was her stalker the same person who had killed Erica and Gabriella's client or was it a secret admirer and someone entirely different? If only the police would find out so they could move on with their lives.

As the water streamed down his body, his mind couldn't help but flash back to the way Gabriella's nightgown fitted loosely around her buxom curves and how she'd flushed when he'd looked at her from top to bottom without meaning to. He imagined what it would be like to kiss the back of her slim neck, pressing his body against hers. Even in anger, she was beautiful, and he could not imagine how he would feel once she returned home. Would he miss her fighting spirit, mixed in with her sensitivity and deep vulnerability?

He ignored his hardness in the shower and soaped himself off. Turning off the nozzle, he got out of the shower and wrapped a towel around his waist. His phone buzzed on the basin. Picking it up, he answered the call. *Joy!*

"Hey, sis. What's up!"

"I wanted to check in with you to see how Gabi's doing. Are you taking her to work this morning?"

"No, Marco's taking her as he wanted to ask a few more questions. I will be glad if I don't see her this morning."

"What happened?"

He shook his head, sighing. "She literally threw me out of the spare bedroom."

"What did you say, Jesse, to upset her that way?"

"Nothing." He thought back to his comment about not looking for a relationship or wanting to meet a girl and being happy where he was. Did she get angry about him wanting to protect her or about not wanting a relationship? Obviously, it was about her wanting her freedom and hating how she had to stay locked up in his house.

"Go apologise to her as you might have said something hurtful you didn't realise. Gabi doesn't get angry easily, but she will get anxious."

"She can apologise to me, Joy."

"Whatever, bro, but I will drop in later tonight and convince her to go out. This is crazy. I hate seeing her this way. There has to be something more we can do, Jesse." She cleared her throat. "Listen, I...might..."

He angled his head. "You might what, sis?"

Joy gave a light chuckle. "Nothing, bro. I will see you later tonight."

He still wondered what she had been about to say. "I'll see you then. Take care."

"I love you, Jesse."

Since when did she use those words? It had been years. "I love you, too." He ended the call. Joy and Jesse had been close, and over the years he'd been protective of her. She was too independent for her own good and felt stifled when he took too much interest in her life.

Getting dressed, he strode into the kitchen but Gabriella wasn't there. He swung open the fridge, took out a nectarine, and bit into it. Filling a glass of water, he drank it down and continued chewing on the fruit.

The doorbell rang and he swung open the door. Marco smiled. "Hello, Jesse. Are you off to work?"

He nodded. "Come in and help yourself to a drink. I will call her and see if she's ready." He knocked on the bedroom door. "Marco's here. Are you ready?" He waited for at least a minute before she replied.

"Yes. I will be there in a minute. You can go."

He drew back at her cold, sharp tone. What was her problem? He shook his head, walked into the bathroom and brushed his teeth. He grabbed his keys, made his way back to the kitchen, and watched Marco pour himself a glass of water.

"She is in a mood, Marco, so tread carefully."

Marco chuckled. "I understand moods all too well. Bella has those too, and in those moments, it's best to let them sulk. Eventually, they'll calm down. Gabriella is going through a lot at the moment, and she's always been independent. She had to be, given her rough background. Give her time."

"I will, and I understand she feels imprisoned, but she has to be careful." He took a breath. "I'll be heading off. Take care of her."

Marco waved. "I will, and know we're doing our very best to find the perpetrator."

He walked out of the house with a heavy chest, wishing he'd at least seen her face. But she made it clear she didn't appreciate him.

***

Jesse leaned forward. He massaged the back of a young man who had short, brown wavy hair and was tall and lanky. The man, Rick, had an inflamed back. He pressed into the taut skin, his mind turning to Gabriella and how he missed not seeing her this morning. "It is pretty tight. I'll work on your other side." He moved around and continued his massage for a few minutes. "Have you been doing the exercises I've shown you?"

"Most days, and it has helped but I guess it takes time, doesn't it?"

Jesse pressed his fingers deeply into his lower spine. "It should improve within six weeks, provided you continue with the exercises every second day." He stopped massaging. "That's it for now, but I would like to show you some new exercises in the gym."

Rick got up and stretched. "Thanks, Jesse. It does feel slightly better after the massage. And I am getting better after resting it too." He pulled down his top and stood up.

Jesse walked over to the gym, and Rick followed. He stretched out his arms with the band. "Do this, then push your right foot forward. Stretch out your arms too." He did this three times before passing on the band to Rick, who appeared distracted. "Is it too hard?"

Rick shook his head, staring through the long glass window. "No, it's just this guy outside. He's staring at us through the window, and it's creepy."

Jesse turned, staring at the back of a man wearing a long jacket, a beanie and dark glasses. He moved off in the opposite direction. "He has nothing better to do."

Rick practised the exercises, then Jesse sent him home with a new appointment in two weeks. He returned to his office, typed up his case notes, and reviewed his next appointment. His mind veered back to the man watching them. If only he could have seen his face. But surely it was a man who was possibly thinking about physiotherapy? It didn't have to mean anything. His phone buzzed on his desk. "Hey Marco. What's wrong? Is Gabriella alright?"

"Jesse, it's Joy. She's been in an accident."

Jesse's body froze as his hand lost its grip on the phone and dropped to the floor.

Chapter Twenty-Nine

CAR ACCIDENT

The boy watched as nausea overcame him. He pushed against the sick feeling in his stomach. His mother gripped the hand of his friend, dragging the knife across his right lower arm.

"No, please. It hurts. No, please." The blood dripped on the carpet as she faced her son with a grimace. She didn't stop there. Pushing him back against the couch, she lifted his right leg, making incisions into the upper part. The tangy smell of blood caused him to run into the bathroom and vomit. Wiping his mouth with the back of his hand, he rushed back into the living room, hoping his mother would stop. She put the knife down and fixed her steely eyes into his own. "Let this be a warning to you, boy. Never, ever ignore me or run away to this boy's home again. Do it again, and I won't be so nice to your friend over here. Now clean up this filthy mess." His friend's eyes closed, his body lying like a rag doll after the pain she put him through.

He froze, believing he could stay in the comfort of his friend's family home to escape his mother's strange ways. If only he had a different mother. But no, he loved her too much and knew she was teaching him great lessons.

***

Jesse rushed into the Williamstown Hospital, sweat across his brow as he almost slipped on the shiny floors of the corridor. He passed by a doctor and nurse wheeling a patient into a room, the scuffling of their feet unnerving him. Where was the damn ward? And how bad was she? Marco hadn't said much but he had an uneasy feeling it wasn't an accident.

The dings of machines rang out as he rounded a group of nurses sitting around a counter, chatting as if there was no tomorrow. When he got inside the room, Gabriella was standing by the window, biting her nails and shaking her head.

A towering nurse held a chart and made notes. She then checked Joy's blood pressure and turned to Jesse, smiling warmly. She looked at Joy whose face was badly bruised with cuts across her arms and upper chest. Dried blood remained on her ear. "I will be back later with more pain medication." The nurse walked out and nodded to them both.

Jesse rushed towards Joy and wrapped his arms around her, playing with the strands of her hair. "Oh, Joy! What the hell happened? You look terrible."

Gabriella moved away from the window, fixing her gaze on Jesse as if she wanted to say something, but held back. "Jesse."

"Gabriella." He angled his head. "What is going on? Where's Marco?"

He sat on the edge of the bed and took a calming breath. Grabbing Joy's hand, he stroked it gently while Gabriella sat on a nearby chair, staring at the floor. What was so interesting down there?

"Take a breath, bro. I am fine, and Marco's on his way. He had a few things to take care of then he'll come by. A couple of officers from Highway Patrol questioned me and I told them what I remember."

He nodded. "You still haven't told me what happened, and you do not look fine."

Joy swallowed. "A speeding car cut me off in my lane on the Tullamarine Freeway as if they didn't see me, but I couldn't make out the driver. I smashed into the car pretty hard, but the driver just drove away with barely a scratch on it. It was a solid car. Then another driver behind me rammed into my car. The windows were tinted. I told the police what I remembered but it's a little hazy. It was just an accident."

He drew back, thankful that she wasn't badly injured. "A crazy driver, I guess. Or is it one of your ex-boyfriends?" He laughed. "What were you doing on the freeway? Didn't you go to work today?"

Joy averted her eyes. "I had a job over there at the last minute. You know my interior design work takes me to different places." She paused. "Anyway, it must have been someone having a bad day. They might've been high on drugs or alcohol, but I never got a look at the driver's face."

Jesse looked over at Gabriella who stared past him towards the corridor. She was quiet. Too quiet, and he was worried about her. Was he thinking what she was thinking? That this was some kind of payback? Was the stalker sending her a message, scaring her into submission and getting his jollies out of hurting her loved ones? No, it was ridiculous. Surely if he wanted to hurt Gabriella, he would have hurt her personally.

They engaged in small talk until Bella, Liz, Jamie, and Claudia arrived. All of them hugged Joy and greeted Jesse and Gabriella.

Claudia leaned forward. "Octavia will be here later. She's in an interview."

Joy grinned. "No worries. I am glad you guys came, but as you can see, I am fine."

Liz gave her a gentle shove on the shoulder. "Listen, girl. When anything happens to anyone, we're here for each other."

"Exactly right, Joy." Bella drew a hand through her hair. "We support each other."Claudia stood upright. "Tell us what happened."

As Joy explained the accident, Gabriella ushered Jesse outside and into a tearoom close by. It was empty, and they sat on the cushioned seats side by side.

"What is going on, Gabriella? You look spooked."

She pressed her lips together and rubbed the palms of both hands. Turning to him, she said, "This was no accident, Jesse."

Jesse knit his brows. "Really? Do you honestly believe it was your stalker? Why?"

She sighed. "Think about it. I move into your place and he probably doesn't like that; he wanted me to be alone, so he did something to get my attention. And what better way than to target my close friend? Someone I'd gladly sacrifice my life for."

Jesse shrugged. "I don't know. Maybe we shouldn't jump to conclusions. I'm sure the police are looking into it and see it as an accident. There are plenty of crazy idiots on the road, Gabriella. We don't know it's him."

"You're wrong." She punched her chest. "I feel it in my heart that this was intentional, and I am no longer sitting on the sidelines like a scared little girl. I am not going to let anxiety get in the way of protecting myself. If he wants me, then I have to use myself as bait and go back home. I have to keep my friends out of this."

Jesse moved forward, ignoring the pain in his chest at the idea of Gabriella getting hurt too. He had to protect her at all costs and now she wanted to leave. "It's madness. You are not going home to be an easy target. No way."

Gabriella glared. "I am sorry, but last time I checked, you were not my parent and you don't own me. This is my mess and no-one else is going to get hurt because of me. I will not allow it. Joy was lucky but it could've been worse."

Jesse shook his head. "No, you are not going to stay on your own. I'll stay at your place if you're more comfortable at home. Please don't do this on your own."

She got up and put her hands on her hips, averting her eyes. "I'll think about it, Jesse. But I don't want this guy to hurt anyone else I care about. He can't." She was fighting back tears as she looked up into his eyes.

Jesse rose, gazing at her, but she still avoided his eyes. He stroked her gently on the shoulder. "Listen. I know you're scared, but Joy is fine. She is one tough girl, and by the sounds of it, she is just like you."

Gabriella faced him. "I know she's fine, but we need to find out who this is before anyone else gets hurt, Jesse."

He nodded. "I know, and we will. You are not alone in this, Gabriella." The softness and vulnerability in her eyes broke his heart in two.

Chapter Thirty

PARANOIA

G abriella drove towards her house after staying at the hospital for another hour with Joy and her friends. She ruminated about her stalker, thinking she wasn't going to stop living her life because of a stalker. But maybe Jesse was right. There was no indication that her stalker had hurt Joy. What proof did she have? She thought it was the timing of it, given that she had moved out of her house to stay with Jesse. The stalker might have been annoyed by not having easy access to her at Jesse's home. But what if her imagination was getting the best of her? What if Joy's accident was only that? Crazy drivers existed everywhere.

She reached her house and parked her car in the driveway. Her eyes wandered in every direction and her body shook. Sneaking towards the front door, she lifted her shoulders at every sound; the revving of cars driving by, the flock of birds soaring, and the footsteps of passersby down her street. With a quivering hand, she unlocked her front door and stepped inside. She glided into the kitchen, picked up a knife from the utensil block, and gripped it tight. Slowly she crept towards her bedroom, holding her breath, then proceeded to walk through every part of the house and backyard. It was empty and she was alone. She was being paranoid. The stalker wasn't here.

Leaving the hospital on her own had been a challenge because her friends had tried to force her to stay with Jesse until her stalker was caught, but she explained that she refused to be weak. She was tired of living an anxious life and had to develop more of a thick skin. With her domestically violent upbringing, she knew it was natural to have anxious tendencies, but she refused to let it continue to dominate her life at twenty-three years of age. She was no longer a scared little girl, having to hide in her bedroom every time her father beat her mother, or hurled verbal abuse because his food was cold, or she hadn't ironed his shirt for a party. No, she was much stronger now, and if this stalker had intentionally hurt Joy, she would no longer hide in the shadows. She would face him head-on and show him she wasn't a highly anxious woman anymore. He had messed with the wrong woman if he intended to target her dear friend, Joy or others close to her.

Moving back into her bedroom, she picked up her laptop from her bed and leaned back against the two pillows. She wondered if the media had picked up on anything new about Erica, and typed in her name on the internet. She skimmed through articles about Erica's death being investigated due to suspicious circumstances, but nothing new appeared on the case. She read about her trips overseas to report on segregation in Africa or the political system in Kenya. What if her murderer was someone who didn't like her reporting on a particular news item? What if someone overseas had taken the time to come to Australia to plot her murder? No, that was a bit of a stretch.

Her mind turned back to the internet searches and a news article came up with a headline—*Journalistic Awards Ceremony*. She clicked on the article from two years ago, outlining the different types of awards handed out, and how talent had been recognised in journalism. Gabriella skipped the remainder of the article and scrolled down to several photos taken of the guests sitting at tables closer to the stage. An image came up of Erica and Derek cosying up at one of the tables, appearing to be having an intimate conversation. Scrolling towards the end of the article, she didn't find any more photos.

Gabriella remembered Erica mentioning how Jesse was sick that night and couldn't attend the ceremony, so Derek had offered to take her. But she had never seen that photo of them together. It might have been innocent. But by the way they appeared in it, she wondered if Derek had been in love with Erica. No, that was insane, as surely Jesse would have known.

Her mind flicked back to Derek and how strange he had acted when she spotted him

near the library. He wanted Jesse to let go of Erica and believed she had killed herself. Did he truly believe she had committed suicide or did he know something more? Did he not want them to investigate? But why? He wouldn't have hurt Erica, surely? She had known Derek for years, and Jesse would no doubt have realised if his friend had been involved. Now that she thought about it, there had been times when she'd visit Joy at home when Erica visited, and Derek would intermittently stare at her with lust. Why hadn't she seen it before? The fact that Derek was possibly in love with Erica? Or was it her imagination? Was she seeing things that weren't there? What if he had killed her to stay quiet? This whole stalking situation was making her paranoid. No, she was being silly.

A sudden banging noise near her bedroom made her jolt. Getting up quickly, she rushed over to her bedroom window and peered through it. Not a soul in sight. She headed over to the rumpus room to make sure her kitten was okay and found Angela sleeping in her padded bed. She exited the room and walked over to the kitchen window, peering outside, staring at nothing in particular. No-one was in sight. *Get a grip!*

Gabriella moved away from her window and paced the carpeted flooring, her mind flashing back to Derek and wondering if Jesse had any idea that he had cared about Erica. She jumped when the doorbell rang. Swallowing, she stared back through the window and breathed a sigh of relief. Did she truly believe her stalker would ring the doorbell? She spotted Jesse's car parked at the kerb and walked to the front door.

Chapter Thirty-One

AWARDS PHOTO

He watched her from a distance, her dark brown hair flowing loosely around her shoulders. He spotted her through the kitchen window until she moved away. Now he wondered where she'd gone to. He waited, hoping and praying he could see her again. Craving her. Wanting her. Needing to feel those slim curves in his large hands as she screamed out his name. He waited until a car drove by and parked in front of her house. No! No! What was that creep doing? She was his. Only his. He owned her, not that waste of space!

Gabriella opened the door, and he hid back behind the tree and peeked carefully, taking a quick glimpse before hiding again. Christ! He wondered if she had seen him. Not to worry. He would only watch her for now, but soon he would send her a nice surprise. He knew how to win her heart.

***

Gabriella opened the door, her body responding to Jesse's stubble over his square jaw, his dirty-blonde hair slightly dishevelled but sexy, and his muscles straining against his tight t-shirt and blue jeans. Her eyes looked past him, thinking she had seen someone watching her, but no, it was most likely someone wandering around in the park and had walked off.

His strong, piercing green eyes caused her to wince as she drew a loose strand out of her eyes. "Hey, Gabriella. I wanted to make sure you're okay. Your friends think you shouldn't be on your own, so I told them I'd check on you. Can I come in?"

Gabriella hesitated but was comforted by his presence. His fresh-smelling musky scent permeated her senses and his eyes bore into hers as if he could read her every thought. He was making it challenging for her to think clearly, and she couldn't afford distractions right now when her life was chaotic. Besides, he would never be interested in another girl after loving Erica for five years. She could never compete with the kind of love they had shared.

She swung open the door wider and ushered him inside. "I am fine, Jesse. Come in."

He walked inside and seated himself on the couch throwing his right leg roughly over his left leg. He watched her in silence with his index finger over his lips. She wondered what he was thinking. *Get it together, Gabriella!* "Joy has to stay in hospital for a few more days, more for observation than anything, but she was in good spirits, don't you think?"

Gabriella sat across from him in the armchair, preferring to keep her distance. "I am glad it wasn't worse. What do the police think about her accident?"

He shrugged. "Nothing against the norm, but they can't locate the driver, and there are no witnesses who remember the car. They think the car might have been stolen." Gabriella gasped. "But these things happen all the time. I don't believe it had anything to do with you."

Why did she not believe his words? Was he having doubts about the accident, too? She couldn't do anything about it now. "I agree. There are crazy drivers out there all the time." Rubbing her hands together, she said, "Thanks for dropping in. I do appreciate it. I know you're busy with your own life, and I feel bad that I am taking up your time."

He lifted an eyebrow and leaned forward while straightening his right leg. "You are not taking up my time. If I had other things to do, I would let you know."

A crashing sound in the back of the house made them both jump. "Stay here." He quickly got up and ran down the corridor, but Gabriella followed him. If there was a man in the house, she had to have Jesse's back. She had to face her fears and overcome her anxiety with the unknown. He scurried out of her bedroom, gave her a strange look then made his way into the rumpus room. Angela had bumped into a cup she had left on one of the cupboards, and shards of ceramic lined the floor. Gabriella picked up a brush and pan and swept up the mess, then dropped them into a nearby rubbish bin.

Breathing a sigh of relief, she patted Angela and watched as she jumped around with a toy ball inside her bed. Turning to Jesse, she followed him out of the room and found him in her bedroom, checking inside her wardrobe and underneath the bed, obviously wondering if the madman was hiding in her home. Oh, no! She had forgotten to close her laptop when she'd heard the noise earlier. And now Jesse had seen that photograph of Derek and Erica. She didn't want to hurt Jesse with her thoughts and regretted finding this photo.

After looking at the open laptop, Jesse's face turned red, and he averted his eyes as if he was ashamed of something. "I couldn't go to that awards ceremony because I had a bad case of gastro, so Derek went in my place. It is no big deal. He did her a favour and she was happy to attend the event with Derek. They were good friends and he helped her out."

Was he rambling? "It was nice of him to do something like that. If I wasn't busy that night, I would have gone with Erica."

Jesse grimaced. "I know they look all cosy in that photo but they were good friends, and in that lighting, it looks different than it really was. I saw that photo two years ago, and Erica said she had a good time with Derek."

She nodded, wondering if he believed his own words. She could have kicked herself for letting him see that photo and hated seeing his mood change all of a sudden. "How about a cup of tea, or would you prefer something stronger?"

They exited the bedroom and he followed her into the kitchen. Then, Jesse looked through her window as she filled up the kettle. "I'll have a coffee."

She reached for two mugs in an overhead cupboard, intermittently watching Jesse who moved and stood awkwardly near the kitchen table. He flicked through a magazine.

As she was stirring the cups of coffee, a shadow flickered in the backyard. Gasping, her hand shook to the point of spilling the hot coffee over her palm. "Oh, Christ!" The boiling liquid scorched her hand and she winced.

Jesse came to her rescue and held her hand out under cold water. "Are you okay? Let me look at it."

Gabriella wanted to say it wasn't okay, but she was a big girl and didn't want him to think she couldn't cope with some hot coffee on her palm. "I'm fine, Jesse." She pulled his hand away and proceeded to keep her own hand under the tap for a few minutes. "It's nothing."

Jesse pressed his lips together and stared out the window. "Okay, but you looked spooked by something. What was it?"

If she mentioned seeing someone watching her behind a tree, he would insist she go back to his place, but she needed to prove to herself that she could cope with her situation and be independent. The shadow outside could have been a stray cat or dog, and she would not read into it. Her father had controlled her, and even Nick did, but now she needed to take the reins on her own life. No, she had to lie. "Nothing, but here's your coffee. I'll stick to water." Jesse picked up his coffee and placed it on the kitchen table. Gabriella joined him with her glass of water. As she sipped it, he sat silently as if processing what was going on with her.

He looked up from his coffee after taking a drink. "How did you come across that article with Erica and Derek in it, anyway?"

She didn't want to hurt him when she didn't have any facts about Derek and Erica. "I was seeing whether the media had any news about Erica's death when I came across that photo. It was the first time I'd seen it."

Jesse's eyes squinted. "Erica kept a lot of things to herself and didn't tell you she was in the paper, did she?" He crossed his arms.

She shook her head. "I had no idea, but she was busy all the time. I am surprised Joy and I got to see her a few times before....."

Jesse stood up and paced in the kitchen, forgetting his coffee. "I never thought about that photo until I just saw it." He returned to his seat. "I am sorry. You have enough on your mind. Why don't I stay tonight?"

Gabriella had to change the subject. "It's fine. The girls will check on me later, and I have my neighbour most likely coming over."

"Okay then. I will get going." He walked out of the house with deflated shoulders and she watched him drive away, then closed the door.

Moving away from the window, she sat back on the couch and closed her eyes. What had she done? Her tense chest and deflated shoulders made her want to fall in a heap on her couch. She had hurt Jesse with that photo, bringing up a lot of horrid memories for him. She hoped that nothing had happened between Erica and Derek as that would destroy Jesse.

Chapter Thirty-Two

POLICE ARRIVAL

The next evening, Jesse drove to Derek's house. He had driven from Gabriella's house with the intention of going home, but then his concern for her overrode his need to be home alone. He ended up driving back and monitoring her house all night, so he'd got little sleep. He was now tired from sleeping in his car.

Seeing the photo of Erica and Derek pained him because a part of him had always wondered whether Derek had been in love with her. He had dismissed the idea two years ago, but seeing that photo again brought his self-doubts up again. A part of him wondered last time if they were too close, but he obviously chose to ignore it. After that event, Erica had been distant for days until she became her normal self.

He couldn't blame Gabriella for wanting to check the Internet, but he still hated seeing that photo again. In spite of his pain over losing Erica, he still needed to protect Gabriella. He couldn't save Erica but he could help save Gabriella. He wished he had been old enough to save his sister, Mia, from getting killed, too. This time he refused to feel helpless.

His mind turned to Gabriella and how she had clenched her hands together in possible annoyance with herself when he had seen the photo on her laptop. She scrunched up her nose when she was in deep thought, and she bit her top lip when she was nervous. He couldn't help worrying that she was underestimating her stalker and taking unnecessary risks. He had called Marco, who arranged for a police officer to patrol her home at nights for the next few days, so he didn't need to worry about her safety in the evenings.

Once Jesse arrived in front of Derek's house, he stopped the car and wondered what he was doing. Was he going to confront Derek about Erica? He took another peek at the news article and photo Gabriella had had on her laptop in his mind on his phone, and looking at it with fresh eyes, he again realised they were a tad too intimate for his liking.

He stepped out of his car when his phone buzzed. He retrieved it from his back pocket and gave a quick reply to his friends Ricky and Martin about not being able to meet them at the local pub. Putting away his phone, he spotted Derek shutting his front door and met him near his car. "Derek. We need to talk. Can we go inside?"

He shook his head. "I'm meeting Ricky and Martin at the pub. Aren't you going?"

He shook his head. "No, I told them I couldn't make it."

Derek frowned. "Okay. What brings you by, man?"

Jesse watched his friend with renewed interest, wondering whether he was hiding any secrets. He had to be blunt and get this over with. "Did something happen between you and Erica? Were you in love with her?"

Derek's face paled as he turned back towards the house as if expecting someone to come rescuing him. "What?"

Jesse explained seeing the news article and photograph of him and Erica. "Were you and Erica ever intimate?"

Derek clenched his hands tight. He later crossed his arms and held tight onto both wrists while averting his eyes. "Listen, why don't we go meet Ricky and Martin. This is ridiculous, man."

Jesse realised he was ignoring the question, but he didn't plan to leave until he got answers. He didn't know how he would feel if something had been going on between Derek and Erica. "You didn't answer the question, Derek. Was something going on between you and Erica?" He pressed his lips together as he watched his friend draw a shaky hand through his hair, averting his eyes. His feet shuffled as he placed his hands in his pockets.

"Listen, why don't we get out of here? Meet the guys at the pub. This is crazy." Jesse stared at his friend, suddenly having an even worse thought. He didn't want to believe that his best friend might have killed Erica to keep her quiet. No, that was beyond comprehension. He would never hurt anyone. Why couldn't they just be friends?

Behind him, the sound of a car revved. Jesse turned and spotted a police car stopping by the kerb. His heart jumped as if he was expecting bad news. Had something happened to Gabriella? Had she been kidnapped, or worse? His throat was parched as he stepped away from Derek and frowned at the officers. The driver exited the car and towered over him but the other policeman was of average height.

The tall policeman gave a curt nod and introduced himself and his partner. He stared at Derek. "Are you Derek Hillcrest who resides at this address?" He pointed to the house directly in front of them.

Derek's face drooped as he turned to Jesse. "Yes, I'm Derek. What is this about, Officer?" Jesse's breathing slowed, his mind churning with possibilities about his friend.

He cleared his throat. "We need to take you in for questioning related to the murder of Erica Hartness. Please come with us."

Derek shook his head. "This is crazy. Why can't you ask me what you want right here?" He avoided his friend's eyes and turned red in the face.

The policeman of average height stepped forward and leaned in. "You can either come with us quietly or we can put the handcuffs on,

Mr Hillcrest. Your choice."

Derek knit his brows and took a deep breath. He shook his head and nodded towards the officers. "Fine. I will come with you. There is no need to make a scene." He faced Jesse. "Can you tell my sister where I am?" Jesse nodded; his vocal cords knotted as if he'd lost his voice. An inner rage-fuelled his insides, wondering if his best friend had hurt Erica. No, this had to be a mistake. Too much was going on and he was having crazy thoughts.

Derek entered the police car in the backseat without turning back to Jesse, and the policemen drove away. He stood there, frozen in his spot, not knowing what to do next. His surroundings looked surreal as if he was in a dream and what happened didn't just happen. His friend couldn't have hurt Erica, let alone kill her. They were close and he trusted Derek, but what if he never truly knew his friend? What if they were having an affair and he killed her so she could stay quiet? What if his lack of response earlier meant more than just an affair? His late girlfriend had been distant for months, and each time he questioned her, she had given the same response. "Only pressures at work, honey. Nothing for you to worry about." But what if it was more than work? She had not only been distant but forgetful too, as if she had too much on her mind. It had to be more than work. He could no longer ask her anything, and he so desperately wished he could get answers.

He straightened his posture, took a calming breath and stepped inside Derek's house to inform Derek's sister of the situation.

Chapter Thirty-Three

INSIGHTS

Jesse rested his back against the chair in the interview room at the police station, shaking his head. "But I told you, Angelo. Derek would not do this. It is crazy."

Angelo leaned forward and clasped his hands together. He lifted up his shoulders as if in readiness for his next question. "I am sorry to put you through this, Jesse, but we have come across a few new leads. It's important we get our facts straight. Now, tell me. What was Erica's relationship like with Derek?"

Jesse cringed after seeing the police take away his friend for questioning. That was earlier in the day, and now it was late afternoon, and he hadn't heard anything from Derek. "Is Derek back home now? He's not under arrest, is he?"

Angelo shook his head. "Derek is a person of interest at this stage, and we are still following other lines of enquiry. Please answer the question."

He shrugged. "They got along, but they weren't that close. Sometimes they fought about trivial things, but that's it. Nothing more, nothing less. Why do you ask?"

Angelo cleared his throat. "Tell us about your relationship with Erica. Did you start to have doubts about your engagement after her behaviour changed?"

Jesse scoffed. "Are you serious right now? I loved her and wanted to marry her. Am I a damn suspect now, Detective?" He jolted at the sound of a knock on the door. The detective stood up and stepped outside, muffled voices sounding like the words, "Gabriella" and "further questioning." The door reopened and Angelo came back inside with Octavia.

He tilted his head. "What are you doing here, Octavia? Is something wrong?"

She sat beside Angelo and pressed her lips together before replying. "Tell us about the relationship between Derek and Gabriella?"

Jesse angled his head. "What? There is no relationship. They're acquaintances, that's all. Why do you ask? I thought this was about Erica's killer, not Gabriella's stalker."

Octavia clasped her hands together and looked to Angelo strangely. "Are you sure he hasn't taken an added interest in Gabriella? She mentioned seeing him at the library and wondered if he followed her there. Apparently, he explained to her that you should let Erica's death go. Would that be a reasonable assessment, Jesse?"

"Yes, she mentioned what Derek had said, but so? He wants me to move on with my life. There's no crime in that." He suddenly twigged. "Please don't tell me you think the killer and Gabriella's stalker are the same person?" They didn't say anything, but he thought about Gabriella and how he didn't want her to experience the same fate as Erica or Nora. The room around Jesse spun.

Octavia frowned. "Listen, Jessie. It is hard to know for sure, but it appears unlikely at this stage. We are still investigating and we will not speculate until we gather further leads."

Who was taunting Gabriella if it wasn't the killer? If it was the killer, would she be his next victim? He shifted his shoulders. "I know that Derek's still a person of interest, but as I said before, he would never hurt Erica. I know the kind of person he is. Whatever you found out about him, you need to tell me."

Angelo leaned forward, scrutinising him and rubbing his chin as if he was trying to figure him out. "I am afraid we can't divulge that information. Anything we tell you can go badly in court."

Jesse flinched. "Court? Do you honestly think it will come to that? I told you he's innocent and whatever you think he did, it has be a mistake. The real killer's probably framing him as we speak. Please think this through. It's ridiculous." He threaded his hands through his hair. "Derek is not a murderer. I am a good judge of character and I've known him since I was a child."

Octavia pressed her lips together. "We are not saying he is anything of the sort. But know one thing: do not underestimate the criminal mind, Jesse. Any psychopath or sociopath has the ability to be two different people and have honed their craft of showing humanity. In fact, they'll show mostly their humanity to manipulate people and get what they want." She took a breath. "We are finding discrepancies, though, as I know Derek is generally messy and disorganised. The issue here is that we're looking at a mixture of an organised and a disorganised personality."

Jesse flinched. "Are you saying there are two people working together?"

Octavia nodded. "It is possible, which is why you need to be on your guard. If the stalker is obsessing over Gabriella, he may not initially want to hurt her if she gives in to his advances. But he might see you as a threat, given your friendship with Gabriella. If there is someone else involved, a more organised person, then that could be a different ball game."

He stared into his hands. "Don't worry about me. I am worried about Gabriella and my best friend. You have to see it's not him. He wouldn't do this." He exhaled and rose. "If you don't have any more questions, can I go?"

Angelo nodded. "Of course, but if you remember anything, don't hesitate to get in touch. Any trivial thing could hold great weight."

As Jesse walked out with Angelo and Octavia, his mind churned at the possibility that Derek fit into that label where he really didn't know who he was. He hoped that Derek had nothing to hide. If he was the disorganised one, would he fit into the category of a love-obsessed stalker? No, he refused to believe that without hard evidence. As the police said, they were still digging into the case.

Walking towards his car outside the police station, he came across Nigel, Erica's brother, glaring at him. He stopped moving. "What are you doing here?"

He shrugged. "I got a call to come here about Erica. What business is it of yours, anyway?"

Jesse scoffed. "I know you and Erica never got along but what's your issue with me? What have I done to you?"

He gestured with his hand. "You think that Erica was a goddess, but she was a first-class bitch and thought she was better than me. She was gutless to kill herself, and that to me, is just weakness and a cop-out." He shoved his car keys into his pocket then stormed off.

Jesse's eyes focused on something that had fallen on the ground. A business card which advertised a Mornington winery. He remembered Erica telling him about Nigel working for a family-owned business, helping out on a seasonal basis while his website business was still getting established. Nigel never liked Erica and Jesse wondered why he was being questioned by the police. What if he was hiding something? The only way to know more was to watch him in his work environment, away from his family. He might pay him a visit at the winery.

Chapter Thirty-Four

NEW LINE OF THINKING

Gabriella sat on the edge of the bed inside Joy's bedroom which featured a tallboy, a large colonial window covered by red lace curtains underneath ash-black drapes, a double bed, and a timber desk with an ergonomic chair over plush white carpeted flooring.

Joy rested her head against the headboard with the blankets tucked over her chest and her right leg in a plaster cast. Her face still had purplish bruising and her forehead had fading grazes. "Thanks for coming by, Gabi, but as you can see, I am fine now."

"Hmm. So fine that you have your leg still in a cast and your face looks a mess too. I am so sorry this happened to you, Joy."

She shook her head. "Do not be silly, girl. You have nothing to be sorry about."

Gabriella took a breath. "Do the police have any idea who ran you down? Did they find the actual driver?"

"No, they haven't. I'm sure it was an accident or someone on drugs who doesn't want to be implicated because of it. I wish I knew more, but it happened so quickly. Then I was out of it."

Gabriella didn't want to assume that her stalker had hurt Joy to get back at her. "I am glad it wasn't worse than it was. But you need to rest. Let me know if there is anything I can get for you. I can call your work or get you groceries. Anything?"

"No, Gabi. I am fine, but thanks." Joy looked at her strangely. "Let's say, for argument's sake, the accident was caused on purpose. I would easily implicate Nigel. He hates me with a passion." Gabriella shook her head. Joy scoffed. "And why wouldn't I say, Nigel? He hates me because I'm so outspoken and always defended Erica against him. He never had one nice thing to say about Erica, and even now he hates her. You'd think he'd feel something after her death."

Gabriella wondered if Nigel could have done this. The last time she had seen him, he had expressed a lot of hate towards Joy. But was Nigel the one stalking her too? No, it couldn't be him. He didn't seem to hate Gabriella, probably because she tolerated his self-entitled nature. "Let's brainstorm and do our research." She placed a finger on her temple and briefly closed her eyes to focus on all those in Joy's and Erica's circle. "Is there anyone at work you don't get along with?"

Joy put her finger on her temple. "No, I get along great with everyone at the company. They love my interior design work and some of them even want to team up with me. But let's focus on Erica, as this was most likely an accident. And what about you? I don't have a stalker, Gabriella, but you do."

Gabriella sighed. "Okay. Let's think about this." She swallowed. "We have Erica's parents and brother, Erica's colleagues at the newspaper, and Erica's news stories which might have triggered hate in someone. It might be a good idea to look deeper into her stories to see whether any of them could have triggered anyone. She might've been targeted because of one of her local news stories."

Joy hugged the blankets over her body. "I think we should start off with the easiest targets. Perhaps look at Nigel first as he's the one with a motive to hurt his sister. He was always jealous of her close relationship with their parents, and nothing's changed now. We could look at her friends at work. If nothing comes from that, then let's look at her stories, particularly the time she went overseas."

Gabriella leaned forward and placed a gentle hand on her shoulder. "There is no 'we' here. I am not getting you involved in this, Joy. This is my responsibility and mine alone. You are still recovering, and I will not let you risk your life by following my hunches."

Joy squinted. "Are you serious? I am involved now, seeing as you think my accident might be related. What if it is connected? Don't you want me to help so we can get results faster? Don't you want the person who might have done this to me to get caught?"

Gabriella scoffed. "Do not manipulate me, Joy. I'm not falling for it." She didn't know what she'd do if another one of her friends died. She wouldn't survive that. "Don't you see? If your accident is connected, the perpetrator might escalate, and I am not having that on my shoulders. This is on me, not you."

She bowed her head. "Fine. If you don't want me to help, then I'm sure my brother would want to be there for you. He has a lot at stake here, too. He won't move forward unless he knows who hurt Erica." She rubbed her arms. "At least now the police know she was murdered and they're finally investigating after one year. What a waste of time. If only they'd known it wasn't suicide from the start." She looked back up at her friend. "Let Jesse help you. He might be able to protect you, too."

She crossed her arms, realising Jesse wouldn't be happy with her researching without him. But she didn't want anyone else getting hurt. "Please don't say anything to Jesse. I need to do this alone as I can't risk anyone else getting hurt."

Joy shifted in bed and winced as she pulled herself up. She reached for her crutch but Gabriella pushed her back down on the bed. "What are you doing? You should be resting your leg."

Joy glared at her friend. "You are unbelievable and stubborn, and I refuse to have this conversation with you. Why do you have to do this on your own when you have willing people who love you to help you, girl? I will not let you put yourself in danger, so if you don't tell Jesse, then I will. It's your choice."

Gabriella sighed, realising Joy wouldn't let up on this. "Fine. I'll tell him." She fixed her gaze on Joy. She thought about doing research on Nigel. "Doesn't Nigel work at a winery part-time?"

Joy nodded. "He does work at a winery, but why don't you visit him at his place?"

Gabriella stared into the distance, remembering something Erica had told her. "Erica once told me she had gone to the Mornington winery to do a promotional piece. She and Nigel got into an argument, but she didn't tell me what it was about. Apparently, a few staff members saw them arguing. They might've heard what the argument was about, and I want to get their take on it."

Joy sighed. "That idiot was always fighting with Erica over something."

Gabriella placed a finger over her chin. "I am not surprised, but let's not jump the gun here. He is a jerk, but we don't know if he hated Erica enough to kill her."

"I wouldn't be surprised one bit, Gabi. Not one little bit."

Could Nigel be cold-hearted enough to kill Erica, hurt Joy, and possibly be her stalker?

Chapter Thirty-Five

HOUSE-WARMING

G abriella got out of Jamie's car with Joy and they stared at Bella and Marco's new house in Spotswood. The grey brick home had a pitched roof and colonial windows. White pillars stood on either side of the front door. Instant turf lawn was short, green, and neat, with a paved pathway leading to the door which featured stained glass at the top and timber down the bottom half. There were two white padded chairs to the side of the house.

The warm wind caressed her cheeks as Gabriella inched her way forward towards the entrance, holding a gift box. Joy and Jamie talked amongst themselves while she thought about Jesse, and whether he would be coming to the housewarming party.

She couldn't stop thinking about Jesse. Lately she'd been distracted at work, but his image flashed constantly in her mind. If only she could wipe him out of her brain as it didn't help her to focus on her mission. She had to fight for justice against Erica and Nora's killer.

"Penny for your thoughts, girl," said Joy. "What's up with you?"

Gabriella rang the doorbell and waited beside her friends. "Nothing, Joy."

Jamie gave her a reassuring smile and touched her gently on the shoulder. "Tonight is a night for fun, Gabriella. I know that I can still have fun without Angelo, and so can you."

Gabriella nodded. "Is he coming later?"

Jamie shrugged her shoulders. "He said he will try, but who knows. He is working on a few priority cases now, and he's been covering for Marco who needs to be here for his own party. Homicides do not solve themselves."

The door finally swung open, and Bella flashed a smile at her friends, then leaned in for hugs. "Hello, ladies. Welcome to our humble abode. Come in. Marco should be here soon. He got called into work unexpectedly, but he shouldn't be too long." Bella opened the door wider and led them into the open space of the foyer and living room with its hardwood floors. A white leather couch sat beside two grey armchairs and a heavy-set timber coffee table rested over a floral rug. A timber staircase flowed up to other rooms upstairs and the living area gave a view of the open kitchen with its long counter and long-legged stools. Suspended lights in the kitchen gave it a modern feel. "How about a tour? I've been meaning to invite you guys over earlier but the renovations had to be done. I wanted it to be complete before you guys saw it."

Gabriella smiled, her eyes roaming the expansive space and her stomach rumbling from the aromas of herbs and spices wafting in the air. Her mind turned to Marco being called in to work. She hoped that it had nothing to do with the current cases involving Nora and Erica. "It is beautiful, Bella. Congratulations." She handed over the housewarming gift while Joy and Jamie did the same.

"Thanks, guys. I appreciate it, but not necessary." Bella placed them on the coffee table then showed them around the home. They wandered through three average-sized bedrooms, including the master room and a spacious sitting area with a small TV, a grey chaise lounge, and two beanbags in it. It was a room to relax and unwind in after a hard day's work, and she could smell the fresh leather of the couch.

When they returned downstairs to the living room, Gabriella sat on the couch and listened to the conversations around her. The doorbell rang. She sat on the edge of her seat, her heart racing and hands fidgeting as she looked at the door. It wasn't Jesse. Hiding her disappointment, she forced a smile when she saw Octavia and Claudia who arrived with a monstrous-sized gift between them. Claudia had her strawberry-blonde hair loose around her shoulders; her grey eyes examining Gabriella intently. Was it silent reassurance about Nora?

A black tight-fitted dress accentuated Claudia's curves. Her petite stature suited her better when she was casually dressed.

"Hello all," said Claudia. "We aren't late, are we?" She handed over the large gift box and Bella put it aside on the table.

"Claudia. Octavia. I am happy you guys came. Come on in." They walked inside the house and looked around.

Octavia's long, brown hair was tied up in a low ponytail, enhancing her high cheekbones and vibrant green eyes. "Hi girls. Where's Marco?" In that moment, her phone vibrated in her bag. She rummaged through it and answered the call. Blood drained from her face and she shook her head. Ending the call, she took a breath. "I am so sorry, Bella. That was the Sergeant. He needs me to go into work regarding a situation. It shouldn't take too long."

Bella huffed. "It's fine. I understand how it works with people in law enforcement. You go do your thing. We'll still be here when you get back."

Gabriella swallowed, staring at Joy whose eyes had darkened. "I hope everything's okay. You will let us know, Octavia?"

She gave them a reassuring smile. "I will see you girls later." Octavia rushed out while Claudia sat herself down on the leather couch in deep thought.

Bella hid her disappointment. "I think we could all use a drink." She turned to the kitchen counter covered with bottles of wine, spirits, a bowl of punch, and assorted juices. She pulled out glasses and they all helped themselves to the wide selection of drinks. Gabriella kept glancing at the front door, wondering when Jesse would arrive. She stared at the door again. Shaking her head, she stopped herself from looking and focused on the current company.

Ten minutes later, the doorbell rang again. Gabriella rushed to the door, her stomach tingling and a smile on her face. Was it Jesse this time? She answered the door and her shoulders deflated as she hid her disappointment again. Where was he? It was crazy to want to see him as badly as she did, but she was still elated to see her friends.

She beamed at Liz and Matthew, welcoming them in with their housewarming gift. Camilla appeared behind them, her blue-green eyes lighting up as her eyes roamed around the house. She wrapped her arms around Liz and Matthew as they stepped into the foyer, then kissed Camilla on the cheek. "Good to see you guys. It has been a while since I've seen you, Matthew." She faced him. "I hope you're not on stand-by."

He shook his head. "Not tonight." He turned to Liz with a gleam in his eye, obviously so in love with her. "I am with my beautiful woman tonight and all you lovely young ladies."

"And flattery will get you everywhere, Matthew," said Liz.

Matthew gave her a wink then turned to Gabriella. "So where are the guys?"

Gabriella leaned in. "Marco and Angelo got called into work unexpectedly, and about ten minutes ago, Octavia was called in, too." Gabriella cleared her throat. "Where's your cute daughter?"

Camilla rubbed her hands together. "Oh, she would've been bored tonight so she's staying the night with a friend."

Liz whispered in her ear as they walked towards the others. "You don't think something happened with the case?"

Gabriella's chest tightened, but she refused to think of the worst. They might have had a lead on the case and were following up. That was all. "I don't know, but we are here to enjoy ourselves, so I am not thinking about that tonight."

Liz's eyes darkened. "I'm so sorry, girl. That was insensitive of me." Gabriella squeezed her hand and smiled. She didn't mean to sound so abrupt.

Liz and Matthew helped themselves to drinks. Bella bent down low to pull out a tray of cheesy vol au vents from the oven, setting it on the stove. She pulled out a tray of meatballs and arancini balls too. Gabriella picked up tongs and placed the vol au vents onto a platter while Bella did the same with the other food. Her mouth salivated at the smell of herbs, cheese, and spices.

"These smell amazing, Bella. No doubt Marco's mum gave you the recipe for the arancini balls."

"No, they're my own recipe but if she was coming, I'd probably have used her recipe. You know how judgemental she can be." She placed the final arancini ball on the tray then started putting the meatballs on a platter. "She couldn't make it tonight as she's still recovering from foot surgery." She wiped her hands on a tea towel. "She has a friend staying with her and helping her out."

Gabriella lay the arancini balls onto a small tray. "That's good. Less pressure on you to look after her and worry about her judgement."

Bella laughed. "I would probably kill myself first. I do care for the woman, but she would drive me crazy, Gabriella. I know her heart is in the right place, but she can be high maintenance." She moved away from the kitchen towards the living room and handed out the food.

Gabriella's chest squeezed tight when the doorbell rang again. She picked up the tray of vol au vents, and her heart raced as she walked around with the tray and glanced at the living room space. Jesse waltzed into the room wearing a dark blue jacket over a tight-fitted shirt. He wore blue pleated pants and a skin-tight white shirt. Her hands shook slightly as she held the tray and made small talk with Joy.

When Jesse finished greeting all the others, his eyes bore into her own without words. He grinned. "Hi, Gabriella." He picked at an arancini ball. "These look delicious." He bit into the ball and watched her as he licked his lips after finishing it off. Setting down the tray on the coffee table, she noticed only one spare seat near Jesse on the couch and sat beside him while Bella, Joy, Matthew, Liz, and Jamie talked about popular movies and shows. The conversation between her friends fled into the background as she took in Jesse's musky scent, his intermittent, soft gaze towards her, and how his thigh brushed against her own, creating a warmth all over her body. Her spine tingled, and she forced herself to focus on Liz and Joy's conversation, not taking anything in. Jesse turned to Matthew and they engaged in banter about football. She admired the way he gestured with his hands and how his body shifted closer towards her as he glanced in her direction with a cheeky grin. Jesse's lips smirked slightly when he noticed her watching him. He paused in conversation and looked at her again, which warmed her face. She heard her name in the distance.

"Gabriella. Did you hear me?" Liz said.

She took a breath and turned to her friend. "Sorry. What did you say?"

Liz smiled. "I asked if you thought I was the most amazing mentor you had."

Gabriella laughed. "Of course you were." She avoided looking at Jesse who she felt was staring at her. Getting up, she walked to the kitchen and poured herself a glass of water. Fanning her face, she sipped the water and stood by the sink for a few minutes before returning to her seat. She took deep breaths to calm her rapid breathing and fanned her face again. Bella must have had the heater on in here. That had to be the reason why she felt so flushed. It wasn't because of her need for Jesse but rather her need to get comfort and protection from him during this trying time; nothing more than that.

At this rate, she didn't know how she would manage to pretend she wasn't all jittery inside. And to think that Jesse had spotted her staring at his mouth. How embarrassing.

Chapter Thirty-Six

ANOTHER MURDER

Jesse's mouth went dry at the way Gabriella swayed her hips as she was passing around the food and offering drinks. She was wearing a figure-hugging red dress that fell above the knees. The cleavage she showed made him want to rip off her clothes, and the wedged shoes she wore accentuated her toned legs. What was going on with him? He was nowhere near ready to be thinking of another woman when Erica's death was finally being looked into. He wanted to find her killer. That had to be in the forefront of his mind, and he couldn't afford to have any distractions. He had to keep his head in the game and focus on at least catching Gabriella's stalker, too, especially if he was also Erica's killer.

Despite the police investigating, he knew that his own powers of observation and familiarity with Erica could speed things up in the case. If he stood by and did nothing, he would not be honouring her memory in any way. He hadn't been able to protect her when she was alive, but he could at least give her a measure of peace in death.

He had to keep his distance from Gabriella, and he knew she wanted that too, so he followed Matthew. He wandered outside into the large backyard with patches of dirt and cobblestones, two towering and tilting trees, a flower bed alongside the back fence, and a small steel shed. "So how have you been, Matthew?"

He turned to Jesse. "Great, man. I'm loving life with Liz and love my job. No complaints. What about you? Liz tells me the police are investigating your late girlfriend's death. How are you doing with that?"

"I'm okay. Apparently, they got a few leads that show a connection between Erica and Gabriella's old client who died in the same way. And now there's someone harassing Gabriella." His chest burned. "I'm thinking it could be someone who doesn't want us finding out about Erica. I wonder why the bastard's not going after me, though."

Matthew leaned forward and pulled up his shirt sleeves in the sunlight. "Yeah, Liz mentioned that, but he might have a certain type. I guess that's what you need to find out. What do they all have in common? Why did he target both women?" He peered into the distance. "One thing Liz mentioned, though. She's been worried a lot about Gabriella after what happened with her father. He was violent towards her mother and she'd been a witness to all that. Retraumatising her. It's social worker talk."

He nodded. "You're right. She can be retraumatised. I just wonder why Marco and Angelo had to go to work today. Do you think something's happened? Another connection or lead?"

"It is possible they got a lead." Matthew looked past him. "I guess we'll find out sooner rather than later." Footsteps behind them made him gasp. He turned to find Marco and Angelo whose faces looked ashen. "Hey, guys. What happened?" They all shook hands.

Marco scrunched up his face. "Another girl died, but that's all I can say at this stage. We'll have to get back to the station in a couple of hours."

Angelo exhaled. "The Sergeant decided to give us a couple of hours of reprieve before digging back into the case."

Jesse's body turned cold as the warm wind suddenly chilled his core. "Is it the same type of murder or different?"

Angelo shook his head. "We can't say more, but once its public news, you'll find out soon enough. Octavia's back but she can stay here for tonight."

After talking about the loves of their lives, Jesse excused himself to find Gabriella. He wanted to see whether she knew more about this new murder. He ambled towards the kitchen and found her bending down to the oven, her dress lifting to show the back of her hot, sexy legs and the full outline of her buttocks. His arousal made him tongue-tied when she placed the tray of spring rolls on top of the stove and turned towards him.

Her face turned red. "Jesse, I didn't see you there. What's wrong?" She pulled out a white platter from an overhead cupboard, took out tongs from a drawer, and placed the spring rolls on the platter.

"Did you hear anything from Marco or Angelo?"

She looked calm as she filled the platter. "No, what happened?"

He hesitated, not wanting to ruin her night. But she had the right to know and needed to stay on guard. She needed to take this seriously as he felt in his gut that her stalker was also the killer. If there were two of them, it was even worse. "Another girl died." His heart palpitated at her pale, deflated expression.

"Dear God!" She closed her eyes briefly and shook her head, lost for words. A vibrating sound came from somewhere, and Gabriella rushed to her bag lying on one of the bench chairs. She dug inside it and checked her phone. Her face stiffened and her hand shook. "What's wrong?"

Gabriella said nothing as she handed him her phone. Scanning the display, it read, *Did you like my roses?*

Jesse pursed his lips, the white of his knuckles showing. "Damn it, Gabriella. What's this guy playing at?"

She shrugged. "He wants my attention." Her eyes roamed as the others mingled and whispered amongst themselves. No doubt, they were talking about the girl's death, thinking it was the same type of murder or suicide. Jesse's eyes locked with hers and he gave her a reassuring smile. He hated having to change her mood when she'd been calm.

"Well, first thing tomorrow, you take this to the police and record everything unusual. Octavia might be able to give you more of a comprehensive profile of this sick bastard."

"I don't think you need to worry, Jesse. This guy seems harmless to me, and I doubt he's the same guy killing the girls."

He leaned forward. "You don't know that."

She stayed quiet. He contained his fury at her careless remark. How could she not be in fear for her life right now? He shook his head at his sense of hopelessness. But he was even more determined to protect Gabriella at whatever cost. They wandered over to the rest of the group with trepidation.

Chapter Thirty-Seven

BREAKING NEWS

Several days later, Gabriella sat in the kitchen of her home with Octavia, a hint of sunlight penetrating through the open blinds as they spoke further about her text messages and stalker. The TV played in the background.

Octavia's green eyes narrowed. "I am glad you showed this latest message to the police. I mean, the fact that he's sending you pleasant messages and gifts sounds to me like he's an intimacy-seeking stalker or love-obsessed. From the way he's behaved, he might think you'll end up loving him, which could also suggest he's someone you know of or have seen before. Although not necessarily. He might've seen you out and about somewhere and has developed this fantasy that you two are in a relationship or will be." Octavia rubbed over her scars as if they itched.

"He sounds delusional. Is he likely to escalate or become violent?"

Octavia hesitated as if attempting to choose her words carefully. "Not always with these types, but if the object of his affection rejects him or humiliates him in some way, possibly."

Gabriella wanted to be sick and felt a strangling pain in her throat. It was obvious what she needed to do. "I can use myself as bait, telling him I do love him and I like the attention. That will draw him in, and the police can catch him."

Octavia shook her head. "He won't buy into that. Most likely, he'll make that final move to be with you. Let us handle it."

"And what about the latest victim?"

"The latest victim should be on the news by now, but the pattern appears similar."

"I'll make us a coffee and you can tell me more." Gabriella rose, her legs feeling like lead as she made her way to the kettle and filled it with water. Setting two mugs on the counter, the rustling of trees in her backyard made her wince. Staring through the window, she couldn't see anything. Most likely a cat roaming her yard. At least Marjorie's cat had returned and wasn't the object of her stalker's affections.

Handing Octavia her cup, she turned to a newsreader's voice on the TV. "We have breaking news today. A twenty-year-old woman has drowned in her home in unusual circumstances. The police are questioning the victim's family and friends and are appealing to any witnesses with any information. The death is deemed to be suspicious. On to other news..."

Gabriella's body stiffened. "Octavia. Is that the woman you guys are investigating? The one you mentioned is similar to Erica and Nora?" Her friend nodded. "What is the connection, and why is he doing this? And is this guy also my stalker?"

Octavia got up from her chair and wrapped her arms around Gabriella. She patted her hair with soothing strokes then pulled away. "Hold up. Answering those questions will take me until tomorrow. Now, I think you shouldn't be staying on your own. Come stay with me."

She shook her head. "No, I want answers about this latest woman."

Octavia sighed then sat back down, gripping her mug while Gabriella picked up her own coffee and set it on the table. "As I said before, it appears connected to the other deaths, and we will investigate until we catch this guy and your stalker. I don't want you thinking about it too much. The only thing you should do is keep yourself safe and stay with someone."

She squeezed her hands. "I am starting to think my intimacy-seeking stalker might be the killer, too. These kills between Nora and this other woman are too close together. It has to be connected. It has to be."

"I don't know, Gabriella. But it wouldn't hurt for you to take precautions. We are looking at all possible leads, and like I said, you shouldn't be alone."

Gabriella fixed her gaze on her friend. "What was her name?"

Octavia's eyes darkened. "Tilly."

"I am assuming this woman had clothes on to make it look like a suicide. I know you mentioned that the woman being naked would be more of a sign she'd been murdered. But if she has clothes on, it would more likely be suicide given the victim would not want to show her nudity. Crazy, though. They're dead, right? They wouldn't be judged in Heaven, but it's possible the killer did that to make people think she killed herself."

Octavia frowned and held a tall, erect posture. "Yes, Gabriella so don't go taking any unnecessary risks. Leave the investigating to us. Now, pack a bag and come stay with me."

Gabriella shifted in her seat. "No, I am not letting this creep take me out of my own home. I will be fine. I am so tired of being anxious all the time. Besides I've got weapons in here to protect myself."

Octavia shook her head. "Do you have an alarm system in your home or a personal safety app?"

She nodded. "I have an alarm system that will notify me if anyone's in here, but how does the personal safety app work?"

"It's an alarm or warning you can set to your phone to alert any of your contacts if something goes wrong. You can add me or the guys at the station if ever you need to trigger the alarm on your phone. A lot of stalking victims use it. Even those who've been hurt in the past. It can keep them safe. Do you have a piece of paper? I'll jot the different apps you can use. At least that way, you've got options."

"Fine." As she went to her kitchen drawer, her hand shook at the thought that she needed to even consider such an app. But she had to do whatever she could to ensure her safety, as she didn't want to end up like Erica, Nora, or this latest victim if her stalker was also the killer.

Chapter Thirty-Eight

INVESTIGATING LEADS

J esse parked his car by the kerb and bowed his head over the steering wheel in deep thought. He couldn't stop picturing Gabriella's stricken face when she'd received that text message about the roses. He assumed she'd notified the police the next day, and knew that Octavia was visiting with Gabriella after he'd messaged her to check in. He wondered if they were talking about the latest murder, which was victim number three if it was the same killer. He sighed with relief that Derek was no longer a person of interest, but something was still going on with him. Jesse still wondered about what had happened between him and Erica, and he planned to coax it out of his friend after he finished with today's visit.

In his dreams, he couldn't stop thinking about Gabriella with her dark, glossy hair, soulful brown eyes, and inviting lips. He wondered what it would feel like to brush his hands through her hair or to stare into her beautiful, troubled eyes so he could soothe her pain. He imagined how soft her lips would be on his own lips, but brushed away the thought. It had not been that long ago when he had planned to marry the woman of his dreams. And now, they would never have that chance to be a family. How could he be thinking about another woman when he wasn't in the headspace for another relationship? It was too painful to love and to lose. No, he wouldn't go through that again for a long time, if ever.

He exited the car, pressed down his shirt, and made his way along the paved concrete path which led to a cottage-style home with ferns and rose bushes lined across the front garden. A rickety chair sat beside the front window, and the weathered security door had several holes in them. Ringing the doorbell, he waited for Erica's mother, June, to answer the door, a part of him feeling guilty for not visiting her after the funeral. It was too hard, and he didn't want reminders of her old family home. Another reason he hadn't visited was because June reminded him of Erica. It was too painful. But now, he needed answers.

The door opened, and his posture deflated at the frail appearance of June, whose short, black hair looked oily and dishevelled; her green eyes bloodshot, and her body malnourished. The tracksuit pants were loose on her. She had lost weight and aged ten years since the funeral. He wondered if it had anything to do with the similar murders and not knowing who killed Erica. "Jesse, dear. What a lovely surprise. Come in, come in." Her eyes, very similar to Erica's, lit up, and he smiled, having sensed he could give her comfort by visiting. But would she welcome his questions? The current murders had most likely triggered her.

Damp, murky smells penetrated his senses as he ambled down the corridor and moved into the living room with its worn purple sofa, dusty coffee table, scratch-marked bookshelf, and newspapers strewn around the carpeted flooring and TV cabinet. He sat down on the sunken sofa and leaned back while June sat opposite on a discoloured armchair. She looked so fragile.

"Would you like a tea or coffee? Perhaps a cold drink?"

"No, I'm fine. Thanks." He took a breath. "How have you been, June?"

The woman shrugged. "Surviving. As much as I love your company, you're here for a reason. What is it, Jesse?"

He frowned. "I hope you don't mind, but I have a few questions about Erica."

June's eyes misted. "Oh, dear. We should be moving on with our lives. It's been over a year, and you have to know she would want that for you. And now let's pray that they find whoever hurt her. For so long, it was ruled a suicide, and I hoped and prayed they would find something suspicious, as my baby would never do that to herself."

"I know." He clasped his hands together."

June looked away, pensive. She touched her throat. "I never wanted to believe she would do such a thing, but the police have come back here to ask me further questions. I told them the same thing; that she would never kill herself. She had a bright future, wanted to win awards in her reporting, had great friends and a supportive family, and planned to marry you. She had no reason to kill herself, Jesse. I never believed that. Not for one second."

"Did she mention anything about Derek to you?"

Turning her head to the side, she gave him a tentative smile. "Why? She loved Derek like a brother. What would she say about him?"

"After they attended that work event together because I wasn't available, did she say anything about him and how the night was?"

June looked away briefly. "She mentioned having a nice time with Derek and that he was a perfect gentleman. I remember waiting up for her as she said she'd be home by eleven, but she didn't get home then. When I asked her what time she got home, she said it was around one o'clock as she went out for coffee with a few of her colleagues. But..."

"But what?"

"I met with Erica for lunch a week later, and while I was waiting at her workplace, I asked the receptionist how the work event was. She said that the work party finished at around ten, and they had all decided to go home because they were exhausted from their long work hours that day. I asked about whether Erica had chosen to go out for coffee with Derek, but she mentioned that Derek was taking her home."

Jesse flinched. She lied, but why? "So where was she between 10:00 p.m. and one o'clock? Did you ask her?"

"I did, and she said that only she and Derek had chosen to stop by for a coffee at the last minute and then he brought her home. When I asked why she lied, she changed the subject. I don't understand why she would lie about that."

He struggled to breathe. "That's a long coffee." He started to wonder why she had been lying about things in those last few months, but then again, she hadn't been herself. Something had changed her, but what?

June rubbed her gnarled hands. "Is there something bothering you about Derek? Or what is it you're worried about, dear?"

He cleared his throat, not wanting to bother the poor woman with his suspicious thoughts. "Can you tell me about Nigel and why he never got along with Erica?"

Her face turned white before she turned away. Was her body quaking? "Oh, you know how it is between brothers and sisters. Always trying to compete with each other. Two strong-minded kids."

"But he feels overshadowed by her. Jealous, even. Why is that? What started it all?"

June gave him a tentative smile. "You know what? I just remembered I have a doctor's appointment. Would you mind if I get ready to leave? I'm sorry, Jesse, but anything about Nigel, you can speak to him. I'm sure he'd be happy to talk to you. But like I said, it's the normal bickering and jealousy between siblings. I'll show you out."

Jesse nodded, resigning himself to the situation. She was hiding something about Nigel. He planned to find out what was going on as he was tired of all these damn secrets.

Chapter Thirty-Nine

AN INTRUDER

Gabriella finished typing up her case notes on the computer then turned it off. She rubbed the tops of her shoulders and winced at the aches and pains in them. She had been the last person to leave the office for the night, knowing she was safe with Joe, the cleaner, a short man with a full beard and bright green eyes who wore baggy jeans and a loose windcheater. She got up and turned to him. "Bye, Joe. I'll see you tomorrow."

"Bye, Miss Gabriella. Can I walk you to your car?"

She shook her head. "No, all good. My car's not far, but thanks anyway, Joe." Bending forward, she retrieved her handbag from the bottom cabinet and swung it over her shoulder while listening to the slow whirring of the vacuum cleaner as she walked outside through the sliding doors. The night air was breezy as she stepped onto concrete ground and passed by a boulder and low shrubs, making her way to the car into the car park around back. Chirping crickets and the zoom of passing traffic filled her ears. Then footsteps. Turning around, she saw no-one. It was deserted with only one car parked; Joe's car. Where was her car? She'd parked it here and now it was gone. Heading back towards the front of the building, she looked around in search of her car. Had someone moved it?

Hair lifted on her nape and arms and her hands turned clammy. Gripping the strap of her bag, she made her way towards the entrance of the building. Footsteps sounded behind her. With a brief look back, she saw no-one. But she was certain she'd heard footsteps. She was only a few metres away from the entrance and rushed back inside the building. She made her way down the corridor and into her office where she'd last seen the cleaner. "Joe, Joe. Help me! I can't find my car." Breathy, her eyes roamed in search of Joe but he was nowhere to be found. "Joe, Joe. Where are you?" A clopping sound made her flinch. Swallowing hard, she sensed that someone was watching her, but it couldn't be Joe. He would call out her name. He would help her find her car, but it was silent in the room.

Rummaging into her bag, she gripped her phone, but a yowl made her look up. The sound came from the staff kitchen. Slowly making her way, she grabbed a pen from her desk. It could be used as a weapon of sorts. Her hand hovered over the desk. A red rose lay on the surface, and it hadn't been there before. She had to get out of here, but no, if Joe was hurt, she had to help him. Sneaking towards the kitchen, Gabriella gripped the pen and put her phone back into her bag. Moaning sounds reverberated in her ears.

As she stood in the doorway, the hem of a pair of jeans stood out from underneath the table. A pool of blood smeared under it. The smell of flowers lingered in the air. An Italian leather shoe protruded from the side of the fridge. "Joe?"

Out of nowhere, a man dressed in an over-sized raincoat and wearing a mask came running towards her. She firmly pushed the pen into his arm. He keeled over briefly, sucking in air with the pain and shock of her attack. Without looking back, she ran for her life towards the front doors and made her way into the street, with beads of sweat over her lip and forehead. She ran and ran until she reached the few shops and a bar but didn't dare look back. Without watching where she was going, she felt strong hands grip her arms and she gasped.

"Whoa there. Are you alright?" Derek's eyes softened.

Her lips trembled as she looked over her shoulder. "Please, I have to get out of here. Anywhere."

Derek nodded, prodding her towards a cafe on the other side of the road. He had his arm around the small of her back, intermittently watching her. "In here. We can talk." She retrieved her phone, making a call to the police. A few moments later, she ended the call after explaining the incident. "Should we wait for the police?"

With dry throat, she said, "I told them I'll report into the police station later tonight and give them my statement. I can't go back there right now."

Smells of greasy food, spices, and herbs permeated the air as they walked inside the cafe. Couples, middle-aged men, and young adults sat around circular tables, chattering and laughing as if having no cares in the world.

Derek leaned over the counter, opposite a server. He turned to Gabriella. "What's your poison?"

"A coffee, thanks." She clenched her hands tight, continually looking over her shoulder and wondering if the man was following her.

"I'm calling Jesse. I know he's worried about you. He can take you to the police station." She watched him make the call then clasp his hands, resting them on the table. "He's on his way. He should be here in the next hour or so. What happened?" Gabriella explained the incident. "Christ! Do you think the dude's dead?"

She shrugged. "I don't think so. I saw blood on the floor and I heard him moan earlier. I really hope he's alive."

"Do you think it's the same guy who sent you those roses? The one who's been stalking you?"

"It has to be, Derek. I wouldn't think I had another stalker as well. But please, can we talk about something else? I need a distraction." Derek looked pensive. "Where were you going when I bumped into you? Don't get me wrong, I'm glad you were around, but this is the second time I have seen you near my work."

"I was out at the nearby pub a few doors down with a friend of mine, and I was walking back to my car. I saw you running and I was worried."

She angled her head, wondering what he was hiding. There had to be more to his story. "Where's your car?" A waiter set down their cups of coffee and he evaded her question. She tried a different tack. "What happened with the police? What did they want?" He looked out through the window as dribs and drabs of customers entered the cafe. "Come on, you can tell me."

Derek leaned forward, fixing his strong gaze on her. "Will you promise you won't say anything to Jesse about this? It would devastate him, and right now, he's got enough on his plate worrying about you and Joy and still pining for Erica. He even visited Erica's mum the other day, but I don't know the details."

She nodded, ignoring the punch in her gut about his last statement concerning Erica. "Okay. Tell me."

Sipping from his steaming coffee, he put down the cup and rubbed the back of his hands. His eyes turned downward. "I was in love with Erica, and...we...we had an affair."

Gabriella's eyes widened and her jaw dropped. Even though she suspected something, it still shocked her, hearing it straight out of his mouth.

Chapter Forty

PROTECTIVE

Jesse hugged his body tight as he sat in on the interview with Gabriella whose hands shook as she recounted her story of what had happened earlier tonight. The police station was quiet and almost empty, and Marco leaned back in his chair with intense focus while Angelo wrote down notes in a small notepad.

He could tell she was putting on a brave front, but he wasn't fooled by the way her elbows pressed into her sides and how her shoulders looked tight. Tendons protruded out of her neck as she recounted the way the assailant started chasing her, but how she had stabbed him with her pen. It demonstrated her courage, and he pushed back his need to hold her in his arms and soothe her with his hands. His gaze focused on her profile as he yearned to brush away that tear that just fell or to keep her wrapped up in a bubble until this creep was caught. What was his motive for going after her, and why? In the distance, someone called.

"Jesse. Jesse. Anyone there?"

He turned back to the present and focused on Marco. "Yes?"

"We're wondering if you saw anyone suspicious as you drove into the area?"

Jesse shook his head. "No, but Derek might know more."

Angelo intervened and looked briefly at his partner as if they were hiding a dark secret. "We spoke to him earlier and he didn't see anyone following." He peered into the distance as if processing something. "You mentioned hearing footsteps behind you. Are you sure?"

"Twice I heard them behind me, but I didn't see anyone," said Gabriella.

Marco took over. "And you mentioned the perpetrator was in the office building in front of you when you heard the footsteps behind you?"

Gabriella's face turned pale as a sheet. "Are you saying there were two people following me tonight? One inside and one outside?" She fidgeted and her body seemed to shrink. What he would do to take her pain away.

Marco looked at her reassuringly. "Listen, forensics are sweeping the area as we speak and they'll find something. Rest assured, we'll catch this guy."

Gabriella took a deep breath, rubbed her hands and peered into them. "Is Joe dead?"

Marco rose. "He suffered some bruising to the back of the head and was stabbed in the leg. He'll need time to heal, but he'll be fine. It looks like the perpetrator only wanted to subdue him. But listen, Gabriella. I'll have a policeman stationed in front of your house for a few days, and do not stay back late at work again. Make sure you leave during the daytime and when people are around. I understand Octavia's given you a list of alarm apps you can activate? Have you done that?"

Her face flushed. "Not yet, but it's next on my agenda."

Angelo got up and touched her on the shoulder. "You need to put safety guards in place, Gabriella. At this stage, we believe this person might have conjured up a fantasy to be with you. Make sure you've always got someone around you. Get that app set up. Set your home alarm, and if anything looks suspicious, call us on our mobiles and we'll get to you right away. Take notes of anything suspicious, even if it's minor." He fumbled with his clothing as if he wanted to say more but turned to Marco who gave him a strange look. Something more was going on, and they weren't sharing.

"I've got a police officer who found your car a few blocks away. They're getting it dusted for fingerprints. We'll let you know when you can pick it up. It was located behind the pub near your work. We can have a police officer stationed at your house for a few days at least, starting tomorrow morning. Can you stay with someone tonight?"

"I'll stay with her so don't worry, detectives," said Jesse.

She gave Jesse a strange look. "Thank you for everything, and I will make sure I'm safe. Don't worry," said Gabriella. Her arms tingled and her throat dried up at the idea of having Jesse keep her company. She was partly elated but also anxious. Did she want him to be so close to her when she couldn't think straight in front of him?

As they exited the police station, Jesse stopped her in her tracks. "As I said before, I'm staying over your place tonight, and no arguments."

"Fine, Jesse. I'm too tired to argue with you."

Stepping into his car, Jesse's eyes roamed in his rear-view mirror a few times and in his side mirrors. Turning on the motor, he drove towards her house and savoured the silence as Gabriella stared out the window, seemingly in her own world. What he wouldn't do to keep her safe so they could live their lives, but this sounded all too familiar.

The look on Gabriella's face reminded him of something he had forgotten about. Erica had received a couple of phone calls where nobody responded. She had hung up after the silence. When Jesse had asked who it was, she mentioned it must've been a prank caller. But she'd been rattled by it. Was more going on with her than she let on? He would ring Marco tomorrow and tell them about this as they might be able to track those calls. Why didn't he remember that earlier? He must have thought they were wrong numbers.

As they arrived at her house, it was quiet in the street. With sluggish steps, he entered her home. No matter what she said, he was not leaving her alone. She turned on lights and moved into the kitchen.

Filling up the kettle, her eyes looked droopy. "I won't be able to sleep just yet. Would you like a coffee?"

Jesse sat at the table and rested his arms over it, fighting his fatigue. "I'd love one." When the coffee was finished, she set the mug in front of him and sat opposite with her own mug. He wondered what was going through her mind as she pressed her lips together and averted her eyes. "I'm glad Derek was with you, but why was he there?"

Gabriella knit her brows. "Oh, he mentioned being with a friend and was walking back to his car."

"Which friend? Our other friends were home tonight. I checked in with them, so who was he with? Did he say exactly?"

"He didn't mention a name. Sorry." She put the mug to her lips and took a sip.

"Do you know what's going on with Derek? I know he's hiding something, and maybe he confided in you."

Gabriella avoided his eyes, cleared her throat, and squared her shoulders. She liked to show loyalty if others wanted things kept a secret. "I don't know, Jesse."

After engaging in talk about work, she answered a phone call from Joy and her other friends and explained the incident. "No, you don't need to come here. Jesse's here, and I am fine." She sighed after ending the call. "They all worry." Picking up the cups, she placed them in the sink and washed them. He wanted to massage her tight shoulders and protect her, but she was putting on a mask of bravery.

Turning around, she walked over to a closet near her bedroom and pulled out a blanket. "I can sleep on the couch and you can take the bed."

He admired her consideration. "Of course not. I'll be fine here. You should get some rest while I'm here." He took hold of the blanket and their hands brushed. Abruptly, she moved away. "Goodnight."

"Goodnight, Jesse. And thanks for staying here."

He turned off the light after she left and rested on the couch with the blanket over him, his mind churning. Thoughts of Gabriella alone in her bed. Of the electricity jolt when they touched, and of the way her eyes gazed over his lips. Did she feel something too?

Tossing and turning on the couch, he struggled to get comfortable, and minutes passed into one hour then another as he couldn't stop thinking about the woman in the next room. He sat upright and placed a hand over his temple, fighting his rampant thoughts. Picking up his mobile phone from the coffee table, the display showed it was two o'clock in the morning. Setting it back on the table, he jolted at the squeaky sound of a door opening. Gabriella stepped into the living room, wearing a dressing gown over a flimsy nightgown, the light of his mobile phone creating an eerie ambience.

She flinched at the sight of Jesse sitting up, and her robe opened up to reveal cleavage under her flimsy nightgown.

It was going to be a problem keeping his hands to himself.

Chapter Forty-One

INSOMNIA

Gabriella smiled awkwardly as she nodded in his direction. "What are you doing up?"

He gave her a cheeky grin. "I could ask you the same thing."

She tightened her robe. "Just needed water." Averting her eyes, she scurried out of his view but he followed her. Prickles on the back of her neck made her hands quake as she filled the glass and brought it to her lips. She sensed Jesse's eyes on her and turned. "Do you want a drink or anything?"

He shook his head. "No, I'm fine. But you don't look fine. You're trembling."

Little did he know that she was shaking because of his eyes boring into her back. The way his jeans tightened around his muscular form and his t-shirt pressed against his biceps didn't help her nerves. Even his smell of a musky cologne made her want to reach out and put her arms around him, just to envelop herself in his scent. What was she doing? She had to be clear in her mind. After all, a stalker was playing havoc with her life and she didn't know if she'd ever be safe again. Losing herself in her emotions could get her killed, and a part of her felt guilty for having feelings for Erica's ex-fiancé and Joy's brother. What would Joy think about her feelings for Jesse? She and Joy were best friends, and she didn't want to complicate things if Joy didn't approve of a relationship between her and Jesse. She had to keep her head in the game now. If she lost herself in Jesse, she could hurt Joy who might not approve of them having feelings for each other. A part of her felt guilty with Erica for caring about Jesse as they had been together a long time. How could she compete with the love they shared over a long period of time? No, she had to keep Jesse at arm's length, given the complications it would cause, especially if the stalker might not want her to feel anything for another man.

Gabriella's hands moistened as her hands slipped on the glass. Catching it quickly, she filled it with water and took a quick sip then put it aside. She held her breath and stroked her arm as if she was cold. Taking a sip then putting aside the glass, Jesse glanced her over from head to toe and thrust out his chest, stepping towards her. She was hyperaware of her exploding heartbeat, and her body suddenly flooded with warmth as Jesse tenderly pressed his hand into her shoulder. Her shoulder tingled with his touch and her breath quickened. She became light-headed until Jesse broke the quiet.

"I take it you can't sleep after what happened. Are you okay?" He shuffled back to give her space as if realising he was too close.

She nodded, hiding her disappointment. As much as her head knew they had to keep her distance, her heart knew different. She was so close to kissing him. "Just seeing Joe on the floor covered in blood. It made me sick. I thought he was going to kill me, but now I realise if he wanted to hurt me, he would have already done it. He has this fantasy about me."

Jesse's eyes turned dark. "He's a sick pervert, which is why you shouldn't be here on your own. My offer still stands if you want to stay with me again."

"No, I won't let this person control my life. This guy has this illusion about us being together, and if I can feed into that, we might all be safe. You included."

He frowned. "Me? Why would he target me? Because I'm trying to protect you or...?"

"Or what?"

He turned his head, looking past her. "Nothing. Never mind. I think you should get some sleep, even if tomorrow is a Saturday."

She remembered something Derek had told her. "Oh, before I got to bed. Derek mentioned you talking to June about Erica. Why would you do that?"

He sighed. "I needed to ask about Derek and Nigel. Erica deserves justice, and I thought she could give me a clue about who might have hurt her. There might be something she remembered."

"I might check something on the computer." She strolled towards her room and Jesse followed. Picking up her laptop, she lay back in bed and turned it on while Jesse walked over to the other side. "Can I sit with you if you're doing research?" She nodded, so he scooted close to her, their shoulders brushing as she entered her password and waited. She did name searches for Erica whose newspaper articles came up, displaying *Woman In Hiding, Research breakthrough Into Chronic Pain, Fighting the Common Cold,* and *The Most Popular Mornington Peninsula Wineries.* Gabriella clicked on the wineries article, hyperaware of how their bodies touched. *Focus!* They skimmed through the article until heading to the part about the winery in which Nigel worked. "I knew she'd written about her brother's winery, but I never read it. Have you?"

"I did read it. It was just a promotional piece about the winery. Nothing sinister about that, Gabriella." His breath was erratic as he stared at her lips. "Hmm. I take it you're thinking that one of these articles might have made her a target? Is that it?"

She nodded. "Maybe." Her head moved closer to the screen. "I guess she was the professional and wasn't bothered by Nigel working there."

Jesse had a thought. "When I visited Erica's mother, I got the feeling she was hiding something, particularly about Nigel. His relationship with Erica was dysfunctional. They were never close, but I sense something there. Something must have happened between them. Something traumatic. Erica hated him with a vengeance but would never tell me why."

"You don't think Nigel would have hurt her, do you?"

"I don't know, but maybe we need to get to him on his own, away from his parents. He might slip up. What if he knows more about his sister than he's let on?" He stared into the distance as if concocting a plan.

"What are you thinking?"

"Do you like wine?" She nodded. "As Nigel works at this winery in Mornington, I was thinking we could visit him there tomorrow. I know he's working. What do you say? Are you up for a long drive?"

She shrugged. "It's not like he's going to tell you anything, Jesse."

"No, but he always liked you as if you understood him better than any of us. You can be my buffer, and we can see how he acts in his own safe environment. He might tell us something trivial that could lead us to a clue."

"Fine, but let's go to bed and get some rest." She thought she spotted a fleeting look of desire in his eyes, realising she'd said the wrong thing. "I mean, I'll go to bed and you get back to the couch." Avoiding his eyes, she said, "Goodnight."

"Goodnight, Gabriella. Sweet dreams." No doubt she'd dream about him now.

Chapter Forty-Two

WINERY VISIT

J esse gripped the steering wheel as he passed by a sign stating "Merrick's Beach" and continued down the road heading to the Mornington Peninsula winery, a short drive from the beach. Gabriella sat in the passenger seat, digging her nails into her skin and appeared to be in her own little world. He eyed her smooth, tanned legs underneath a light, cotton floral dress which covered her above the knees. She placed her hands over her legs, unintentionally drawing his attention to their smooth skin and shapely curves. Lavender and musk permeated his senses. They'd been mostly quiet on the trip down here. He would have to do something about this tension between them, but right now, they had a job to do.

He came to a stop inside the parking space of the winery and turned off the motor. The building was clad in grey weatherboard, and as they made their way towards the entrance, he was in awe of the greenery surrounding them. The fresh air smelled amazing. Rectangular timber tables with timber slatted chairs were raised over a Merbau decking, with a view of grapevines row after row. Towering green trees stood in the distance. Steel posts lined the front outdoor open-plan area, furnished with several rows of tables, seating guests who shared wine and snacks. Huge boulders sat opposite the seating area and close to a concrete path leading towards another outdoor seating area on the other side.

Gabriella walked alongside him as they moved up the steps and passed by a few tables with seated guests. "What are you into? Sweet or dry wine?"

"Sweet mainly, but you can try whatever you like. I don't mind."

Heading to the front counter, Jesse smiled at the buxom older woman who leaned forward with a smile. He picked up a card with their range of wines and scanned through them. "Hi, I am wondering if we could taste your moscato."

The lady's eyes lit up. She grabbed two glasses with one hand and set them in front of them while pouring the wine. "This is a very popular wine that pairs well with spicy foods and comes from the muscat grapes. It's famous for the sweetness of peaches and orange blossom. And did you know it has less alcohol than other sparkling wines?"

Jesse gave Gabriella a look. "I did not know that." He sipped the wine while Gabriella did the same.

"Mmm. Very nice. Refreshing," said Gabriella.

The lady brought out a jug of water and two short glasses. "You can cleanse your palate with the water and then try our range of riesling wines. Even prosecco is nice, but quite fruity and less sweet, whereas moscato is more fragrant."

Jesse accidentally brushed his hip with Gabriella who moved away. "Sure."

By the time they tasted the other wines, Jesse was feeling a little light-headed with a spring in his step. Behind Gabriella, he spotted Nigel holding a tray of drinks and heading over to one of the tables a few metres away. When he was returning to the counter, Nigel froze then glared.

Gabriella walked towards him and whispered something. Nigel had a hint of a smile then nodded. She approached Jesse. "He has a break in about twenty minutes and said we can talk to him at one of those tables outside on the grass."

Jesse wondered what she'd said to him to make him smile. "Okay, but I wanted to buy you some wine. Which one do you prefer, or would you like all three?"

Gabriella rummaged into her bag and pulled out her wallet. "I'll get one for me. You don't need to do that unless you want it for yourself." He grasped her wallet and put it back into her bag. Her hands were warm and smooth, and he felt his body respond to the touch.

"My treat. Please."

She shook her head. "I am perfectly fine to get my own wine, Jesse." She grabbed her purse again and turned over to the lady who was serving a man and a woman.

"No, it is my honour to pay. Put your wallet away."

Gabriella ignored him and pulled out her card, but Jesse beat her to it. He slipped his card into the server's hand and gave her a cheeky smile. "I cannot believe you, Jesse. So stubborn, but remember we are not in the olden days here. Women can actually pay for themselves, you know?"

"No doubt. I admire your tenacity, but I beat you this time."

Gabriella turned to the server. "I'd like to buy a bottle of moscato and your prosecco as well." She stared hard at Jesse. "Did you want a bottle?" He shook his head.

"Of course. I'll get you those bottles." The lady handed her the two bottles and swiped his card.

He turned to her. "How about a light lunch while we're waiting for Nigel?"

She nodded. "Fine, but at least let me pay for that."

He waved her away and focused on the server who was smiling at their exchange. "Let's try the tapas. It looks pretty good here on the menu."

He flicked through it when the lady at the counter stood up straight. She took out a notepad and pen. "Now, what would you like to order?"

Jesse took out his wallet. "What do you recommend?"

"Well, the homemade lamb sausages and meatballs are nice. And our dips are made with herbs and fresh vegetables from our garden. We also have a tasty garden vegetable frittata, as well as a variety of cheeses from Victorian farms. We support the farm community here on the Mornington Peninsula." He turned to Gabriella, and they both selected a couple of cheeses and everything else she'd recommended. They also ordered assorted dry crackers to pair with the cheeses. "Great. Take a seat in the sun outside. Anywhere you like, and I'll bring it out to you."

Once Jesse paid, they walked into the blinding sun and sat at a table shaded by a tall, wilting tree. He took his seat opposite Gabriella and stared at her lips which she was licking. Their legs touched briefly. He swallowed a few times and fumbled with his clothing. Why was he hot around his neck all of a sudden? He looked away and focused on the view of the vineyards, the wind blowing strands of hair over her eyes as she stared past him, watching new customers coming in as small groups. Waiters circled other tables, holding trays of food and wine glasses. "Do you enjoy coming to wineries?"

She nodded. "I do. Anything that takes me out of the city and into nature is the most healing thing for me. For anyone. What about you?"

"I love it. Sometimes Erica and I would come to wineries around here, in Red Hill mainly. We never came to this one together."

Gabriella pushed aside a tinge of jealousy. "Would you like to move out into the countryside one day?"

"One day, but not now. I much prefer living in the city. I'm sure in my old age, I'll probably like the quiet and move. And you?"

Gabriella beamed. "I feel the same. I think when you're young, you prefer to be in the midst of events and excitement, close to facilities and services. But I'm sure I'll get tired of the noisy life and want to settle somewhere like here. It is so beautiful and calming."

Jesse wanted to tell her *she* was beautiful, but he held back. "Yes, breathtaking." He wished she realised the double meaning in that.

The lady arrived and set down their tray of food and two plates. She returned with two glasses of moselle. "Oh, I noticed you talking to Nigel. It is tragic about his sister. If only they hadn't fought the way they had that day. Such a bad way to leave things."

Jesse leaned in. "What do you mean?"

The lady forced a grin, ignoring his question. "Enjoy. And if you'd like anything else, please let me know."

"Thank you," said Gabriella. "I guess we can ask Nigel about the fight. Quite heated by the sounds of it."

They dug into their meatballs first. Sauce dripped down Gabriella's chin. Picking up a napkin, he leaned forward. "You have sauce on your chin. Do you mind?"

Gabriella fixed her gaze on him. "No." He wiped her chin, wondering what it would feel like to be that napkin pressed against her chin. She bit her bottom lip and turned away, cheeks flushed. Was she feeling it too? "Oh, here comes Nigel."

Their moment was broken as Nigel made his way towards them. Jesse refocused and wondered if his deep-seated anger towards Erica would have been enough to hurt her.

Chapter Forty-Three

MYSTERY

Nigel lifted a chair towards them and sat close to Gabriella. A little too close. Jesse's stomach churned at the way Erica's brother was staring at Gabriella. It wasn't like he had any claim to her, so she could like anyone she wanted to like, but the idea of Nigel and Gabriella made him sick. "So why are you here, Gabriella? What's going on?"

"We wanted to talk about Erica." She faced Jesse briefly. "I know she promoted this winery for her work and wrote an article. You must be proud of that."

He shifted in his seat. "Whatever. It was part of her job. So what's with the visit?"

Gabriella squeezed her hands tight, watching Jesse whose glare was obvious. "We had some questions about Erica. The police would've questioned you about her, didn't they?"

He scoffed. "Yeah, some garbage about suspicious circumstances, but if you ask me, she was weak and could have easily killed herself. She had no enemies and she hated her life." His eyes steered towards Jesse. "No offence, but she wasn't ready to be engaged to you, and I wondered why she rushed into a commitment with you in the first place."

Jesse clenched his teeth. "Seriously? We were engaged for five years so we didn't rush into anything. Why did you hate her so much?"

Nigel looked over his shoulder as if he was concerned about anyone listening in. He swallowed while Jesse bit into cheese and a cracker. Gabriella used a toothpick to fork a lamb sausage then bit into it. "What's with that question? We just didn't get along, that's all. It happens to a lot of siblings. Personality clash, you could say."

"No, I think there's more to it. What happened between you two over the years?" Jesse turned to Gabriella who must have wondered the same thing.

His face paled as he picked up a cracker and shoved it into his mouth. He touched Gabriella on the shoulder. "Erica loved you, Gabriella. She talked about you all the time."

Gabriella smiled. "Listen, we heard you had a fight with Erica the day she came here for her article. What happened?"

He averted his eyes. "Nothing." He rose. "I have to get back to work. See you."

"No, wait. I have more questions," said Gabriella.

"I have to go. Take care, Gabriella." He ignored Jesse and scurried away.

Jesse's eyes roamed. "He's hiding something, but what?"

She turned to Jessie. "Siblings fight all the time, but how bad could their relationship have been? I don't remember ever seeing much love between them when he was home."

Jesse watched Nigel head through a door near the front counter. "I don't know, but why don't we enjoy this tray of food for now and chill. Maybe we can talk to that lady again. She might be forthcoming with a bit of a nudge."

Gabriella's heart warmed. "You might be right. Good thinking."

He chuckled. "You haven't seen me at my best. I am quite the smart one when I'm in the mood."

Gabriella threw a piece of cheese into her mouth. "Right, so does that mean you're always in a bad mood?"

"Ha ha, very funny. But seriously, I do love solving puzzles. It's like physiotherapy, where you're looking at a range of ways to manage a chronic condition. You come up with a program which fits everyone in different ways based on their individual cases."

"Is that one of the reasons you became a physiotherapist? To solve mysteries and puzzles?"

He shrugged. "Kind of. I guess after my sister died, I hated the way things were swept under the rug. We never talked about her, and I found that it affected Joy a lot. I helped her to feel better with a massage and exercise and came up with a daily program for her. She could manage her grief a lot better after that. I got such a high helping her that I thought this is what health is about; movement, exercise, and taking care of the body. Such a science and an art to it all. So, I decided to study and here I am." He paused. "What about you? Why did you become a counsellor and soon-to-be social worker?"

Gabriella munched on the vegetable frittata. She stared up into the sky in thought. "I didn't want anyone going through what I went through—so much pain, violence, and humiliation. I even lost an old friend who was my babysitter. She died in a horrific way, and I don't want that kind of violence in this world. I have to stop people from coping in destructive ways through drugs, alcohol, and more violence. If I can help one person, that person can pay it forward and influence their community and family life. It' so rewarding when people succeed by reducing their drug intake gradually and through sheer willpower. I wish I could have helped Nora. If she was scared for some reason, I should have been able to see that." Her eyes dimmed and she downed the remainder of her wine in one gulp. "Anyway, sorry. We were meant to talk about positive things, and here I am ruining the mood."

His heart warmed at her vulnerability and how much she'd shared. He wanted to wrap his arms around her and assure her she was safe. "It's okay. You do amazing work, Gabriella. Working in crisis and thinking on your feet. It takes courage and a thick skin. I doubt I could do what you're doing, handling emotional problems and dealing with crises."

"And I doubt I could be a physiotherapist. But we're both in the helping professions and each has its own rewards. We all have our own strengths and passions."

"Hmm." He patted his stomach. "I am so full right now. We can get the rest to go."

She nodded. "Sure. Let's go talk to the lady." Turning around, she said, "It's quiet."

Gabriella started to rise when the lady approached them. "Can I put these in boxes for you?"

"Yes, please," said Gabriella.

When the lady returned, she handed them several boxes. "Here you go."

Pushing a hair strand away from her eye, she asked. "Can you tell us more about the fight between Erica and Nigel?"

The lady seemed to process the question. "Listen, Nigel is my employee and I don't want to be talking behind his back. I'm sorry."

"Please," said Gabriella. "We're trying to give her family closure about her death, and if Nigel knows anything that could help explain who could have hurt her, it would give us closure too. I was one of her friends. Besides, we will not mention your name."

The woman frowned and looked over her shoulder. She sat down, whispering, "I thought she killed herself?"

Gabriella looked to Jesse, but she continued. "Her case was reopened due to similar murders, so anything you can tell us, would be great."

The woman's eyes darkened at the news. "It was a screaming match between them; something about crossing the boundaries. He slapped her hard, and I thought for sure she wouldn't write anything great about the winery in her article. Luckily, she did. I wasn't happy with the way Nigel was treating her, but he mentioned apologising to her later."

Boundaries! What did that even mean? "Was there anything else you can remember?" said Jesse.

"He told her that she needed to know the truth, but when she asked him what he meant, he backed off and got back to work. That's it."

"Thank you," said Jesse.

The woman smiled and wandered back to the front counter.

"What do you make of that, Jesse?"

He shrugged. "I don't know. What did Nigel mean by boundaries? Was Erica doing something she wasn't supposed to be doing? And what's the truth?"

"It looks like we need to do a bit more digging."

Jesse wanted to shy away from the truth as he got the feeling it could shatter him.

Chapter Forty-Four

A BETRAYAL

In his garage, Jesse slipped on gloves. He picked up a sander, bent down over an old car he was restoring and glided the sander over the body to remove the paint. Derek pulled out the bumper and threw it roughly on the ground, narrowly missing his toolbox.

"Hey, careful. If you knock over the toolbox, you'll be the one getting all those nails." His old Ford Mustang would be a work of art once they finished restoring it, but it had a long way to go.

"Sorry. Butterfingers." Derek gripped a wrench and removed a nut from the wheel. He clenched his teeth, overexerting himself and almost dropped the wrench. His consistent sighs and breathlessness were distracting him. His mind was not on the job.

Jesse continued to sand, thinking it was about time Derek told the truth. It wasn't only Derek who was hiding something, but Nigel too. Yesterday at the winery, he had refused to tell them why he had hated Erica with a passion. "Gabriella mentioned you were out with a friend the other night. Who were you with?"

Derek's veins protruded as he clenched his teeth again to remove the nut. He took a deep breath. "No-one you know, man. Just another panel beater work friend you've never met. I have other friends, you know."

Jesse shook his head and stopped his sanding. "I know when you're lying to me, Derek. You're lying about this and you're lying about Erica." He bent over and lay down the sander. "I spoke to Erica's mum and we talked about that awards event you went to with Erica. June mentioned that you guys were out late that night." He took a breath, not sure he wanted the truth. "What happened between you two? And don't think about lying to me because I'll know it."

Derek threw the wrench roughly back into the toolbox and removed the wheel. He rolled it over to the side and grabbed the spare tyre to replace the old one. His brows bumped together in a scowl as he placed the new tyre on the wheelbase of the car. "Why can't you let the damn past go, Jesse? I told you we were just friends. Leave it alone."

He scoffed and wiped his sweaty brow. "Damn it, Derek. The fact that you're telling me to leave it alone means there was more to it."

He shrugged. "Ask your damn girlfriend."

Jesse's body stiffened. What was Derek talking about? Gabriella wasn't his girlfriend and what did she know that he didn't? "What are you talking about?" He put aside the sander and approached Derek who was tightening the lug nuts on the tyre.

Derek wiped his dirty hands on his overalls and stood up straight. "Your girlfriend knows the truth, so leave me be. Ask her."

Jesse put his face inches from Derek's. "Will you stop calling her my girlfriend? Gabriella is a just a friend." His eyes fixated on his. "What is it that she knows, anyway?"

Derek kicked the wrench sitting on the concrete. "Give me that damn sander. It doesn't look like you're doing any damn work."

Jesse crossed his arms, shaking his head. He was tired of all these secrets. Secrets with Erica. Secrets with Derek. Secrets with Gabriella— if she knew what Derek was hiding and didn't tell him. He had to keep pushing until he was sick of him asking. It was the only way.

"Listen, Derek. I don't care what you tell me. I just need the truth."
He steeled himself, knowing the look in Derek's eyes would give him
the answer with just one question. "Did you sleep with Erica?"

Derek's shoulders slumped, looking defeated. He avoided Jesse's
eyes and picked up a rag then started wiping the driver window. His
focus was on a particular spot on the car which didn't look dirty to
Jesse. It was obvious he didn't want to respond, but he had to know
the truth. "Answer me, or I swear to God, I will beat it out of you."

Derek gripped the rag and scrunched it into a ball. His eyes closed
briefly, but when he opened them, it was as if he was fighting back
tears. Was that guilt in his eyes? Shame? "I'm sorry, man," he
whispered.

Jesse tasted bile in his throat. "What did you say?"

Derek knit his brows. "I loved her."

Jesse sagged against the wall, frozen. Another betrayal. Another
loss. How could he be friends with someone who had betrayed him in
the worst possible way? He thought about the times Erica had wanted
to delay the wedding. The times that she had looked at Derek a few
seconds too long. The times she had visited Derek without him and
didn't tell him. It was all a lie, and the guy he had trusted with his life
was now a stranger. A poor excuse of a friend. Why had he chosen to
ignore the signs that were staring him right in the face? "How could
you both do that to me? I loved her. She was my fiancée, not yours."

Derek sat on a chair, his body slouching and his hands clenched.
"We didn't mean to hurt you, but if it's any consolation, Erica broke it
off with me. We only slept together a few times. It didn't last long. She
chose you in the end."

Jesse chuckled and planted his legs wide. He glared at his friend
and approached him. With a rough hand, he grabbed him by his top
and shoved him, causing Derek to fall out of his chair and lie on the

ground. "As if that excuses your behaviour. Only a few times." His eyes bore into him with fury. "You bastard. When did it stop?"

He pushed himself up and remained sitting on the ground. "About four months before she died. She wanted to tell you, but she didn't because she realised she loved you more than she loved me. We couldn't help what we felt."

Jesse stomped, his muscles quivering. Heat flushed through his pores and his pulse sped. "Get out of here or I won't be responsible for what I do next. I am containing myself right now, so get out. Now!" Derek moved to his knees and stood up, grabbing his phone and rushing out of the garage without looking back.

Jesse moved to the chair and sat down for the next ten minutes, ruminating about what he had done wrong in the relationship. Why had she looked elsewhere for pleasure? Why wasn't he enough for her? This must have been what Derek disclosed to Gabriella the other night, and he hated her for not telling him. He had a right to know, but they had both kept it a secret.

Bowing his head, he let the tears fall. He had loved Erica with every fibre of his being, and he had lost her twice. He would have done anything for her. He wanted to marry her, but she didn't love him enough to stay faithful. She could have broken up with him instead of cheating on him, and now he could never confront her. He would never understand why she had looked to Derek for love.

Pushing aside his thoughts, he got up and gripped the sander, circling the machine around the body of the car. Working with his hands was a great healer for him, and in this moment, he was tired of being in his head. He had to keep busy and get his body moving.

Moments later, he turned at the sound of footsteps, wondering why Derek had returned. "If you're back here, I'll hurt you, Derek. Get lost." No-one appeared. It must have been the next-door neighbour, as sometimes his noise sounded like it was happening in his own backyard. His eyes focused on the specks of paint coming off, a pattern of wiggly lines and dots. The car would be a work of art with new paint. His rage dissipated as he continued to glide his hands over the surface.

A noise stopped him. It sounded like a laugh, but when he looked over his shoulder again, it was deserted behind him. He put down the sander. Jesse peeked outside, but nobody was out there. The wind blew the trees and the sun blazed down on the ground, creating multiple shadows.

He imagined things because he was too much in his head, carrying all this heartache and pain. If only he could have shaken the truth out of Erica when she was still alive, but now he would never know what had been on her mind. He would never know why she betrayed him when he worshipped her. Maybe that was the problem. He had stifled her when she wanted freedom. The freedom to travel and to enjoy other men. They had been together a long time, and he never realised she had been unsure about marriage. If only she had talked to him. They could have worked it out.

Jesse made his way back inside and neared the car but the sander had disappeared. He was sure he put it down in this spot, so where was it? He wandered towards the toolbox, thinking it must be near there but it wasn't. When he made his way to the other side and looked underneath the front of the car, he spotted two black shoes. His heart raced. Derek didn't wear those shoes so who was in here? "Who's here? Show yourself." Standing up slowly, he picked up a wrench and made his way around the other side. There were footsteps behind him.

As he slowly turned around, a hard knock on the back of his head brought him down to the ground, the scuffling of feet reverberating in his ears. "No," he heard. Then he saw black.

Chapter Forty-Five

A MOTHER'S SECRET

The day after her winery trip, Gabriella stood outside June's front door with her hands in her jeans pockets as she waited for her to answer the door. She had called Erica's mother to ask if they could meet, hoping to get answers about Nigel. His hatred for his sister went way beyond sibling rivalry and jealousy.

June smiled awkwardly as she touched her neck with one hand and opened the door wider with her right hand. "This is a surprise, Gabriella. Come in, dear."

"Thanks, June. It's been a while." She stepped into the foyer and made her way into the living room. Smells of cinnamon and chocolate filled the air as she sat on the couch, her back sinking into the cushiony comfort. "I am sorry I haven't visited earlier, but it's been busy and I didn't know what to say. After the funeral, I was in shock, as I know you and your family were, and I needed time to clear my head."

June drew a hand through her short, black hair and leaned forward in the armchair beside the couch. "Oh, dear. You have nothing to apologise for. We all needed to clear our heads and try to move on as best we could. You are here now, and that's all that matters. This moment."

Gabriella swallowed, a sense of guilt causing a sick stomach. She hated being here on the pretence of a normal visit when she had questions. But she needed the truth—for justice and to get answers. She had to focus on the big picture and find out what Nigel was hiding. What his family was hiding. "How have you been in the past year, June?"

She shrugged. "Still working and focusing on my family." Her eyes turned away. "Would you like a tea, coffee or a cold drink?"

"No, thanks." She smiled. "And how is Nigel doing?"

Her eyes darkened and she touched the base of her throat again. "He is managing as best as he can. Keeping busy at the winery and trying to get his web design business established. He has a few clients and is building this up."

"I wish him luck with that, then he can do it full-time." She wondered if Nigel mentioned their visit to the winery and decided to test it out. "Jesse and I took a trip to the winery where Nigel works. Did he tell you that?"

June rested back in her seat with her head tilted. "No, dear, he didn't. But then again, Nigel is busy rushing around and he will probably mention it tonight."

It was strange how she didn't ask why they visited. "He has taken Erica's death pretty hard, hasn't he? I mean, I saw him in the city a while ago, and he seems very angry about her death. I hope I'm not overstepping here, but why is he so angry, June?"

A timer rang out and interrupted their moment. "Excuse me. I've got chocolate cookies in the oven. Nigel likes these. We could have some."

"Of course. I will have that coffee now too."

June rose and stood frozen as if in her own thoughts. "I'll be right back, dear."

Gabriella wondered how she would get June to open up about Nigel or Erica as she didn't see her being forthcoming about her son. The way she sighed with relief when the timer went off concerned her. She knew something was off.

June returned, carrying a plate of cookies on a tray, with two mugs of coffee beside it. "I hope you like them." She put a cup down in front of Gabriella on the coffee table and brought her own cup to her lips.

"They smell amazing. You always were a great cook. Erica hated going out sometimes because it meant she'd miss out on your home-cooked meals."

June's eyes lit up. "Thank you for saying that, dear. It means so much." Her eyes looked past her as if she remembered the good times. Gabriella hated to push her for more, but she reminded herself of the bigger picture.

She returned to her original question and sipped a bit of her coffee. "I don't want to make you uncomfortable, June, but the more I know about Erica, the more chance there is that the police can find her killer." She knew the police had explained their investigation to Erica's family. "Why is Nigel so angry? He was angry with Erica when she was alive, and even in death? What was going on between them?"

The white of June's knuckles showed as she tightened her grip on the cup. Her green eyes squinted. With a resigned sigh, she said, "Oh, dear. There is nothing to find out here. It was pure sibling rivalry, that's all."

"Please, June. I get the impression there is more going on here." She had to give her the whole truth. "When we saw Nigel at the winery yesterday, he became agitated when we asked him about Erica. I know he's hiding something. The more we know, the more likely it is that the police will find Erica's killer. Every little thing counts."

June's eyes turned downward as if she was processing her statement. "Please, Gabriella. Can you please leave? I'm not feeling well." She rose.

Gabriella knew when she'd overstayed her welcome and would respect her privacy for now. She could resort to other ways of finding out. She sipped her remaining hot drink. "Thanks for the coffee, June." She gave her a reassuring smile. "I'm sorry if I upset you."

When she reached the inside of her car, her phone buzzed. Clicking on the notification, she read the text message from Joy. "Jesse was in an accident. He's at the Williamstown Hospital." Frozen in her seat, the pain in her chest was unbearable.

Chapter Forty-Six

AN INJURY

G abriella entered the ward, the smell of antiseptic and flowers prominent. She approached Jesse who shifted in bed as Joy held his hand. His face looked haggard. His head was bandaged, and he had bruising around his forehead. Instead of saying hello, he averted his eyes and stared at the covered window. Why was he acting that way?

Joy rushed into her arms. "Thanks for coming."

She nodded. "How are you feeling, Jesse? And what happened?" He kept staring out the window.

Joy looked at Jesse strangely, then turned to her friend. "Someone he didn't see attacked him in his garage." He remained silent.

Behind her approached their friend, Jamie who was a doctor. She was clad in her white coat with a nametag reading Dr. Porcellin." "Hello, ladies." She picked up the clipboard at the end of the bed and jotted down notes then turned to Jesse. "Are you in much pain, Jesse?"

He shrugged. "A bit dizzy and I still have this headache." His face suddenly changed colour, and Jamie wasted no time in picking up a bedpan from underneath the bed and putting it underneath his mouth. He vomited. Gabriella looked away, not wanting to become nauseous herself. Jamie wiped his mouth with a towel resting on a chair then walked to the bathroom.

Jamie returned. "I'll give you something for the nausea and perhaps something stronger for the headache. Your symptoms shouldn't last too long. We'll keep you here overnight for observation."

"Thanks, Jamie," said Jesse. "I'll be glad to get out of here."

Joy wrapped her arms around Jamie who patted her on her back. "Thank you for looking after my brother. You've been amazing." They pulled away.

"It is my pleasure, Joy." She neared Gabriella and touched her shoulder. "Jesse will recuperate fairly quickly. There is no need to worry. Luckily, the hit on the head didn't do much damage, but it could have been worse."

Gabriella's eyes remained fixed on Jesse who had not once looked her in the eye. He was upset with her for some reason, but what?

"I'll be back later with the medications." Jamie walked out.

Gabriella stood by the window while Joy held her brother's hand, talking to him about Derek, who had stepped out for a drink and would be returning any minute now. The tension in the air was thick, and she needed to let Joy and Jesse talk through things. When she'd heard that Jesse had been in an accident, something shifted inside her. A terror she had never known ravaged her, and it almost triggered a panic attack on her way over to the hospital. His sad, soulful green eyes broke her. Her chest tightened at the sight of the bruising, and she wanted to take away his pain. First, Joy had been in an accident and now Jesse. Both incidences were not accidents, and this was all her fault. She swept a hand across her forehead to get rid of sweat. A voice in the distance brought her back to the present.

"Gabriella. What's up with you, girl?" Joy got up from Jesse's bedside and pulled her towards Jesse. "Here. Take a seat."

She addressed both Joy and Jesse. "Can you guys tell me exactly what happened here?" Jesse bowed his head, saying nothing.

Joy intervened, giving her brother another strange look. "He was in his garage with Derek, restoring one of his cars when someone hit him in the back of the head with a rock. The police questioned him earlier but so far, no leads."

Gabriella nodded. "Where was Derek? Who found you?" Joy remained silent.

With a stern look, he briefly focused on her then turned to Joy. "Derek left, then he came back and found me."

Light-headedness made her body sway and her stomach felt rock hard. Who would do this to Jesse? It couldn't just be a random attack. It had to be her stalker. Maybe he'd seen Jesse as a threat to his desires. An obstacle to reaching Gabriella. "Do you know who could have done this to you?"

He scoffed. "Why do you even care?"

Joy neared her brother on the other side of the bed. She leaned forward and touched his chin so he was facing her. "What is with you, Jesse? Why are you being rude to Gabriella? What has she done?"

"Listen, Joy. I need to be alone. Can you guys please leave?"

Joy stood cross-armed. "I am not leaving here until you tell me exactly what's wrong. I know something must have happened today because you and Gabi went to the winery yesterday. So spill." The quiet in the room was awkward and Gabriella stared into her lap, waiting for a response but Jesse said nothing. Derek walked into the room and broke the quiet. One look at his face and she knew what had happened. Jesse must have confronted Derek who must have told him about his affair with Erica. It surely wasn't Derek who had hit him with the rock after their possible argument, was it? No, that was crazy. Derek was Jesse's best friend and whatever happened, they would sort it out.

"How are you feeling, man?" Derek asked.

Jesse avoided his eyes. "You get the hell out of here, Derek. I can't talk to you right now." He faced the window and clenched his hands. It was as if he had to contain his fury.

"I am so sorry, Jesse." He put his hands into his pockets with slumped shoulders and ambled out of the ward.

Gabriella got up from her seat and looked at Joy. "Did they find any prints on the scene or on the rock itself?"

"Crime scene's investigating the scene as we speak, Gabriella, so I guess we'll find out soon. How about we go grab a coffee and let Jesse settle down. I'll talk to him later."

Gabriella didn't want to leave. She needed to make things right, but he was too enraged to have a reasonable discussion. "Okay, let's go."

Joy put up a hand. "Hold up." She kissed Jesse on the cheek. "Last chance, bro. What happened between you, Derek and Gabriella?"

He stared up at the ceiling. "I need to be alone, Joy. I can't deal with more pain right now, so please just give me time to process it myself. I love you."

Joy nodded. "Okay. I'll give you your space, but I will be back tomorrow to pick you up. Have a good night, bro."

"Goodnight, Jesse. I hope you get to relax a bit," said Gabriella. He nodded in response, which was a slight improvement. But what had she done? It then hit her like a ton of bricks. It had to be about her knowing about Derek and Erica's affair.

Chapter Forty-Seven

THE TRUTH

Gabriella drove all the way back to June's house a few evenings later after she'd contacted her to help sort out some of Erica's possessions for charity. But she hoped the real reason June asked for help with her belongings was to talk to her about Nigel.

Brushing off the thought, she parked by the kerb and rubbed the back of her neck as she sat there for a few minutes, wondering whether June would reveal whatever Nigel was hiding.

Gabriella got out of the car and rang the doorbell. Within seconds, June answered as if she'd been standing by the door. "Hi, June."

"Come in, dear." She swung open the door wider and led her to Erica's room. She touched her on the shoulder. "I know it's been a long time. I just couldn't bring myself to give them away, but it's time." A tear fell. "I thought you might like some of Erica's things in the walk-in-robe. I've seen you wear similar kinds of styles so you might want these. I've sent off other clothing to charity stores, but you can have these ones. They've been washed."

Gabriella stiffened, not comfortable taking these. "No, I'd rather you give

them away." She smiled. "I am glad you asked me to help sort these."

June gave her a reassuring smile. "Take a look, and it is fine if you don't want anything. I still need help to send them to charity. We'll have a conversation once I've made tea. Take a few minutes, and then join me in the kitchen." She walked away.

Once June left, Gabriella winced looking at her dead friend's room. It had been so long since she'd been in it, talking about boys when they'd met in high school and sharing clothing and perfumes. She stared around Erica's room which hadn't changed much with its mahogany dresser containing assorted creams and perfumes and a double timber-based bed with a grey comforter and matching pillowcases. A lone chair rested near the bed, and a walk-in-robe stood ajar and displayed a few scarves folded on a shelf, a rack of shoes on the floor, and several jumpers and t-shirts on hangers.

Gabriella approached the window, drew open the lacy curtain, and stared outside into the street, her mind on Erica and how secretive she'd been in those last few months. Glen 20 smells filled the air as she breathed in the air and wandered over to the walk-in-robe. Two garbage bags lay nearby, and she sorted through the clothing and placed the ones she thought were too ratty in one bag and ones for charity in the other.

Half an hour later, she had filled two bags and decided that she didn't wish to have any of Erica's things. Disadvantaged people out there needed them more than she did, and she wasn't comfortable taking her dead friend's possessions.

Gabriella placed the bags near the door and wandered around the room. She touched the silky fabric of the comforter then flicked through a magazine lying on the dresser. On the last page of the magazine, a few A4 printed pages of articles fell out and dropped to the floor. She bent down, picked them up and stared at the three headlines: *Sydney Woman Missing*; *Suspicious Murder Of Sydney Woman*; *Parents' Press Appeal.* She skimmed through the first article which indicated that the woman had been stalked and later went missing. The second article questioned if a woman's suicide was staged, and the final article mentioned the parents' belief that their daughter would never commit suicide and had been murdered.

She clutched at her stomach, fighting nausea and sagged into the chair near the bed. A wave of cold hit her chest and her head spun for a moment. A voice in the distance brought her back to the present. Standing up, she made her way to June in the kitchen while carrying the articles. A mug of coffee and shortbread were on the round table, and she sat back, holding the articles before placing them on the table.

June sat opposite and took a sip of her hot drink. She frowned, leaned forward, and picked up the articles. Scanning through them, her eyes darted in all directions. A glassy stare indicated that she was focused on a memory.

Gabriella needed her attention. "I'm happy to take the clothing bags to the charity store. I've filled up both bags."

June looked up. "No, it's fine. Nigel or my husband can do that." Her eyes dampened up as she fixed her gaze on Gabriella. "I never saw these. Where were they, dear?"

"Inside a magazine. I was flicking through it when they fell out. Why would Erica have these articles hidden inside a magazine? Was this something she was writing about?"

Her mother shook her head. "No, it can't be. The last thing she was working on was about garbage disposal sites. She had never reported on young women's deaths, but I know it was her ambition to write more serious articles, more local, human-interest stories. After her work overseas, she wanted to do more serious reporting in the local area. But these? I don't know why she had them or why she didn't mention these to me."

"I'd say she wanted to bring them to the attention of her editor so she could be the first to investigate these and do them as part of her work."

June sighed. "These articles describe what I was feeling with the parents' press appeal. It's as if they're talking about us. Do you think she knew something about these deaths? Was she doing research?"

"I don't know, June. But I can take these to the police. Do you mind?"

June's glazed look made Gabriella worry. What had she done? She didn't mean to upset June, but she couldn't take these articles without her knowing. As hard as it was to bring all this stuff up about Erica, she needed answers and June knew more than she was letting on. Focusing on the big picture about getting justice for Erica was primary. "Yes, of course. I would like to know why she had them. But before I forget, I need a favour, dear." Her eyes misted. "I could never bring myself to pick up Erica's belongings at her workplace when she first died. Would you go for me if I ring them and give my consent for you to pick up her things?"

Gabriella nodded. "Of course, but I thought the police would have collected her things as part of the investigation."

June nodded. "They did visit her workplace recently, but the few things in storage were personal and they didn't believe those had any relevance to the case."

Gabriella nodded. "Right. Well, I'm sure the local police here are aware of these unsolved cases." Downing her hot drink, she brought up her next topic of conversation. "Was there something else you wanted to talk to me about?"

June got up and rubbed her hands as if fighting the cold. She paced the kitchen floor and bowed her head. Her bottom lip trembled. She swallowed, looked briefly through the kitchen window, then sat back down. "I'm sorry. I need to work up to this, as I have struggled with it for so long. Give me a minute."

June pushed her body forward, hands clasped tightly together. "I know now that we may have given Erica more attention than Nigel, but there was a reason for that. We could never find the courage to tell her the truth." Her eye twitched. "Erica was adopted, so she wasn't Nigel's biological sister."

Gabriella flinched and placed a quaking hand across her chest. That she hadn't expected.

Chapter Forty-Eight

NEW LEADS

Jesse touched the back of his head, which still ached slightly from his attack as he stepped onto the uneven concrete path towards the police station. He slowed down his steps, wondering what more the police wanted to know about his attack. All he knew was that he hadn't seen his attacker as he was hit from behind, but the police might have had new updates.

Walking inside, he approached the counter, nodded to the elderly policeman manning the office, and asked for Marco and Angelo. Jesse had taken a week off work to recuperate from his injury but didn't expect to be spending part of it talking to the detectives again. But if they had leads, it would be worth his time.

As he sat in the waiting area, an image of Gabriella flashed through his mind. He hadn't spoken to her since seeing her at the hospital but knew her place was monitored by the police. He missed her like crazy. The only issue was that she had betrayed him and he couldn't forgive her for that. She knew about the affair and kept it to herself, and he hated people who kept secrets. Erica had had a lot of them, and he would no longer put up with them from another woman he cared for. Not that he planned to do anything about that, especially after realising that she kept secrets too. No, he was better off single.

Angelo interrupted his thoughts. "Jesse. Come on through." He followed Angelo down the corridor, passing by cubicles and other policemen talking on the phone or face to face with people. His head exploded at the loud, angry voices of people making complaints or shouting with their hands punching the air.

Jesse made his way inside the interview room with Marco looking down at a file in his hand. In his other hand, he held a photocopied note. What was that? "As much as I like seeing you guys socially, I really don't want to be in this place unless you have leads. So why am I here? I told you everything I remember about the attack. I don't know what more I can say."

Angelo sat across from him, beside Marco, with a worried look in his eyes. He turned to Marco briefly. "We have news and thought we'd share it with you. Gabriella called and explained how she found something noteworthy. She'll be here any minute now. I'll be back." Jesse's chest tightened at the thought of Gabriella's presence.

Marco cleared his throat and pulled out the note. "I'd like you to read this note we found at the scene. Jesse picked up the note, saying, "*Gabriella is mine. Always has been.*"

Jesse collapsed in his chair, his heart beating a mile a minute. He threaded his hand through his chair and calmed his breathing. "Are you serious? Her stalker attacked me?"

Marco nodded. "It appears that way." He took a breath. "I want you to close your eyes for a minute and see if you can remember anything else. Any small detail. Even a smell or the sounds of the footsteps can reveal a lot. Go back to the last time you were working on the car. Retrace your steps."

Jesse closed his eyes and flashed back to the day. He had fought with Derek when not long after that, he was attacked. "The footsteps were light, and I...I smelled something like lavender and maybe oranges or lemons? A kind of citrus smell." He took long, calming breaths. "Not long before my attack, I was having an argument with Derek. But I'm sure it wasn't him. We've been friends since we were kids."

"You can open your eyes now." Marco leaned forwards. "Derek claims to have been in his car at the time of the attack, and he's right. We were able to track his car through automatic number plate recognition and he was driving his car at the time. He mentioned turning back to talk to you again, wanting to apologise. We know he had an affair with Erica. I am sorry about that, but we are sure he didn't hurt her nor you."

Jesse breathed a sigh of relief. "I already knew that." The door opened and both Angelo and Gabriella entered, her eyes gazing into his. Her tight, white jeans hugged her body to show her curves, and her light and pink woollen jumper pressed tight against her chest. Why did she always instil a physical reaction in him? She sat next to him while Angelo took a seat opposite them.

She leaned forward and he smelled her floral-scented shampoo. "I have these articles that Erica kept in her bedroom. I believe she might have been researching these stories."

Marco put out his hand and retrieved them from her. "We interviewed her colleagues, and apparently, she didn't investigate deaths or suicides." He faced Jesse. "Did Erica ever talk to you about these cases?"

Jesse shifted then sighed. "No, she never did. I know she wanted to write more serious articles and had ambitions, but Erica made it a habit to keep things to herself. I need to find out what else she was hiding from me."

Angelo intervened. "Please leave the investigating to us. The killer might not be working alone." He turned to Gabriella. "We'll need to keep your house tracked and make sure both of you don't do anything to compromise the investigation. And Jesse, that note..."

Gabriella winced. "What note?"

Angelo showed her the note and she slouched in her seat. "This was found at the scene. So I want you to think back to anyone who might be doing this. Any ex-boyfriends, acquaintances, people you might've bumped into in the street. Anyone who you can think of who might believe you're their fantasy girlfriend?"

"I have racked my brains, Angelo. But no, my last boyfriend is in prison and the other ones would never do this. They might have been jerks but they would never do this."

Jesse wondered about her last boyfriend. Why was he in prison and what had he done to her? His protective instinct kicked in and he wanted nothing more than to keep her safe. "Have you questioned her ex-boyfriend? What if he sent someone after her?"

Gabriella glared in his direction. "How dare you? You know nothing about him, so get your facts straight before you go accusing him. He would never do this. In spite of what he did, I know he loved me." Jesse looked away and squirmed in his chair.

Marco put up his hand. "Let's stay calm." He stared at both of them. "We have questioned Nick and he was surprised about Gabriella having a stalker. He claims to still love you. We don't think he's connected with this in any way. There is a connection that starts with Erica. And as for your attack, we believe there were two people in your garage. The stalker is working with someone else. Octavia believes that one is submissive or less dominant than the partner. Now you mentioned hearing the word 'No' before you blacked out. Is it possible that someone tried to stop the other one from bashing your head in?"

Jesse flinched. "Of course. That has to be it. What if the stalker's got a bit more of a conscience than the dominant one? What if the dominant one's the killer and the submissive one is Gabriella's stalker."

Gabriella replied. "You might be right, Jesse."

Marco and Angelo looked at one another, remaining silent. They changed the subject when Jesse and Gabriella answered a few more questions before walking out of the police station in awkward silence. He ambled towards his car while Gabriella did the same, but he turned back and stopped her. "Can we talk? Your place is the closest."

She nodded. "Fine. I'll meet you at home."

Chapter Forty-Nine

HEATED MOMENT

G abriella sat on the couch with her arms crossed while Jesse stared into his lap with a worried frown. His aftershave drowned her senses and she yearned to have him hold her. All this new information was making her sick, and Jesse made her feel safe. She was falling in love with him. The way his hand clenched loosely over his lap, the way his eyes softened whenever she opened up to him, and the way the shape of his full lips tantalised her with arousal. Her chest warmed at how he had been protective of her all these months, and how in spite of the secret she had kept from him, he was still trying to protect her. How could she tell him how she felt when they would never work? When she no longer believed in relationships? Not to mention needing to keep Jesse safe from her stalker. She would tell him to stay away after this final meeting.

He broke her out of her thoughts. "How did you get those articles?"

Gabriella explained her meeting with June and the news that came with it. He jolted in his seat. "I'm sorry. If it's any consolation, Erica didn't know she was adopted. But it gives Nigel motive to hurt her, particularly out of jealousy and because he got less attention than her from his parents."

"But we don't know if Nigel's your stalker. Why would he want to hurt you? If anything, he'd most likely go after Joy who he hates with a vengeance."

Gabriella shrugged. "She was in that car accident, and if we have two people working together, maybe the dominant one tried to hurt her. What if Nigel's the angry one and my stalker's the nice one. "I don't know, but Nigel looks good to me. And I figure the new leads the police have might be linked to Nigel. I get the feeling he has some other secret, other than the adoption. He's hiding something else."

Jesse frowned. "I wonder if it's worth me going to Erica's work. Someone at Erica's work might know something. She might've confided in her friend, the receptionist. It's worth a try."

Gabriella shot him a dirty look. "No, stay away from this. Don't you see that the stalker can escalate if you're by my side? I can go to her work and ask questions."

He scoffed. "Don't pretend to give a damn about me after what you pulled." His eyes averted, he shifted in his seat.

Gabriella drew back. "What are you talking about?"

He turned his head to the side. "You kept the secret about Derek and Erica's affair. How could you betray me like that? Why didn't you tell me?"

Gabriella's thigh brushed against Jesse, and she ignored the heat in her loins. "I'm sorry, but Derek told me in confidence, and it wasn't my place to say anything."

"Your place? I thought we were friends, Gabriella. I trusted you, or at least I thought I did, and you go and do this to me."

"What's really going on here, Jesse? This is more than just me not telling you the truth. Let's look at the real issue here."

Jesse got up from the couch, peeked through the blinds, then paced the rug. "Don't go psychoanalysing me. The fact is, you lied, and I don't trust you anymore."

Gabriella joined him on the carpet with her hands on her hips. "You don't trust me? I'm not the one who accuses their ex-boyfriend of being their stalker without having all the facts. That was out of line."

Jesse moved his body towards her, his face within inches of hers. Any closer and they'd be meeting with their mouths. "Hardly on par with you knowing about Derek's lies. At least I'm looking to help you, and all you can do is get angry about such a trivial thing. All women are damn crazy, and I have given up trying to understand you all."

Gabriella glared. "Do not generalise and put me in that basket. I am an open book, so don't go thinking I'm just like Erica. I'm not. We are two different personalities, so don't go judging me without really knowing me fully." She hated him and wanted him at the same time. His hand accidentally touched hers.

Jesse pressed his lips together. "I am so angry with you right now. I cannot breathe. I want to trust you. So much." His lips parted, and he lifted his chin upwards as his eyes glanced from her head down to her toes.

Gabriella was strongly aware of her own heartbeat and her body flooded with warmth. Her fingers tingled with the need to touch him as Jesse shifted closer towards her. Was he going to kiss her? She shivered, whispering, "You can trust me." As if that clinched it, Jesse brought his body close to hers, his lips crashing against hers. His tongue penetrated her mouth as he wrapped his arms around her and caressed her back, the kiss deepening as Gabriella moaned in arousal. What was she doing? This could get Jesse killed and she had to keep him at a distance. She wasn't looking for a relationship, not with all of this going on. Quickly, she pulled away and averted her eyes. "I think you should go." Gabriella turned away from him and stared in the other direction. "Please."

His voice lingered in the background. "I'm sorry if I crossed the line." A few seconds later, the front door slammed. She fell onto the couch and bowed her face into her hands, hating her emotions right now. What had she just done?

Chapter Fifty

WORKPLACE VISIT

Gabriella walked up the steps, facing the huge rectangular glass building of the newspaper where Erica had worked. She held on to the steel rails and pushed herself through the revolving doors. Surrounding her inside were women wearing corporate dress suits and men sporting collared-up shirts or suits with matching smart, casual pants. In the foyer, a middle-aged woman with vibrant red hair and a slim physique sipped a hot drink from a disposable cup as she sat on a yellow swivel chair at a white round table. It was that female reporter, Janey, who had shown up when Gabriella's house was broken in to. Looking up, the woman nodded in her direction, and Gabriella smiled back. She walked along glossy grey floor tiles and spotted a range of pastel-coloured couches in pink, grey, and yellow.

She had had trouble sleeping these past couple of nights since seeing Jesse at her place. The kiss penetrated her mind like a disturbing flashback. It warmed her heart, but then she realised that he'd only kissed her with Erica on his mind. He had most likely kissed her as a way of dealing with Erica's affair. What if he was only hurting and needed a distraction out of his pain? She didn't want to be his distraction, but she knew he had projected his deep feelings towards Erica onto her. They had been together for five years, and she had been a woman that nobody truly knew, with all her secrets. She had never spoken about her research into these girls and had hidden her affair with Derek. Why couldn't Erica open up to Gabriella or Joy? She guessed it was a shame at what she'd done with Derek. At least he was no longer a suspect in her murder, but something linked all these women together. Perhaps she'd get answers today. She had taken the day off and would hopefully get answers.

Approaching the counter, she explained her visit to the blonde receptionist who looked at her with suspicion. She must have been replacing Erica's friend today. "Take a seat. The senior editor, Riley Minthy, will be with you shortly."

"Thank you." She made her way over to the yellow couch and crossed her legs. Janey watched her with curiosity then disappeared to the elevators.

As she rubbed her hands, with her mind on Erica, the voice of a woman startled her. "Oh, sorry. I'm Gabriella."

"Hello, I'm Riley Minthy, the senior editor. Follow me." The woman appeared to be in her sixties with grey hair tied up in a bun, wearing a grey dress suit. She attempted to keep up with Riley's large strides towards the elevator until she waited for her to step inside and push a button. "Erica's mother explained how she wanted you to pick up her personal things. But I must say, it's been a long time, so we had them in storage. The police didn't want them." She glanced at her long fingernails. "But for today, I've put her belongings on her desk."

"Thank you." As no-one else was in the building, Gabriella fished for answers. "Erica loved working here with the interesting stories she was working on."

"If you count stories about council policies and animal protesters as interesting, then yes." The woman looked straight ahead without eye contact; her posture rigid.

"Erica never spoke to you about wanting to work on other stories of interest, such as crimes, homicides, that sort of thing?"

Riley looked at her strangely. "Of course. Erica was highly ambitious but she was also distracted with personal issues, and I couldn't trust her to write the facts on those. I encouraged her to get help, but she claimed to be fully focused."

Gabriella watched her curiously. "What personal issues are you talking about?"

She sighed markedly. "Getting ready for marriage, and whatever else distracted her. I don't know what it was. She never mentioned specifics, but she was making mistakes and doing sloppy work not long before her death."

Gabriella nodded. "Were you close with Erica?"

The woman curled her brow. "We had an amicable working relationship."

"Was she close with anyone else here, apart from the receptionist?"

The woman looked away. "What is with all these questions? I thought you were Erica's friend. She would have told you all this, surely?"

The ding of the elevator stopped and Riley pushed on ahead. She fixed her gaze on Gabriella as she kept up the pace towards a set of stairs, the sun's glare through colossal, bare windows reflecting in the interior of the building. "She mainly kept to herself, but she was ambitious and quite the talented reporter. If only she had sorted out her personal challenges, which led to mistakes in the end." Riley put up a hand. "And no, as I said before, she never confided in me about those challenges."

Climbing the stairs, Gabriella held on to the steel beams, with each landing providing a view of the city through the large windows. She spotted several offices as they walked up a few flights. They ended up in a room featuring open-planned offices with a range of cubicles and staff members working on their computers, flicking through papers, or handling phones. A few of them looked at her with curiosity, and

Janey was sitting a few metres away, intermittently watching her. Opposite Gabriella's desk, a young man with glasses peeked over his shoulder and smiled. It was the other reporter she'd met when her bed was filled with roses. It was Arthur. Riley stopped at a cubicle that consisted of an ergonomic chair, a computer monitor, a set of three-layered in-trays devoid of documents, with a low set of white cupboards opposite. Flung over the chair was a brown dress jacket.

Riley broke into her thoughts. "Sorry. I'm not sure whose jacket that is. A few casual staff have used her desk so one of them must have left their jacket behind. We'll have to contact them. With funding cuts, we haven't had anyone replace her permanently." She picked up a box and handed it to her. "These are all her things. I trust you don't need anything else?"

Gabriella eyed the reporter who appeared to be approachable. If he'd sat close to Erica, he might know things about her, particularly if she was anxious about anything. "Is it okay if I give her desk another check?"

"Of course. But please be quick about it as we have a business to run." Before Gabriella could reply, she scurried off into the distance.

Arthur walked over to her. He drew a hand through his ginger hair then played with his moustache. His suit was at least one size bigger than his actual body. He had a nice smile. "Hi, Gabriella. About that story. We never ended up writing it as my boss had another pressing story that overrode it. But I did read the story from another reporter who wrote about it. Did they ever catch the guy?"

She shook her head. "No." Taking a breath, she said, "I'm here, just collecting Erica's things. I shouldn't be too long."

Arthur nodded. "She was very suited to her role here, and it is a crying shame she is no longer with us. You must miss her."

"I do. She was one of a kind. Did you know her well?"

Arthur touched the rim of his glasses, shifting them underneath his forehead. He looked over his shoulder to peer at his fellow workers, but they all appeared to be busy typing away or chatting on the phone. He leaned forward, whispering. "I did know her well. Sometimes we worked together on projects, but she was ambitious and wanted to do more scandalous type stories. I do miss her laugh, particularly."

"She was so young. Did you know whether she talked to you about other stories she wanted to work on, given her ambitions? Did she confide in you about anything?" Janey stared again in her direction then left her desk and disappeared.

Arthur looked upwards, pondering. "Hmm. Not really, no. She wanted to write stories about deeper world issues but never got the chance. I got the feeling she was having issues with her boyfriend, and that distracted her. But she had talent, for sure."

That was exactly what Riley mentioned. Distractions. "Did she have any enemies here or someone she didn't get along with?"

Arthur shook his head and toyed with his tie. "Not that I know of. She was loved by everyone and had no qualms at all. But..."

Her eyes lit up. "But what?"

"I remember her brother, Nigel, coming here once and they argued about something. It was quite heated. I overheard him say she would regret it, but I have no idea that was about." He exhaled. "Do you think he would hurt her?"

Gabriella shrugged, not knowing what to make of that. "I had better go. Thanks for your time."

"Any time, Gabriella." He ambled back to his desk and clicked keys on his computer, appearing to be the only friendly person in the building. Was that why Erica hadn't been close to anyone except the receptionist? Because they were generally cold people, apart from Arthur? Both Riley and the temporary receptionist appeared to be standoffish and aloof, but she shouldn't judge as she didn't really know them.

Gabriella retrieved the box of items. She walked back down the stairs with a view of the other offices when she saw Janey having a heated discussion with Riley whose hands leapt into the air as if she was upset about something. Janey inched close to Riley and shook her head then stormed out of the room.

Walking to the underground car park after a ten-minute walk, Gabriella finally entered her car, placed the box on the passenger seat, and rifled briefly through it.

Digging deep into the box, a set of photos popped up. One of them had Erica standing with Riley, a few other staff members she didn't recognise, and Arthur, and Janey. The red-headed reporter looked more attractive with her wide grin. Who were these people truly, and why were Riley and Janey arguing? From what Arthur just mentioned, was Nigel guilty of hurting his own sister?

PANIC

Gabriella and her friends ambled along the Southbank promenade with a view of the river, city's buildings and skyline on Friday evening. The sun shone and the calming wind made her forget her troubles as she linked arms with Joy and Liz on either side. Octavia, Claudia, Bella, Jamie, and Camilla lagged behind as they chattered amongst themselves.

She wasn't in the mood to socialise, but Joy convinced her that she needed respite from all her issues and that, until her stalker was caught, she would fare better interacting with friends. Turning to Joy, she asked, "So how's Jesse doing?"

Joy kept up her walking pace as Liz turned in her direction. "He's still processing what happened with Erica and Derek. But he's gone back to work and has fully recovered." She frowned. "What is going on between you two?"

Gabriella blushed. "Nothing."

Liz squeezed her arm. "Oh, come on, girl. We all know you have a connection with Jesse. Is something going on between you two?"

The women behind them stopped as if listening in on their conversation. "Oh, leave her be, ladies," said Claudia. "It is her business."

Claudia was not one to be tactful with her thoughts, but Gabriella appreciated her support. She turned and smiled at her new friend. Claudia threaded her hands through her strawberry-blonde hair while Octavia watched Gabriella with a worried expression.

Joy prodded a few of them over to one of the restaurants. "They're advertising cocktail hour over there. Let's go, ladies."

They'd enjoyed a fine meal at BearBrass and decided to settle on drinks and snacks before they went home. They entered one of the restaurants to enjoy a cocktail hour, and the waiter ushered them over to a large table outside with a view of passersby strolling. He returned five minutes later, and Gabriella browsed through the drinks menu. "I'll have the Margarita, thanks."

Jamie leaned forward in her seat, her posture straight. "I will order the espresso martini. Thank you." One by one, all of them ordered their drinks with a round of cheese, crackers and dips. The waiter walked off with a curt nod.

Jazz music played in the background. Gabriella rested against the steel-backed chair, watching Bella scroll through her phone, Liz whispering to Joy, Octavia and Claudia ogling a few young men who had walked inside, and Camilla talking to her brother, Matthew, on the phone.

"Penny for your thoughts, Gabriella," said Bella.

"I'm just enjoying my amazing friends, that's all. I needed this." She touched her neck and choked up, thankful that she was able to get respite. Her neck and back ached from lack of sleep, and her throat dried up thinking about how she would deal with Jesse and her stalker.

Camilla leaned forward. She was well-groomed with her black, glossy hair and blonde highlights. Her blue-green eyes showed a hint of sadness, with arms crossed over her body and her eyes darting as if she was looking for someone. Something had spooked her. "Thanks again, guys, for making me a part of your group." She uncrossed her arms.

Jamie said, "We love having you with us, Camilla. Is everything alright? You look somewhat rattled." She frowned but didn't respond. "I am sorry. I didn't mean to pry."

She shook her head. "No, it's fine, Jamie."

Liz sat opposite her, watching as the waiter brought over their drinks and left. She sipped her vodka cocktail then placed it on the table. "You can tell us anything, girl. We have your back, whatever it is. Matthew mentioned that something did happen, but he thought it best that it came from you. But don't feel you need to say anything. No pressure, girl."

Camilla bowed her head and gave Liz a reassuring smile. "I don't want to be a bother. It's fine. I can deal with it. My counsellor's been a great help, but things can trigger me."

"Maybe we can help," said Octavia.

Jamie intervened. "We can talk another time, Camilla, if you're not comfortable sharing it. There is no judgement from anyone here."

Bella nodded. "I agree. You can open up whenever you're ready to." She downed her espresso martini and gave Camilla a warm look.

Camilla's face flushed and she started to open her mouth then closed it. She wondered what Camilla was worried about. "I am enjoying this cocktail," she said as a way of possibly easing into the subject of concern. She eventually blurted it out. "I got a call recently from a detective in Queensland, asking me questions. When I lived there, a friend of mine died a few years back. It was ruled as a suicide and...I wondered if it was more of an accident." She faced Gabriella. "Jill drowned in the bathtub and seemed to have been heavily medicated. So she might have died of an overdose. The police are trying to decide whether it was an accidental death or something suspicious, given these current deaths. It's just something I never got over. We were close back in Queensland, but then we lost touch. She was still drug-affected and refused to stop. I tried to help her back then, but she wasn't open to it."

"It could have been an accident if she was still taking drugs," said Claudia.

"I don't know." She frowned. "It sounds suspicious as she died in the same way as your friend, Erica, and those other two girls."

Octavia gave Claudia a strange look. "What do you think happened?"

Camilla shrugged. "I honestly don't know. It could go either way, as she was still taking drugs and couldn't control it. But she kept her distance a couple of months before her death, and I hadn't been able to reach her. She kind of disappeared."

Joy knit her brows. "Did the police find anything at all suspicious?"

Camilla shook her head. "I doubt it. She kept moving around, and if she had a stalker then, knowing Jill, she would have thought nothing of it. She was too out of it most of the time, and I wasn't in the best shape either."

Liz touched her hand. "Listen, girl. We all make our choices, and Jill made hers. You were not responsible for what happened to her." Camilla smiled back.

"At least now they're looking into it. This killer must be transient to avoid detection," said Bella.

Gabriella wondered how many poor girls had to die before they caught the killer. In her gut, she knew without a doubt now that her stalker was also a killer. And that he was most likely working with someone else. What if she knew who it was? Nigel, possibly. She smoothed down her clothing and bit her bottom lip. Her knees and legs remained tightly together. She clutched at her chest, and her breathing accelerated. Her palms felt sweaty, and her heart palpitated as she abruptly rose from the table without looking at anyone, and ran to the other side with a view of the water. She stared out over the Yarra River and grounded herself. Towering trees, the soft breeze against her cheek, the sounds of laughter from a group of people passing by, and the city's skyline soothed her. No, she was safe right now. He would not ruin her night. It was her time with her friends.

"Gabriella." She turned around and Joy hugged her from behind. "Are you okay?"

Gabriella nodded. "I'll be fine. Don't worry."

Joy pulled away from her and stood by her side. She prodded her over to a bench on the promenade. "The police will catch your stalker. He might not even be a killer, but you have to keep yourself safe. Let Jesse be there for you." She smiled. "We're here for you too, Gabi. You know that, right?"

Her heart warmed. "I know, and thanks. But what if my stalker is the killer? What if he's the same person?"

Joy twisted her body around so she could face her head-on. "Now, you listen to me, girl. We've got your back, and nothing will go wrong. The police have leads so do not worry. We will not leave you alone until this prick is caught. You hear me?"

Gabriella wrapped her arms around her. "I hear you, and thanks, Joy." She had an afterthought. "Oh, and please apologise to Jesse again."

She put up her hand. "Oh, he'll get over it. Just give him a bit more time to stew, but he's only upset with the situation, not with you." She smiled. "Are you ready to go back in? If not, we'll leave and I'll come home with you." Before turning back, Joy asked, "Jesse's been distracted recently. Did something happen between you two?"

Gabriella swallowed, not wanting to have secrets from Joy. How would she react to what had happened between them? She couldn't lie. "We kissed and then I threw him out."

Joy's eyes widened. "Right. And why did you throw him out?"

She took a breath and rested back against the seat. "He kissed me after knowing that Erica had an affair, and his mind was on her."

Joy nodded with understanding. "Do you think he was projecting?" Gabriella nodded. "Let me tell you something, Gabi. Jesse would not kiss just anyone, and he has not had any interest in anyone else. I can see how much he cares about you."

"But he loved Erica. And I don't know if you approve of this thing between us."

Joy frowned. "And? So what? He loved more of the idea of her, and she had a lot of issues that even we couldn't fix. If she'd been open with us, we could have helped her, but she made her choices. And in the end, I think Jesse had started feeling differently about her. He would never admit it, but I believe he fell out of love with her when he realised she wasn't this idealised version of what he made her out to be." They remained silent for a minute. "And for the record, I do approve. You and Jesse are more compatible than he ever was with Erica. I loved that girl, but they had grown apart and only stayed together out of obligation."

Gabriella pushed back tears, comforted by Joy's approval if anything should happen between her and Jesse. "Let's go back. I'll be fine." As Gabriella followed Joy back to the bar, her chest squeezed tight at the thought that Jesse might truly care for her. But how could she be having erotic thoughts about him when things would likely escalate with her stalker?

Chapter Fifty-Two

AN APOLOGY

Jesse sat opposite Gabriella inside the Spotswood restaurant for Sunday lunch, with the permeating smells of cinnamon, spices, and coffee beans. Dribs and drabs of customers walked inside the place, which featured a spacious and cosy ambience with round tables and steel-back chairs. Vases of artificial flowers rested in the middle of each table, and the crowd was buzzing with noise, muffled voices, and laughter.

He rested back against the chair and dug into a slice of fish. Gabriella's lips wrapped around a chicken thigh, the juices dripping down her chin. He was curious to know what it would be like to lick the liquid over her lips and to penetrate his tongue inside her mouth again. He'd had a taste of her full, luscious lips and he craved for more. Was he falling in love with her?

After the way they fought last time, he didn't know if he could learn to trust again, but he so desperately wanted to trust Gabriella. It showed her loyalty to Derek to keep the truth to herself. It was Derek's responsibility to disclose the truth.

He squared his shoulders and wiped his mouth with a napkin. He sipped his beer. "I asked you here to apologise for the way I treated you the other day. I'm sorry."

Gabriella pursed her lips, her eyebrows drawn inward. Her smooth hands clasped together and she leaned in. "It's fine. I know it must've been a shock to hear about Erica, but I didn't want to come between you and Derek. I was keeping his confidence. He trusted me with his secret, and I assumed he would have told you eventually."

He nodded. "I took it out on you, Gabriella, projecting all my anger on you when it should have been placed on Erica and Derek. They're the ones who betrayed me, not you. I needed time to process it all, and I understand you were only being a good person. Loyal to Derek. Not that he deserved it."

Her eyes darkened. "Have you spoken to him?"

Jesse fought back his tight chest, his gasping breath. "I don't know if we'll ever get past this. He's called me a few times, but I haven't answered. He's even texted, but I've ignored him. I can't talk to him right now." He sighed. "My friends have tried to help, but I don't know if I'll ever be able to forgive him. The trust is gone."

Gabriella forked a baked carrot and softly chewed. She downed a few sips of sparkling wine and left a lipstick mark on the glass. Her strongly-scented perfume filled the air, and he couldn't take his eyes off her own fixed gaze, as if she wanted to tell him a secret but was holding back. "You'll need to have a heart-to-heart with him eventually, Jesse. Otherwise, you'll never get closure. Either way, you'll need to talk."

"I know." He finished off his beer and gestured to the smiling waiter, who approached. "Can I have another one, please?" The waiter nodded then returned a few minutes later with another beer. "Joy mentioned that you guys went to Southgate Friday night, and that you panicked about something. She didn't give me the full details, but I got the feeling it has something to do with your stalker. What happened?"

"Camilla knew one of the girls who was killed in Queensland. They used to be friends, and she died in similar ways to these current deaths."

Jesse gasped, his hands shaking underneath the table. He wanted to stay in control and give her his unwavering support. He had to be strong for her. "Jesus! This is bizarre. We're all somehow associated with all these women getting killed. What is the connection?"

Gabriella shrugged. "I don't know, but Camilla's friend was a drug addict, so it might have been an accidental death. Who knows?" She peered into the distance. "We know that Erica was acting strangely in the last few months. Nora was on drugs intentionally and so was this latest girl, Tilly. So, could drugs be the connection? What if he's a counsellor or has had contact with these girls?"

"It's possible. But we know that Erica was investigating those similar murders interstate, so the killer must have wanted to stop her from investigating further. Have you heard anything more from the police?"

"No, nothing. It is so frustrating." She averted her eyes for a moment. "I shouldn't be seen with you, Jesse. You got hurt because of me, and I can't have that on my conscience."

"I was careful coming here. No-one was following me. Besides, as long as you're not on your own, you should be safe. I told Joy that tonight I'd be your babysitter. She's told all the others too."

"No, I can't let you risk your life. You need to stay away from me. Don't you remember you were hurt? And if we're dealing with two people, that's even worse."

He shook his head. "We cannot let this creep control our lives. I couldn't help Erica, but I can help you now. She would want me to protect you at all costs. Let's honour her memory and do the right thing." He wanted to bring up the kiss but it wasn't the right time. It would probably never be the right time.

Moments later, Jesse got up and paid the dinner bill. He touched the small of her back as they opened the door to be met with a mild breeze and glare from the sun's rays. It was early afternoon, so they took a short walk to the Albert Park Lake and strolled along the walking tracks in silence, the tropical trees lining one side of the track as men jogged past them. A woman walked her dog, and a young teenager stretched close to the rippling lake. Views of the city skyline were picturesque, and overhanging trees stood over the lake, creating reflections in the water.

Jesse turned to Gabriella who clutched her bag, looking over her shoulder. "Relax. No-one's here." He had to distract her. "How is work?"

"It's great. Since the incident, I've had a lot of support, and I got a huge apology from the board members about Nora's assumed suicide. The staff make sure that I'm never in the office alone, and I no longer stay back."

"That's good. And are you getting any interesting cases?"

Gabriella nodded. "Sure, but none I can talk to you about. I must say that my university degree's keeping me busy. I can do some units online, but the number of assignments I need to do before I get into my work placement is mind-boggling. I don't even have time to sleep."

Jesse had an image of sleeping alongside Gabriella, his lips trailing down her entire body. He had to stop having these erotic thoughts. "But you'll be a fully qualified social worker. It is such an achievement to be working full-time and studying. You have your own place, and you made your own life after the way your father treated you."

"Thanks, Jesse. What he did to me was nothing compared to what your family had to go through with your sister. Besides, my mum bore most of the violence, but it was still hard to be a witness to it. He ruined my life back then but he won't ruin it now." She stared at a young woman pushing a stroller as they kept up their pace around the lake. "My mum has finally found happiness with my stepfather, and he's like my real father. I am grateful to have him in my life. He helped me with a deposit for my house and he keeps helping me financially with my studies. He's a godsend. He gets me, and he understands our background because he was a witness to the same kind of violence growing up."

Jesse yearned to draw her into his arms as she expressed a part of her life that made her vulnerable. He wanted to protect her and keep her safe. He'd make sure that nothing happened to her, even if it was over his dead body.

Jesse stopped her in her tracks, turned her body around and pulled her into his arms. "I am sorry you had to face that." Stroking the small of her back, he breathed in her fresh apple shampoo and lavender perfume. Gabriella hugged him back and buried her face in his shoulder. He could feel her rapid heartbeat through their clothing and skin. He could never get enough of her touch. All he wanted to do was kiss her again, but she had made it clear she wasn't interested. He wanted to be closer to her, and it was killing him that he couldn't. He hadn't felt this way about anyone, not even Erica. He wasn't ready for it, either. Jesse broke their hug and kept a few feet between them as they finished their walk. He couldn't trust himself around Gabriella.

Chapter Fifty-Three

SHOCKING PHOTOS

Later that day, Jesse parked by the kerb in front of Gabriella's house. They had recently stopped police surveillance as there had been no further incidences. He wondered if things would get worse before they got better.

Gabriella's friends had been staying with her overnight, and tonight was his turn. If the stalker was watching him, he would be ready for him this time. He would never let anything happen to Gabriella, and he sure as hell wouldn't let the bastard keep him away.

Gabriella parked in her driveway and stepped out of her car. He was close behind, scanning the area for anyone lurking or out of place. She stepped to the front door and bent down. An A4 size envelope lay in front. Picking it up, she unlocked the door, and he followed her inside before scanning the outdoor surrounds. No-one appeared to be watching them.

His heart did a flip as he locked the door behind them. "Wait here. I'll check on Angela too." He searched the rooms, laundry, kitchen, bathroom, and backyard, and came up empty. No-one was around. Then he peered through the window, but not a soul was in sight. Entering the rumpus room, he patted the kitten who was drinking water from the bowl, then made a beeline for Jesse. He patted Angela again before she scurried over to her bed to play with her rubber toy bone.

Jesse returned to the living room. "All clear, and Angela's fine."

Gabriella nodded. Her hands shook as she placed the envelope on the kitchen table. "We need gloves just in case it's from him. I'll get some from the laundry." She returned a couple of minutes later and handed them to him. "Would you mind?"

He shook his head. "Of course not." With trepidation, he put on the thin gloves and ripped through the envelope. Out popped a clear, large photo of two people kissing. Who was that? Picking up the photo, he gasped and dropped one of the photos to the floor. Turning to Gabriella, she paled, and drew back as if being burnt.

"Oh, my God! Jesse. I am so sorry. This has to be photo-shopped. It can't be real. Surely whoever took these must have fabricated them? It can't be what it looks like."

Jesse turned away, realising that he had never known Erica at all. None of them had. She had had this whole private side to her, and hadn't shared anything with them. A photo underneath revealed Erica slapping him across the face. The second photo showed his face within inches of her own, as if they were about to kiss, but Erica looked confused. The last photo had them kissing. "These look real to me. Erica kissing Nigel." Bile in his throat and abdominal pain made him wince. "Erica never knew she was adopted so how could she kiss her own brother, for God's sake? This is sick. So sick." He wanted to get his hands on Nigel and rip his damn throat out. The fire in his chest was hard to contain as he gripped the edge of the table.

"Jesse. This looks like Nigel kissing her, and not the other way around." She cleared her throat. "This other photo shows her slapping him, so she would have stopped it."

He forced himself to look up at her. "Nothing could excuse this, Gabriella. Nothing."

She pressed her lips together, and her eyebrows drew together at the same time. "He obviously liked her but she didn't like him back. It shows in this photo."

Jesse sat on the chair with his shoulders hunched. "So many secrets. So many things we didn't know about that family. And I was planning to marry her. What a mistake that would have been." He shook his head. "Not only did she hide this from me, but she also had an affair with Derek. She had a whole different side to her, and I never really knew her at all. Joy was right. I didn't truly love the real Erica, only an idealised version of her. I had this illusion about her, and I realise now that I could never love someone like this. Someone who lies and cheats, and has no real heart. How could she keep these things from me? What else was she hiding?" A soft touch on his shoulder brought him out of his thoughts. He looked up at Gabriella, who remained silent with a soft expression. "This implicates Nigel in her death."

Gabriella joined him on the chair, sitting beside him. "How so?"

He scoffed. "The bastard must've been in love with her, and when she slapped him, she rejected him. That's why he hated her so much. He felt abandoned and unloved. They were always fighting. I had never seen any kind words between them."

"Now you're assuming things. I know that Nigel was jealous of her getting most of the attention, but it makes sense now. She was adopted and probably had no real family, so they felt sorry for her. But even if he didn't like the competition, that doesn't make him a killer. We need more evidence than this."

He got up from the chair. "We need to take these to the police, Gabriella."

She shook her head. "I don't think we should just yet. Let's talk to Nigel and explain these photos, and see whether he has an explanation."

Jesse sighed, drawing a hand through his hair. "Are you mad? What if the bastard's your stalker and Erica's killer, and we set him off like that? No, unless we know for sure, we'd be taking a risk. I'm taking these to the police. For all our safety."

Gabriella swallowed. "These photos had to have been sent by either the killer or my stalker. It wouldn't have been Nigel unless he wants to show himself. It doesn't make sense."

He shrugged. "Whoever sent them can give the police further clues. If Nigel's innocent, then we've at least ruled him out. It has to be this way."

"Fine, but first thing in the morning. I'm too tired to go now."

Jesse nodded. "Good. I'm glad you're seeing sense."

Later that night, after they watched a bit of TV, Gabriella rose. "I'll make us some dinner. Are you happy with steak, sweet potato, and salad?"

Jesse nodded. "Sure. I'll help." He followed her to the kitchen. Gabriella took out iceberg lettuce, tomatoes, cucumber, and two pieces of steak. She set them aside on the kitchen counter. "I'll wash the lettuce and make the salad."

"Thanks, Jesse. But Joy says you're not much of a cook, so don't ruin the salad."

He frowned in her direction, putting his arms by his sides. "Oh, come on. That's not fair. I can make a few things."

"Sure. Like what?"

Jesse put a finger to his temple in contemplation. What could he cook? "Let's see. I can make a mean pasta, and a cheese omelette."

Gabriella chuckled. "Okay, perhaps next time I'll let you cook those for me."

His heart warmed and her face blushed as she turned away from him and tenderised the steak on a chopping board. "You're on, lady." He proceeded to rinse the lettuce leaves underneath the tap then dried the leaves with paper towels. They stood side by side near the bench when he turned to her. "Where are your bowls?"

She bent down to reach for a bowel in the bottom cupboard, her dress lifting high enough up to display her smooth, toned thighs. What would it feel like to rub his hands over them until he reached higher up? He stood frozen to the spot, watching her curves and cleavage displayed. She was sexy and he had to push back his arousal.

Gabriella got up and handed him a bowl, their hands brushing. "Here you go." He smiled then broke the lettuce into pieces. He placed them into the bowl while Gabriella finished tenderising and seasoning the meat. "I'll fry the sweet potato. Is that to your taste?"

"Sure. Sounds good." Needing to take his mind off her body, he asked, "So what's it been like spending every night with one of your friends?"

"It's been good, but I feel bad too. I know they have their own lives, and I'm getting in the way of that. I just hope this'll be over soon."

He wondered if they'd still see each other once it was over. Surely, they were friends, and could keep in touch. He yearned to see her every day, but what good would that be when he didn't want a relationship? He still felt the need to protect her. "I'm sure the police are getting closer to the truth. Have faith."

After eating dinner, they sat on the couch side by side, watching a movie. The sex scene on the screen was hot and raunchy, and Jesse could see in the corner of his eye that Gabriella was staring into her hands. Very slowly, she turned towards him and blushed. Jesse scraped his hand over hers and brought it to his lips. He moved closer to her, their legs touching. Turning his face towards her, he leaned in and gently brushed his lips over hers. The kiss deepened and he wrapped his arms around her and caressed the back of her neck, moaning in arousal. Without warning, Gabriella pulled away from him.

"I'm sorry, Gabriella."

She averted her eyes and rose. "I think we're a bit too emotional right now, and we're both not in the right headspace."

"You're right. We've just discovered something shocking, and we need time to process that. I didn't mean to take advantage of you."

"It's fine, Jesse. I think it's best I go to bed. I don't want Erica to be on your mind when you're kissing me."

"Wait, what? That's not what this is."

She stood, arms crossed, squinting. "You are kissing me because you're hurting over Erica. And besides, you're endangering yourself by kissing me. It has to stop. I won't be your rebound."

"Are you serious right now?" How could he explain how his feelings for her ran deeper than he cared to admit? "I care about you, and you alone. This is not about Erica. It's about me feeling drawn to you, connected. I know you care about me too."

She nodded. "I do care about you, Jesse, but I feel like we're too emotional right now, and need to process things. We need to be sure that what we're feeling isn't just about Erica or me being in danger."

"It's not about that. This runs deeper for me, Gabriella. I might not be ready for a relationship, but I would like to explore if there is anything between us."

"Goodnight, Jesse." He watched her scurry out of the living room and towards her bedroom, the tightening of his chest prominent. Why the hell did he say he wasn't ready for a relationship? He was starting to think he might be, but he couldn't admit that to her.

Chapter Fifty-Four

RUDE AWAKENING

Gabriella and Jesse sat inside the interview room, talking to Marco, Angelo, and Octavia. Jesse watched all three of them look at each other strangely as they stared at the photos of Nigel kissing Erica. Something was going on here, and it had to do with Nigel.

Gabriella eyed Jesse curiously as she bit her bottom lip; that one act alone leaving him undone. He couldn't get that kiss out of his mind, in spite of their lives literally being in danger with a killer and stalker in their midst.

"What's going on here? Is there something we should know?" Jesse threaded his fingers through his hair and leaned forward, watching Octavia, who took a deep breath.

"These photos don't surprise me, actually," said Octavia. "We spoke to his mother, and she admitted to his little infatuation with his adopted sister. He is now a person of interest in this investigation."

Jesse's breathing accelerated as he fixed his gaze on Gabriella. "Because of these photos or is there something else?"

Gabriella answered for them. "You mentioned having leads, so I assume it's about Nigel. What else has he done?"

Octavia pressed her lips together. "We have police officers bringing him in for questioning as we speak."

Marco intervened. He undid the top button of his shirt as if he was too hot. "Gabriella. We believe he might be obsessed with you, as he was with Erica."

Gabriella's face paled and her body slumped. "But he wouldn't have sent these photos to me when it could implicate him. It just doesn't make sense."

Octavia nodded. "You're right. It doesn't make sense, but we have other information that connects him to your workplace and to the latest victim. Why he would send these to you could be to make you think he's not involved. But the evidence is there. We have nothing that connects him to Nora as yet. But we are thinking it's a drug angle."

Angelo's face softened. "Listen, we're going to question him, and will keep investigating, but in the meantime, stay with Jesse or one of your friends. Do not stay alone until we're sure he's the one."

Jesse rubbed his chin. "But how was Nigel connected to Gabriella's work?"

"All we can say is that we found his fingerprints inside Gabriella's car and inside your garage," said Angelo. "And another thing." He stared at Octavia. "If Nigel is obsessed with Gabriella, then he hurt Jesse out of jealousy. We'll see if he talks about who he's working with. He'll most likely have a partner."

Octavia reached forward to grab Gabriella's hand. "Listen, I want you to keep yourself safe, and be on guard, because Nigel does have violent tendencies. Otherwise, we wouldn't normally tell you guys this much if we didn't think you were in danger." She took a calming breath. "Why you had to visit him at the winery still boggles my mind, but you shouldn't have got yourselves involved. Anyway, his mother explained...mentioned how Nigel had once tried to drown Erica in the baby pool not long after she was adopted. If it wasn't for his mother catching him in the act and Erica screaming for help, she'd probably be dead. If that doesn't count as motive for a deep-seated hatred, I don't know what does. But it's also the fact that Erica rejected him, and he obsessed over her for years. The jealousy and his frustration and anger at not being able to have her may have drove him to kill her." She took a breath. "And if he truly did kill her this time, then he finally got his wish to destroy her."

Jesse slumped in his seat, pushing back tears. Why didn't he realise that Nigel was a threat? How could he not see that he was dangerous and violent? He always thought that Nigel was an annoying pest, but to know now that he had tried to kill his adopted sister, it changed things.

Gabriella reached out for him and held his hand. "I'm sorry, Jesse. I wish I had seen it, but I still find it hard to believe he's a killer. What if he's being framed?"

Marco frowned. "We don't know with certainty that he's the one, but a lot of these incidences point to him. His jealousy, her rejection of him in these photos, the near-drowning, and the constant bickering over the years. But we have evidence against him. In the meantime, keep yourself safe, Gabriella. You too, Jesse."

Jesse fixed his gaze on Marco. "What about those deaths interstate? Do they implicate Nigel or someone else?"

Marco shrugged. "We can't say anything about that. We're in communications with those detectives." He stood up. "Listen, we'll keep you in the loop with anything new that comes up. But please don't go talking to anyone. Stay in your zone and do not get involved in police business."

Jesse got up, as did the others. "We'll behave, don't worry."

As Jesse and Gabriella walked towards the exit of the police station, passing by other officers at their cubicles, either on the phone or talking to members of the public, Nigel walked alongside two policemen.

Nigel angled his head. "Well, fancy meeting you guys again." He glared at Jesse. "I still wonder what I'm doing here."

Jesse glared back. "You're a sick bastard. Sending those photos of you kissing your own sister." He rushed towards him, but Gabriella and the officers tried to pull him away. "No, he's a bastard and deserves prison."

Nigel drew back. "What are you talking about? Prison? I didn't do anything wrong, you prick."

Jesse scoffed. "How could you try to drown your own sister? You wanted her dead, and you make me sick. If I ever see you near me, I'll kill you, you loser."

Nigel knit his brows, his face turning pale. "No, I...I loved her."

Jesse shook his head. "You bastard."

Gabriella prodded him towards the exit and touched the small of his back. The fresh air made him breathe easy, even though his chest tightened at the thought of that creep trying to drown his own sister. It had to be him. Too many coincidences for it to not be him.

Chapter Fifty-Five

AN ARREST

Gabriella gripped the steering wheel and peered at a white van parked outside her house, wondering if it was meant to be in the neighbour's spot. She pulled into her driveway and hesitated to get out, when in her rear view mirror, she spotted a man and a woman. *No, not damn reporters.*

It had been two weeks since they questioned Nigel, and more recently, they arrested him for Erica's murder. It appeared he'd also been Gabriella's stalker as she hadn't been harassed since Nigel became a person of interest. Was he as obsessed with her as he was with Erica?

She could no longer stay in the safety of her car and threw open the door. In a few moments, they made a beeline towards her, both holding notepads. Those reporters she knew. The nerdy guy with the glasses was Arthur and the older lady was Janey, Erica's coworkers. Was this about Erica?

Arthur shifted his glasses up his face, holding a pen above his notebook. He stood close to her near the car while Janey stared at her curiously. "Hi, Gabriella. It's good to see you again." He took a breath. "You must be excited about the police finally catching Erica's killer. Finally. After all this time."

She wasn't in the mood for this, but then again, she hated to be rude. "I am."

He lifted his shoulders. "We'd like to ask you a few questions about Nigel and his arrest for Erica's murder. Can you share your thoughts about what he did to you?"

Gabriella couldn't believe what they were asking. Why didn't they just go to the police and get their facts? "Please, I cannot comment. You should speak to the police as they have all the information."

Arthur pulled at the collar of his shirt. He wore a grey suit with an unbuttoned jacket, which was again, one size too large. "Do you have an opinion about his motive? Was it out of love, obsession, or pure hate?"

He was in full reporter mode this time, but Janey peered at the ground. Did she even have a voice? Wearing a flimsy, transparent blouse, her cleavage was on full show, and her black, pleated skirt was quite short.

Gabriella frowned. "Listen, Arthur. I appreciate that you have a job to do, but I don't have any comments and no opinions. I just finished work and I'm tired. I'd like to get inside my house."

Janey leaned forward. "We are sorry to bother you, Gabriella. We just wanted an emotional piece for the article." She turned to her colleague. "Come on, Arthur. Let's leave the girl alone. I'm sure the police will have a press conference soon."

Arthur beamed at her. "I guess you're right." He turned to Gabriella. "We are so sorry to trouble you, but we thought you might have an opinion. We'll be on our way."

Gabriella was about to go inside when she turned to watch them head to the van. Arthur touched Janey's bottom and squeezed it, then when they got inside the van, he leaned forward and kissed her hard on the mouth. They were lovers? Such an unlikely couple. A beautiful older woman and a nerdy, plain man.

***

Later that evening, her doorbell rang. She peered through the window and spotted Jesse's car parked outside. Her heart soared as she missed his presence, and needed to see him tonight. They needed to celebrate.

She swung open the door. Jesse had the widest grin as he stood outside. "You're free, Gabriella."

"Yeah, and I already had Arthur and Janey coming by for a report on my opinion about Nigel's motive. Their police consultant must like to give them tips about my life. I didn't say anything. And get this. He kissed her when they got back into the van."

"Who would have thought a nerdy guy would hook up with a beautiful older woman? Strange combination."

"Come in." Entering her house, she closed the door behind them, but before she turned around, he wrapped his arms around her waist and his fingers trailed both sides of her waist. His mouth traced the outline between her neck and shoulder, his breath hot on her skin. Moving his arms up higher, he traced underneath her breasts then turned her around. He pushed her against the wall, holding up her arms and kissing her hungrily. Gabriella reciprocated as she moaned in his mouth, circling her tongue in his mouth and deepening the kiss. Her hands swept through his hair as she couldn't get close enough to his body. She wanted more. Needed more.

Jesse pulled away from her. "I think we should talk before this gets out of hand."

Gabriella's shoulders deflated, needing the intimacy but realised they needed to make sure they were both on the same page. She nodded and they moved over to the couch beside each other. "I want us to talk about this thing between us."

"Right, and what is this thing between us, Jesse?"

He picked up her hand and stroked the centre of her palm. It endeared him to her, and she beamed in his direction. "I don't want anyone else, Gabriella. It's only you. I loved Erica for a long time, but in that last year before she died, I started seeing her differently. I felt we had grown apart, and I stopped loving Erica a long time ago. Even when I was with Erica, I wanted you then too. I was attracted to you, but I knew it was wrong to explore something because of Joy and Erica being your friends. We only stayed together out of obligation, but even back then, I wanted you. It's always been you, Gabriella. I stopped myself because it wasn't right then, but things are different now."

She fought back tears, overwhelmed with how much she yearned for him. Now that she was free due to the police arresting Nigel, she wondered if it was truly over. Something still didn't sit right with her. "Are you sure you care about me, or is it the guilt over not being able to protect her? She was a damsel in distress and I'm that now too. How do I know I'm not just a replacement for Erica?"

Jesse rubbed her knuckles. "Because what I feel for you is different. More mature and real. I have grown up a lot since then, and I should have broken up with her instead of staying with her out of pity. And you were never a damsel in distress. You are strong, a fighter, resilient, and you no longer have to worry about your stalker. Nigel won't hurt you anymore. I am certain he'll talk to the police about who he's working with." He stroked her cheek. "What we have is real. Can't you see that? You are not a stand-in for Erica, because I realised that what I felt for Erica might have initially seemed like love, but I know now it was only a strong lust, not true love. I was too young to know the difference. What I feel for you doesn't even come close to what I felt for Erica. Isn't what we share worth exploring, Gabriella?"

Gabriella stared at him, needing to process things. She gave him a reassuring smile and squared her shoulders. "I need to think about this, Jesse." Turning away, she said, "How about you help me make dinner."

He nodded. "I would be happy to help you with dinner."

She walked to the kitchen, wondering if they could have a future together.

Chapter Fifty-Six

INTIMATE MOMENTS

G abriella tossed and turned in her bed, her thoughts on Jesse and what he had told her about Erica. She flashed back on the times he would intermittently watch her while standing next to Erica, or the times he would touch her affectionately when they shared a joke in their group. At the time, she didn't like how she might have had a tad of attraction towards him, thinking he was not only her best friend's brother but her other friend's fiancé too. It was wrong to have these feelings for him, so she put him out of her mind and got on with her life. When she'd been with Nick, she had always had a small part of her that cared for Jesse, and what she thought she had with Nick wasn't real anyway.

What stopped her now from exploring something with Jesse? Joy seemed to approve of a prospective relationship, and Erica was dead. He made her feel so much more than Nick ever had, and she could no longer deny that she had fallen in love with Jesse. Would it be so wrong to explore their deep-seated emotions, which had started with a strong attraction years ago?

Staring at the digital clock, she pulled the blankets off her. It was two o'clock in the morning, and her throat was dry. She got up to get a glass of water, passing by the living room, not wanting to wake up Jesse sleeping on the couch. Tip-toeing to the kitchen, she grabbed a glass from the overhead cupboard and filled it with water. She drank down the whole glass then put it inside the sink.

Footsteps sounded behind her and she stood there with tingles down her back, fighting her yearning for Jesse. But why did she need to fight it? She wanted him, craved for him, needed him.

"Gabriella, are you okay?" Jesse said behind her.

Slowly, she turned around and licked her lips. "I couldn't sleep."

He moved closer towards her and brushed his fingers down her arms. "I couldn't sleep either. It must be the heat in this house."

Gabriella chuckled, understanding his double-meaning. She could see the intensity of emotions in his eyes. He hungered for her and craved her as much as she did him. She beamed at him and grabbed his hand to lead him to her bedroom.

"Are you sure about this?" asked Jesse.

Gabriella nodded then lifted the quilt and sheet off the bed and lay on top of it while pulling Jesse on top of her. He stared at her with such tenderness that she thought she was in a Utopian universe. It couldn't be possible to be this content, could it?

Jesse pulled off her t-shirt and trailed his hands down the side of her upper chest then moved over her bottom lip. She sucked on his finger as his lips tantalised the outline of her breasts. He freed his finger from her lips and cupped her breasts gently with both hands. Moving his mouth back up, he licked his way into her mouth, and she felt his manhood harden. He gathered her closer, kissed her deeper as he ran his fingers over her underwear, in between her thighs. She was soaking when he slowly pulled off her underwear and probed with his fingers. She pressed herself harder against his hand. "Oh, Jesse."

His hands captured her face with such tenderness. "Come for me, Gabi. Let me see you come." He watched her closely with such yearning as he kept pressing two fingers inside her, massaging her clitoris in rhythm until she climaxed.

He took off his jeans and underwear and grabbed a condom from his jeans pocket. Gabriella placed it over his manhood. Together they writhed and fell into a rhythm as he stroked her cheeks and moved his finger over her brow. Gabriella lifted her hips for him and squeezed her legs around him to get even closer. Her body was on fire and she knew without a doubt that she loved him. They moved in sync as they stared into each other's eyes, seeing the expression of joy in his eyes. With a single hard thrust, she buried him as deep as she could. The blinding ecstasy and pleasure she experienced as he continued to move against her deepened her love. They reached that climactic ending and lay in each other's arms for a long time, relishing their closeness.

***

Jesse stretched out in bed, the sunlight shining through the bedroom from a gap in the curtain. He fully opened his eyes to see Gabriella's leg draped over his. She wore a flimsy nightgown, the upper part was transparent and showed the outline of her nipples. Jesse became hard again as he stared at how beautiful she was in sleep. Her mouth was slightly parted and her hands stretched out on either side of her. He could never tire of looking at her sleeping so peacefully.

The way they'd made love last night was like nothing he had ever experienced. Her glossy hair, the fresh lemon scents around her body, the way her body felt against his, and the things she could do with her tongue. He was getting aroused thinking about it again, and he knew without a doubt that he loved her with a passion. This was real, and he was excited to explore a deep abiding love with Gabriella.

She was finally safe from Nigel, and Erica's killer would finally be brought to justice. One thing bothered him, though. He could understand him killing his adopted sister out of jealousy and rejection, but why target Gabriella? They'd always got along well, and he wasn't convinced that he would hurt Gabriella in any way. But then again, it seemed to be all over, and the police had arrested Nigel. They were still looking for his partner, but the police thought he was long gone by now and running scared. But he needed answers. He needed to understand from the police whether Gabriella was truly safe.

Stirring from sleep, Gabriella slowly opened her eyes and smiled up at him. "Hey, stranger."

He chuckled. "We weren't strangers last night. In fact, I am thinking we might do it again." He reached over and stroked her upper thigh, gliding his fingers between her centre as she bucked and leaned into his hand. Her moans aroused him further as she licked her lips and closed her eyes.

"Oh, Jesse. What are you doing to me?" She rolled over and their lips met with hunger and need, tongues dancing and bodies mingling. Heat enveloped his body as he rubbed her clitoris, savouring her moans as he delved deeply into her mouth. Holding her face in his hands, he nibbled at her bottom lip and kissed her with ravenous hunger, exploring, tantalising, and following her tongue, her mouth warm and sweet. He pulled away from her inviting mouth and trailed her upper chest, circling his tongue around the outline of her breasts while gently squeezing her nipples. She arched her back and caressed the back of his head.

"It's always been you, Gabriella." He moved down to her waist and kissed the side of her hips until reaching her abdomen. He pushed two fingers in between her thighs again until his mouth reached her mound, tantalising her with his tongue as she pressed his head gently against her. With legs widening, he looked up at her flushed cheeks and held her gently by the hips as his tongue rotated inside her, growling, yearning, and needing to get closer to her. It was never close enough as he kept probing and prodding her open with his fingers. Her climax brought him to a stop as he pulled off his underwear, found her spot, and pushed himself inside her while staring hard into her eyes. She gazed back and they both climaxed together. "I love you, Gabriella."

She caressed his cheek. "I love you too, Jesse."

***

He peered through photos of their love-making and became aroused. Unzipping his jeans, he placed his hand in between his legs and masturbated while closing his eyes, the juice coming out thick and fast. Why did she always make him come? He could never get enough of her, and yet he could never have her.

The front door slammed and jerked him out of his arousal. Zipping up his jeans, his companion stared at him for a moment then walked to the bedroom. Smashing noises reverberated in his ears, understanding the anger being taken out on the lamps and vases in the other room. He'd have to go back to the flea market and replace those that were now broken.

Not long to go now to claim his prized possession: Gabriella.

Chapter Fifty-Seven

THE TEXT MESSAGE

Gabriella tossed and turned in bed and eventually fell asleep deeply.

A young girl lifted up both palms out. "Help me. Please help me." Gabriella ran towards her, hands sweaty and blood dripping from her cheeks; her stomach tightening as she reached the girl. Stretching out her arms, the girl vanished. "No, no. Wait." Body turning in all directions, her nightgown dampened at the ends as she trudged in water. Splashes of water sprayed around. She walked towards a narrow corridor, eyes roaming as she pushed forward with her arms by her sides. Knocking into the walls, she flinched at the stickiness and pulled away, but the room was getting narrower with each step. Remaining still, Gabriella listened, waited, and watched, but the room was empty. In the near-distance, a man appeared but she couldn't see his face. It was faded out. A woman appeared. She approached the girl, grabbed strands of her hair and threw her against the wall. Gabriella ran towards them but they were getting further away. "No, please don't. Take me. Please. Take me."

Gabriella gasped under wet sheets as she abruptly opened her eyes and looked around. Just a dream. It wasn't real, but it seemed real and so vivid. Nigel had been arrested and he had been her stalker too. Surely she was safe.

Pulling away the sheets, Gabriella walked to the kitchen and put on the kettle. With a shaky hand, she poured boiling water into the mug and dropped half of it on the counter. Wiping it away, she filled up her mug and sipped her tea. Sitting down, she thought about her dream, realising that she couldn't save the girl. Was that girl Nora, or someone else? And why would she have this dream when they at least caught one killer? Was it the dominant killer? The one that got away? She pushed aside her uneasy feeling when she suddenly remembered something. The brown jacket at Erica's workplace. It smelled of lavender and fruit, like lemons or oranges. Wasn't that the exact same smell she'd had in her car at Bella and Marco's wedding? If someone had been in her car with that kind of scent, then was it someone at Erica's workplace that was involved in all this? Maybe her dream was telling her that this wasn't over.

Her phone buzzed on the coffee table. Rising, she looked at the display and answered with a smile across her face. "Hi, Jesse."

"Hey, beautiful. Are you going to work today?"

"I am, but I didn't sleep well so I might leave work early. I'll see how I feel later. Do you have a busy day?"

"Very busy, but I will catch up with you tonight. I can take you out for dinner."

"I would love that."

"Then I'll enjoy my dessert with you. Very much, and maybe even lick it off you."

Gabriella's heart raced as her inner thighs dampened with arousal. "You're a cheeky boy, aren't you?"

"Only when I am with you, Gabriella. I miss you already."

Her heart warmed. "I miss you too, Jesse. Have a great day, and I'll see you tonight."

"Is everything okay? You sound strange."

Gabriella realised she was overthinking things and pushed her uneasiness aside. "I'm fine. I will need sleep tonight so don't keep me up too late."

"No guarantees, beautiful. But take it easy today, and I will see you tonight. I love you, Gabriella."

"I love you too, Jesse."

She ended the call with love in her heart, then finished her tea and washed her mug. The hairs on the back of her neck stood on end for no particular reason. It was just a bad dream, nothing more. Moving to the bathroom, she showered and dressed, then got her bag and keys ready to leave for work. Her phone buzzed again in her bag, thinking it was Jesse texting her, but the display said, "Swap Janey for you. Come to this address alone. We have another girl too. No police or she dies."

Gabriella stood frozen in her spot, dizzy with head pain as she realised it was not over. Not by a long shot. Which only meant that Nigel was not her stalker, so who was?

She stepped into her car and floored the accelerator to the address twenty minutes away, but with congested traffic, it would take her twice as long to get to Laverton. Oh, hell! What if she didn't get to her in time and he decided to hurt Janey? He mentioned having another girl. She had to save her.

Gabriella refused to think of the worst and realised that the stalker wanted to play games. Otherwise, he could have picked her up without involving Janey. She had to save her, but the traffic was slow. She didn't want another dead body.

Criss-crossing through lanes, she was making some headway but then got stuck behind a truck. Taking a breath, she realised she was close. Very close. She had to get a clear mind and not be distracted. If this was a joke, then so be it, but if it wasn't, she could save Janey.

She ended up near an industrial area, close to a bunch of warehouses, and stopped. The area was deserted. This was the address she was given, but she didn't see anything. As she walked out of the car, she made her way to the warehouse, but stopped in her tracks and turned when a car slowed behind her. With tinted windows, she couldn't make out the driver as he stopped the car, leaned over, and pushed Janey onto the ground. The older lady had bruising around her face and deep scratches across her arm. Leaping for Janey, she leaned over her. She was sleepy and looked weak. Putting her arms behind Janey's back, she dragged the older woman towards her car while the driver of the other car drove in the opposite direction. Reaching the back of her car, she heaved and breathed heavily due to the weight of Janey. Her arms were killing her as she opened the back door and pushed the woman inside. As she made her way back to the driver's seat, the other car returned and was accelerating towards her. She moved out of the way and got inside her car as the driver continued to drive ahead. Where was he going? As she turned on the motor, a sound came from behind her, then a needle penetrated her arm. She blacked out.

Chapter Fifty-Eight

MISSING

Jesse walked inside the police station and approached the front desk. "I need to speak to either detectives Marco or Angelo. Are they in?"

The towering police officer nodded. "Wait here, please."

His hands shook as he reached for his phone and dialled Gabriella for the tenth time in two days, but she still wasn't answering. Even her friends and family hadn't heard from her. He had reported her missing the day earlier.

He looked up when Marco approached. "Marco, have you heard anything?"

He shook his head. "Listen, we will find her, but you can't keep coming here, Jesse. Let us do our job."

"Any new leads?"

"Yes, but they might not pan out."

He sighed. "Come on, Marco. I love her and I'm worried sick. Please tell me something. I will not go spreading anything around."

He pushed Jesse down the narrow corridor and into an interview room, pursing his lips together and shaking his head. "We have officers scoping an address but we can't be sure it's anything yet. We're on stand-by." His phone rang. "Hmm. Right. I'll be right there." He turned to Jesse. "We found a place that had displays of a few women on the wall; one of them being Gabriella, but she's not there." He cleared his throat. "Now, sit tight and let us do our job. I've got to get to the area as it might give us more leads."

"Can I come with you?"

He shook his head. "No, you're a civilian and not thinking straight. I can't have any loose cannons to worry about too." He walked ahead of Jesse while he followed towards the exit.

He walked back to his car with deflated shoulders, racking his brain about who the perpetrator might be. Turning on the motor, he wondered if this person was someone she knew and who had been in her life. He walked to nowhere in particular until he remembered a few things about Arthur, and how he had tried to get involved in Gabriella's life. First at the house, then again after Nigel's arrest. Arthur had even spoken to her at Erica's workplace.

Parking his car by the side of the road, he retrieved his phone resting on the passenger seat. He typed into the Internet for a search on any articles Arthur might have written, but he came up empty. Nothing of significance, and no stories about Gabriella. He clicked on a few more links and found something interesting. Scanning the article, he realised that the story was about Nora. It had to be. Her name wasn't mentioned, but he identified her as a youth worker, living in the local area, abstaining from drugs, and having counselling at a community centre. It couldn't be a coincidence. That gave him a connection to Nora, and a connection to Erica through work, and now a connection to Gabriella. But all this didn't lead him to Gabriella's whereabouts either. By the time the police got further leads, she'd be dead. He couldn't let that happen. Time was ticking. But something else niggled in the back of his mind. Something important. A memory.

Resting back against his seat, he closed his eyes and thought back to Erica's Christmas party. He had dropped Arthur off at his home because he was drunk. But what had he said? Pressing a finger to his temple, he remembered Arthur whispering something about having another house. He had said, "Fifty doors down is the real prize." What if he meant the prize to be a house or another building? Did he even remember where he lived?

He made a call to Derek as he had no choice. He was a mechanic and would be able to track his GPS history from a couple of years back. Making the call, he said, "Derek. I need your help."

Chapter Fifty-Nine

DRUGGED

G abriella's eyes drooped as she lay on the bed. Her hands were bound with chains and her legs ached. She looked at her body, noticing bruising and pain in her upper chest. She was short of breath and her head weighed heavily.

Over her stood a familiar figure, who approached, leaned in and slapped her hard across the face. She moved over on the bed and sat on top of her, pulling hair strands out of her head. "You fuckin' bitch. You're filth just like the others." The woman proceeded to wrap her hands around her throat and squeezed.

Gasping for breath, she shook her head. She was about to die. The woman was choking the life out of her as the room spun around her, slowly blacking out, almost feeling like she was in another world. It was surreal.

"Stop it, Mother. Enough! She is mine, not yours."

Gabriella opened her eyes, becoming more alert. The woman who got off the bed was still blurry, but Gabriella was sure she knew her. If she could just clear away the haze, she could figure it out. Who was she and why did she hate her so much?

The woman neared her son, who leaned forward. "Maybe we can give her a show, Son. That would be fun. One show before we drown her in the bathtub."

Gabriella became nauseous as her vision cleared.

Janey was one of the killers, and had pretended to be a victim earlier. She had tricked her.

Arthur gazed at Gabriella whose head continued to spin. "Come on, Mother. We have a guest and I love her. Maybe later, but you've had your fun, and now I want mine."

The lady shook her head. "If only this one could love you. But she's like the other bitches who don't appreciate you."

"But, Mother, you never appreciated me when I was young."

The woman leaned forward and kissed him hungrily on the lips, then she placed her hands in between his legs. "You have proven yourself, Son, and you are my master now." He moaned in arousal and pushed her against the wall, his hands squeezing her breasts. Gabriella wanted to be sick. Mother and son about to have sex? She looked away but couldn't stop hearing the sick sounds of arousal as they became intimate.

Moments later, she looked up at the man who was buttoning up his shirt with a satisfied smirk on his face. "Sorry about that, Gabriella. But she drives me crazy with desire, and if I could have you, I wouldn't need her."

The woman came up from behind him and shoved him. "You bastard. You will always love me, even if you had another girl. She could not compete with me."

He turned to her. "Of course, Mother. I don't think I will ever find someone that matches you, but I can still try."

"Let me find another girl for you, Son. We can get that other girl from Altona, the one who just got sober last week. She is pretty."

He shook his head. "No, we still have the other girl. There might be hope with that one. We only took her the other day. If we take too many, the police will get suspicious. No, Mother. We wait and see."

Chapter Sixty

FIGHTING FOR LIFE

Gabriella attempted to open her eyes as her head rested back against the bathtub, wearing a flimsy nightgown with her right hand bound by a chain. It was digging into her skin and her wrist was red-raw. Her eyes closed again out of sheer fatigue. The water level was up to her stomach but he was filling it up with more water. She had to think of a way out of here, but so far, he had enjoyed watching her suffer.

It was only on the first day that he had kept her on a bed. On the second day, he'd undressed her and put her in this nightgown, moved her into the bathtub, and chained her. At least the water got warmed every couple of hours, but she was shaking out of fear right now rather than the cold. She had no chance of escape.

This was what had happened to Erica and Nora. Both drowned in the bathtub.

Jolting in her position at the sound of footsteps, she forced her eyes open. "Please let me go. I promise I won't tell anyone about this. About you."

"I'm sorry, my dear Gabriella, but I love you. I can't let you go. We were meant to be together, you and I. But it won't work out now, and I have to let you go, at least emotionally. This would never have happened if you didn't betray me with Jesse. We could have had a life together. You could have given me a chance."

She tried to play along earlier, but perhaps she needed to be more convincing. What could she say to convince him? Or she could stall him so the police could find her. "If you get me out of this tub, I can show you my appreciation. Would you like that?"

He chuckled and threw his head back. "As if you would. And even if you do, you'll just leave again. They all do. At least this way, I can keep an eye on you and watch you die peacefully like a work of art. Don't you want to be an angel in Heaven?"

This guy was crazy. "Why did you kill Erica? What did she ever do to you?"

He turned away briefly as he sat alongside her near the tub. "She didn't love me when I asked her nicely, and neither did Nora and the others. My mother explained how Erica was getting to the truth about those girls interstate. She was snooping and we had to stop that. I had to convince the others I could be the man for them, but they turned me away time and time again. I had to take them."

"But why kill them if you loved them?"

"They hurt me too many times to count. They belong in another world, and eventually, I will join them." His eyes peered into the distance. "It is such a work of art to watch the life being snuffed out of each of them. Beautiful."

Gabriella felt sick. "But I didn't hurt you, Arthur. I could learn to love you if you give me the chance."

"You hurt me by loving Jesse. No-one can have you. If I can't have you, then no-one can. It is just how it has to be. Besides, better this way in water than the other way. I'm saving you from a life of suffering. The medication will help make it easier."

Her throat was dry and her skin wrinkly. Even her legs went numb as he filled it up with even more water. If she could just lift her left arm, she could pull him inside the tub with her, but he kept his distance and had a gun trained on her.

Arthur sat back against the wall and watched her as her head tilted slightly out of exhaustion and dehydration. With one hand, he unzipped his jeans, placed his hand inside and masturbated. "Oh, this is so exciting. You excite me, Gabriella. So much."

The drug injection was wearing off. "Let me excite you with my hand. Unchain me and I can pleasure you even more. Please, Arthur. You're a handsome man and I think I can love you. Come to me." He stopped before climaxing, his gaze fixed on her as if weighing up his options. She had to strengthen her argument and lie. "Erica mentioned you at work and I told her to give you a chance. She didn't listen to me, so it was her loss. Such a bitch not to notice you. If I worked with you, I would have noticed you. I love men with moustaches and glasses. They are such a turn-on."

He scoffed. "Fuckin' Jesse doesn't look like me, so why are you with him?"

She shrugged. "I am...starting to notice you more. Jesse's not the man for me. He's too rough, and I like men who are more analytical. I looked you up online and I noticed you, Arthur. So let me pleasure you. Or we could do more if you like."

His eyes squinted. Rising from the ground, he left the bathroom and returned five minutes later. In his hand was a key and he unchained her slowly. He put down his gun, but she wouldn't know how to use it. "Don't let me regret this."

When her hand was free, she grabbed him by the scruff of his shirt and knocked him into the tap. He fell unconscious. Quickly, she leapt out of the tub and picked up the gun, so he wouldn't have it. He didn't need to know she couldn't use it, but she'd pretend she could. Rushing towards the front door, she fumbled with the knob then realised the screen door was locked. Where was the security key? Using the butt of the gun, she knocked it against the latch and it broke. Taking a deep breath, she pushed open the security door but strong arms dragged her back. She dropped the gun. "No, no. Let me go. Please, Arthur."

"You bitch. I knew I couldn't trust you, just like all the others." He pushed her back into the bathtub, but she screamed, flailing her arms around. With her right foot, she kicked him in the groin from behind as she leapt out of the tub. "Oh, God!" He stood up straight, holding on to his groin area, but he trapped her and held the gun, pointing it towards her. "Get back in the tub." Gabriella was short of breath as she stepped back in the tub.

Footsteps sounded behind, and in walked Janey. "This one's different. She has to die my way, Arthur."

Arthur shook his head. "No. She has to die my way, Mother."

Janey ignored him and reached up into a cupboard and pulled out a jagged knife. "My way now. She'll be too out of it so we won't need to secure her with the chain."

Chapter Sixty-One

SAVED

Jesse peered through the windows but he couldn't see anyone inside. The door was locked but he was able to break the window with his baseball bat. He had called the police on the way, but he couldn't wait for them. The bastard normally killed them after two days, and Gabriella's time was up. He had no choice but to get here as fast as he could.

Jesse crawled through the window, sped through the living area, and ran straight to the bathroom. He saw Arthur pointing a gun at Gabriella while his fellow reporter, Janey, cut into Gabriella's leg as she screamed in pain. "No, please. No."

His heart breaking at her pain, he quickly lifted up his right arm and swung it hard at Janey's head. She fell back, seemingly unconscious. Arthur was staring at the woman's still body. He swung the bat again but missed when Arthur became alert and pointed his gun towards Jesse. He hit Jesse with the butt of the gun against the side of his head and pushed him against the bathroom cabinet. A multitude of tablets fell out and into the basin. Jesse saw stars but came to when Arthur, again, pointed the gun at him. Gabriella knocked into him and pushed him in the bathtub, but he quickly recovered and ran headlong into her. She hit her head against the door and moaned.

Jesse found the gun sliding across the floor and picked it up, but Arthur moved fast and wrestled him for it. The man was strong, and he was struggling with the gun as it flicked in all directions, his hand gripping it but not able to grasp it completely. The gun fell and Arthur punched him as Jesse fell back and bumped his head. Where was the gun? His eyes searched, and even Arthur was looking for it. Bending his head down, he found the gun in the corner of the room and reached for it. Arthur beat him to it, and Jesse pounded him hard in the face, forcing him to let go. But Arthur wasn't deterred. The gun went off.

***

Gabriella came to when the gun went off. "Jesse. No!" Fighting for breath, she pushed herself forward at the sight of Arthur lying on top of Jesse. Blood seeped into the floor, but she didn't know whose blood it was. Making her way forward, she pushed him off Jesse, noticing a bullet wound in Arthur's stomach. "Bitch!" he said while his eyes closed. Checking his pulse, she found he was dead.

Turning to Jesse, she helped him up from the floor and wrapped her arms around him. "Thank God you're okay. Oh, Jesse." Stroking the small of his back, she finally felt safe.

He hugged her back with a weak arm. "I love you, Gabriella. Are you okay?"

They pulled apart. "I will be. Thank you for saving me."

He crawled to the towel rack, picked up a small towel, and wrapped it around her leg wound. "I would do it all over again." He beamed. "The police are on their way."

She suddenly remembered. "There's another girl here, Jesse." She winced at her stinging leg and clenched her hands.

Jesse pointed to Janey and handed her the baseball bat. "Watch her. If she wakes up, hit her with this. I'll be back." He rushed away, but she later realised that he was taking too long, so she forced herself to limp to one of the other bedrooms. She saw a young blonde girl in her twenties. Her head drooped. Her face was gaunt and her body malnourished. Her hands were chained to a bed and she was naked. Jesse was rummaging through the drawers looking for something.

"I can't find the key to this chain. It has to be here somewhere."

Gabriella approached her. "It's okay. We'll get you out of here. You're safe. The police are on their way."

The girl nodded, whispering, "Thank you."

Sirens in the distance alerted them to the police, and within minutes, car doors closed and footsteps resounded in the house. Marco and Angelo rushed towards them and the girl.

"Gabriella, Jesse, are you okay?" Marco asked.

She nodded. "I'm fine, but this girl needs to get loose." A policeman later joined him with bolt cutters and freed the victim. He and Marco helped the girl out of the room.

Jesse nodded. "I was trying to find the key, but the bolt cutters did the trick." He fell back against the ground, his head bleeding from his wounds. Angelo rushed towards him and lay him against the bed, while Gabriella walked to his side and put an arm around him. She gasped in fear. Was he going to be all right?.

Angelo turned to the paramedics scurrying inside. "I need you two to tend Jesse's wounds and check Gabriella here too.

Marco handed Gabriella a bottle of water and she sipped it fast. The female paramedic checked her blood pressure and vitals, then placed a gauze on her graze and tended to her bruises."

As they later walked out of the room, past the bathroom, they stood and watched Janey stir while the same paramedics tended to her wounds. Angelo approached Janey and cuffed her. "You are under arrest for multiple murders, Janey." She took one look at Arthur's dead body, and she screamed. "No, my boy. My boy. No..."

Turning to a police officer, Angelo said, "Take the woman away." She was hauled out by a police officer, whimpering. Who knew the woman had a heart?

Gabriella turned away from Arthur's body, realising how close to death she had been. If only they could have saved Erica and Nora.

Jesse faced her. "I had to get here, Gabriella. I knew that after two days he would have tried to kill you. I had no choice but to get here."

"I am glad you did, but you risked your life too."

He scoffed. "Are you kidding? I would risk my life for yours any day. I couldn't save Erica, but I could save you. I'll deal with the detectives later, but I'm sure I'll just get a reprimand. All that matters is you're safe."

Jesse tucked her against him, keeping her close. She leaned into him. Gabriella wanted to go home and sleep for two days. It was finally over.

Chapter Sixty-Two

EPILOGUE: TWO MONTHS LATER

Gabriella sat with Jesse on her living room couch. Chairs surrounded the space as Joy, Bella, Liz, Jamie, Claudia, and Camilla sat with drinks in their hands.

She leaned forward as Jesse stroked her hand while she addressed her friends. "I called you all over here to explain everything. Marco, Octavia, and Angelo are working on another case. I know you guys wanted the details about everything, but Marco wanted us to hold off on telling you anything until they prepared all the evidence for the upcoming trial. But that won't be for at least another six months."

Liz gripped her wine glass and looked concerned. "Gabriella. You don't need to get back into it if you don't want to. As long as you and Jesse are okay now, that's all that matters. I don't mind being here for a free drink."

Joy chuckled. "I'll drink to that." She turned away, staring at the ground as if she had something on her mind.

"Are you okay, Joy?" asked Gabriella.

"Couldn't be better, girl. Why don't you start?"

Bella sat between Jamie and Camilla and squeezed Camilla's hand. She wondered if Camilla should have been here, given her traumatic history. "Take your time, Gabi. It's still early in the day."

She took a deep breath. "Okay, I know you guys know some of what's been happening, but I'll start off with the murders in Queensland." She took a quick sip of her wine and placed it on the coffee table. "Arthur and Janey committed three murders while they lived there; all drug addicts who had told their story, either officially or informally to Arthur. Arthur became obsessed with me after stalking Nora who came to see me for counselling. He sent me the text messages and the love notes at my front door. He sent photos of Nigel and framed him with his fingerprints in my car. Apparently, he stalked Nigel at the winery and got his fingerprints from a glass. Janey attacked Jesse in his garage and might have killed him if Arthur didn't stop her. He didn't want Jesse dead but only incapacitated until he could get to me; not that it worked out that way." Gabriella cleared her throat and steeled herself.

"She also moved my car at my workplace. Arthur and Janey did things together, and thought this would throw off the police with the method of kills. It was her idea to get the women to cut themselves as she had a sick obsession with seeing people suffer. It was her idea to stab one of the women in Queensland because she preferred violence. Arthur preferred seeing women die in the water." She lifted her shoulders. "He followed me when I went jogging and sprained my ankle, and Janey sent that social media text. She was the dominant one, who seemed to show a lot more anger than Arthur, and liked to humiliate people. He even put roses on my bed after getting the idea from his mother's ex-boyfriend. The boyfriend had written 'I love you' on Janey's bed with the rose petals, and Arthur liked that idea. He followed me at university." She took another deep breath, pushing down a tension headache. "Janey put a tracker in my car on the day of Marco and Bella's wedding, and I did smell lavender and citrus. It's her favourite perfume." She looked at Jesse, who squeezed her hand. "That's about it."

The room was silent for a few minutes until Camilla broke the quiet. "I am sorry for what you went through, Gabriella. I thought my dad was a sick bastard, but nothing beats those two."

Claudia shook her head. "If I could get my hands on that psychopath, Janey, I would fulfil my greatest wish. I am sorry, Gabriella. If ever you need to talk one on one, call me."

"Thanks, Claudia. Camilla. I am so glad it's over. Finally."

Jamie leaned forward. "What is the story of Arthur and Janey? I know they are mother and son, but what did she do to him?"

Bella turned to Gabriella. "I'm curious too. What made their relationship so dysfunctional?"

Jesse took over. "From what Octavia was saying, Janey started sexually abusing her son from primary school age, and over time, he developed sexual feelings towards his mother. The father was abusive and left Arthur as a child; not sure what age. When Arthur got too chummy with female or male friends, Janey would punish them by cutting marks into their legs. After that, he had no friends left and was basically a loner in high school. She forced her son to become a reporter like her, and she'd only started working with Erica six months before she died. They started killing in Queensland, going back at least five years."

Claudia shook her head. "That is so sick." She faced Joy. "What about Joy's car accident? Was Janey involved in that, or Arthur?"

Gabriella swallowed. "No, Janey said they weren't involved in that accident, so maybe that's all it was. An accident." Staring over at Joy, she wondered why her friend stayed quiet. She would chat with her later. Something was on her mind.

Liz crossed her legs. "And how did you find Gabriella, Jesse?"

He took a breath. "I found the house where Arthur lived, and he told me about another place he owned when he was drunk at a work

Christmas party. Derek tracked my GPS history of the location of his house, and I won't bore you with the rest."

Joy's spirits lifted. "My God, Jesse. If you didn't get there in time, she might not have survived. Didn't Janey have a knife?"

He nodded. "She planned to use it when Gabriella fought her way out of the tub. Janey doesn't like disobedience. At least Arthur's dead, and she'll get to rot in prison after the trial. Justice has been served for Erica, Nora, Camilla's friend, and the other girls." He leaned in towards Gabriella and kissed her briefly on the lips. "And I love this beautiful woman right here and will never let her go."

She yearned to spend alone time with him. "I love you too, Jesse."

A scream of applause spread around the room, and the girls got up and wrapped their arms around both of them.

Joy moved back to her seat. "I hope you're sorting things out with Derek, bro."

"We're not where we used to be, but we're working things out slowly."

Joy's phone buzzed. She looked at the display and her eyes turned a shade darker. Answering the call, she said, "Hey, Octavia. What's up?"

Her face turned pale and her hand shook as she held the phone. "Okay, I'll be right in. Thanks." She got up from the chair. "Listen, I have to get to the station. A co-worker of mine is missing, and I need to answer some questions." All the girls stood up, including Jesse and Gabriella.

"We're coming with you," said Bella.

"I'm coming too," said Gabriella.

Liz pushed her back down on the couch. "No, you've been through enough. Stay here with your man."

***

Later that day, Jesse and Gabriella were lying in bed after making love. She fell into the crook of his arm. "I love you so much, Jesse."

"I love you too, beautiful." He gently glided his fingers down her arm until it trailed down to her waist. Her body tingled with desire. She could never get enough of him. "Maybe we should go another round."

"You're crazy." She remembered Joy. "Do you think Joy's okay? She did look worried earlier."

"She'll be fine. I'll check in on her later and let you know." He fixed his gaze on her. "I was thinking, maybe...perhaps, you could move into my place? Or I could move in here. We could always get one of our places rented out if you like. What do you think?"

Gabriella's eyes lit up. "I think it sounds like a great idea, but can we hold off on that for a while? Let me settle into a routine first. We've been through a lot."

He nodded. "Of course."

She stroked his cheek, hopeful about their future. "I just need a bit of time, that's all."

Jesse beamed. "I am never going to give up on you, Gabriella. If you need time, then I will give you time. You're it for me."

Leaning in, she pressed her lips to his and wrapped her arms around him. She was exactly where she was meant to be.

ABOUT THE AUTHOR

Lucy Appadoo is a prolific reader and author of the Friends In Crisis Series. After a childhood spent reading and imagining escapist worlds, Lucy has put her imagination into stories. Her work as a rehabilitation counsellor, and
former work as a counsellor in private practice, have led to an interest in writing inspirational stories about authentic, driven women who manage adversity with strength and heart. She writes in the genres of romantic Suspense/thrillers with significant life themes and contemporary romance.

Lucy's interests include researching crime stories and news to inspire her work, watching crime thrillers and suspenseful movies, travel, exercising, reading for entertainment or knowledge, meditation, and spending time with friends and family. She also appreciates her Italian background and culture, which has inspired her to write imaginative stories about her parents' childhoods, leading to The Italian Family Series novels.

Reviews are gold to authors and allow Lucy to keep writing. If you enjoyed this book, please consider leaving a review on Amazon.

Check out Lucy's website and sign up for a FREE romantic suspense novel here: www.lucyappadooauthor.com.au

ALSO BY LUCY APPADOO

<u>FICTION</u>

Women Of Strength Series – Romantic Suspense/Thriller

In Rio's Shadows (Book 1) - http://mybook.to/InRiosShadows

Shadows Of The Past (Book 2) - http://mybook.to/shadowsofthepast

The Friends In Crisis Series - Romantic Suspense/Thriller

Haunted By The Past (Book 1) -
http://mybook.to/HauntedbythePast

Twisted Obsession (Book 2) - http://mybook.to/TwistedObsession

Web Of Lies (Book 3) - http://mybook.to/EbookWebOfLies

The Hearts Series - Romantic Suspense

Rising Hearts (Book 1) - http://mybook.to/RisingHearts

Forbidden Hearts (Book 2) - http://mybook.to/ForbiddenHearts

Kindred Hearts - (Book 3) - http://mybook.to/kindredhearts

Broken Hearts (prequel to Forbidden Hearts) - http://mybook.to/Bhearts

Short Story Thrillers

Evening Interrupted - http://mybook.to/Eveninginterrupted

The Dreamcatcher - http://viewbook.at/Thedreamcatcher

Red Flags - http://mybook.to/Redflags

Collection of Short Story Thrillers - http://mybook.to/collectionofthrillers

The Italian Family Series - Coming of Age Family Drama/Romance

A New Life - http://mybook.to/ANewLife

The Beauty of Tears - http://mybook.to/TheBeautyofTears

Dancing in the Rain - http://mybook.to/dancingintheRain

A Life By Design - http://mybook.to/Alifebydesign

NON-FICTION

Grief & Loss

Moving Beyond Grief - How To Shift From Grief & Loss to Joy & Peace - http://mybook.to/MovingBeyondGrief

Stress Management & Anxiety

Holistic Spiritual and Mental Health - Building Resilience and Creativity by Conquering Anxiety and Managing Stress -http://mybook.to/Holistichealth

Career Guidance

Your Holistic Career Path - Create Career
Change, Satisfaction, and Work/Life Balance -
http://mybook.to/YourHolisticCareerPath

Journal and Record Of Books You've Read (with Quotes)

Readers' Journal - http://mybook.to/ReadersJournal